Catching Cara

Amy J. Hawthorn

Dedication

To all the Caras of the world! You rock.

And to my own little warrior princess. To be so strong, persistent, and yet sweet, you awe me.

Stubborn? Hell yeah! That's the way we roll.

Three weeks ago…

Boyd Campbell finished wiping down the sparse motel room, erasing his prints. He threw his laptop and charger on top of his clothes and zipped the duffle closed. Slinging the bag over his shoulder, he grabbed his weapons case. A quick onceover assured him the room was empty.

Travel light, move fast, and leave no footprints behind.

The simple lesson served him well over the past few years, so he'd be a fool to ignore it now. He'd laid Preston Hayes' murder on his crazy uncle's head. There'd been more than enough evidence to put the good senator away for the rest of his years, but when you added the Senator's drama at Walker Farms, no one in their right mind would believe his uncle's raving protests of innocence.

Still, Boyd had a burning need to get the hell out of Riley Creek and Potter County. It was too close to his home, Bourbon County, and those Dark Horse assholes. If he lingered any longer, he'd feel the heat of Rick Evans breathing down his neck. While he'd like to go head-to-head with the prick, it wouldn't be smart. He couldn't afford the attention a confrontation would bring.

He opened the door with hem of his shirt and walked into the evening humidity.

Fuck. Me.

He stopped dead in his tracks.

Marcus Sutton leaned against the driver's side door of Boyd's SUV. He inhaled a long pull of his cigarette before he flicked the butt at Boyd's feet. "Campbell."

He met Sutton's dark, menacing gaze and silently held his ground. What could he say when a ghost from the past appeared on his doorstep?

Only this ghost was no Casper.

"Fine. I see how well you appreciate my favor. We'll skip the small talk and get down to business. You owe me." Sutton pinned him in place with eyes so dark, they might as well have been coal.

Ages ago, Boyd had needed safe passage and not many people had the resources or the balls to provide him with the kind of assistance he'd needed in BFE, Afghanistan. He'd known eventually the day would come when the price he paid would be a steep one. Then again, expecting it didn't make swallowing the pill any less difficult.

Boyd remained silent, waiting.

Cold, dead eyes, bored into him. "Let's go somewhere and have a chat."

Chapter One

She flinched as a flash of white light split the sky in two. Gripping the wheel tighter in one hand, she used the other to increase the speed of her windshield wipers before gripping the wheel again. Water roared down from the sky even faster, making the blades nearly worthless, even though they swiped back and forth at warp speed.

Thunder boomed, and she choked back a cry of terror. Her palms grew slick and her heart fluttered against her sternum. Dark spots swam in her vision.

She drew in a deep, stuttered breath and told herself it would be okay. There was nothing to be afraid of. Crazy intense summer storms boiled up in Kentucky all the time. As a perfect example of their fury, this one was wild, dramatic, and violent. She knew that, nine times out of ten, they blew themselves out just as quickly as they appeared.

But it wasn't the storm itself that scared her so badly. The thunder that came with it turned her normally confident and in control self into a whimpering mess. She hated that more than anything else. After all she'd been through, something as simple as a summer storm shouldn't still contain the power to cripple her.

Her shoulders ached from the tension of holding the steering wheel in a white-knuckled death grip. She focused on slowing her breathing. In through her nose. Out through her mouth.

The cascade of water slamming against her car slowed to an almost manageable rainfall.

She drew in another deep breath. Exhaled. She was fine.

Until gunfire hit her car.

Bang! Bang! Bang bang bang!

No. She was fine. It was hail beating her car to death, not bullets. She was in Kentucky and headed home. She saw the blur of rolling green fields out the window to her left and a forest of madly waving trees out the right. This was not Afghanistan.

She slowed her already crawling car even more and prayed that no one came up too quickly behind her on the country road. *I can do this. I'll be okay.* The winding road straightened out in about another mile and a half. She could make it that far then pull over in the little church parking lot.

A blinding flash of blue-white light arced above her. She closed her eyes and flinched. Less than a second later, the world around her exploded as thunder boomed, shaking her car. She opened her eyes just in time to see a tree crash on the road ahead of her.

"Shit!" Adrenaline rushed into her bloodstream, and Cara's heart jumped into her throat. She jerked the steering wheel to the right as the wet gray and green scenery blurred. The road curved left, and she slammed on her brakes as the asphalt ended. The world around her shook as the frontend of her car dipped. She gritted her teeth, bracing for impact.

A loud thump shook her, and she winced at the sound of spinning tires. She looked up and turned her head to the left and right, trying to get her bearings.

Dropping her head to the steering wheel, she gave into her terror, releasing a whimper. She didn't hear the violent storm throwing a tantrum around her, but a war that raged years ago. Gunfire and explosions. Shouts and screams.

One scream in particular stood out from the rest.

Justin.

Frozen in horror as the IED detonated between them—maybe fifty feet away—the distance had felt like miles when she couldn't get to her friend.

She fought to break free of the flashback. That was a long time ago, and she couldn't do a damn thing about it. She hadn't been able to then, and she sure as hell couldn't now. She focused on her breathing. She could do this. She'd survived a war. She could make it through a crazy summer storm.

She opened and closed her hands, easing the tension.

The rain softened to a drizzle. Thunder rumbled in the distance but in a low, subdued growl. She could handle that.

She took another deep breath and focused on the here and now. She needed to get out and see about her car. She looked in the backseat and found an old sweatshirt. It'd have to do. She cursed her clothing choices as she stepped out of the car on shaky legs.

What she wouldn't give to be in a pair of ACU pants or even jeans. But no, she hadn't wanted to listen to her mother's harping. What had it gotten her? Stuck in the rain, wearing a flimsy skirt and strappy sandals.

She focused on the mess in front of her and cursed.

After nearly completing the four-hour drive back, she wrecked her car less than thirty minutes from home. She was a mere fifteen miles from the Bourbon County line. She couldn't say she was surprised. With her track record, she should probably be relieved no one was hurt.

Damn it all. How would she get home? Thanks to a fall and hip surgery, her mother couldn't drive, and it had been so long since she'd been home that she was virtually a stranger. She had no one to call.

She brushed her damp hair from her face and steadied herself. She'd been in far worse situations. She drew from her past and took another steadying breath. Hell, it might have been ages ago, but she'd spent a year in Afghanistan. She could walk home if she needed to. Of course she was wearing the wrong shoes. She looked down to the lavender polish on her toes. Well, if she were wearing boots, she could have walked, but she couldn't leave her car.

Knowing it was useless, she felt compelled to at least try to get her car out of the ditch. She got back inside and shifted into reverse and crossed her fingers. She eased her foot onto the gas pedal. The car did a little shimmy and made an ugly sound.

She dropped her head to the steering wheel and groaned. Who could she call?

She'd come home to take care of her mother. Now she had a mess of her own.

***

"Daddy, can we go to Twent and Katie's today?"

Joe set another plate in the dishwasher and looked at the bar. On one of the stools, his daughter's little legs swung back and forth. Bright hope shined in her green eyes.

He gave her the exact same answer he'd already given her twice in the past hour. "Not today, pickle. We've got work to do. The house is a mess."

Her long brown curls covered her face when she looked down at the picture she was coloring. He'd fixed her hair into pigtails that morning, but they never seemed to stay in place for the entire day. Even after years of practice, he couldn't make a damn ponytail or braid like his sister could. When Kylie looked up again, he could see her disappointment. She visibly brightened, a sure sign she had a new idea. "Can we go tomowow? I wanna feed Bonnie and take a wide on

Scawlet. Pwease?" Thanks to therapy, his daughter's speech had improved a great deal, but from time to time, she slipped back into her old habits.

"Sweetheart, it's *please* with an *l*. And we'll see. I have to work tomorrow."

"Awww. You always have to work." She enunciated her words carefully. *Funny how her speech improves when she wants brownie points.*

"I know, pickle. I wish I had more time to play, but this is just the way it is right now." When had he become his father? Not a single day went by where he didn't find himself repeating something one of his parents told him. He'd didn't know how many times he'd rolled his eyes at their little bits of wisdom, thinking all the while that he'd never do the same when he was a father.

Then again, he never dreamed he would become a single father of a little girl whose entire world rested on his shoulders.

No pressure.

"It's almost finished raining. How about, when it stops, we take a walk by the creek and then we'll go get some ice cream before your bath?" A list of chores waited for his attention, but some things were more important than folding a load of laundry.

The sound of cowboy boots banging against the barstool answered his question. She hopped down from the chair and bolted through the house as fast as her feet could carry her. "Yay! I need my bucket! Maybe I can find Fwank!"

He hung the dishtowel on the oven door handle and prayed they didn't find any animals, wounded or otherwise. His daughter, who wasn't bigger than a minute, had a heart larger than any adult he'd ever known. She'd gone toe-to-toe with a cousin not too long ago in defense of a snake. Frank, the snake, had been moved to a safe location, but she still worried about it weeks later.

His phone rang at his hip, and he looked to the ceiling in frustration. He longed for the day he could pitch it into pond. When he saw the caller ID, he frowned. Rick Evans wasn't the kind of man to make random social calls. A call from the head of Dark Horse Inc. likely meant trouble.

Shit.

"Rick. What's up?" Joe's belly sunk as Kylie barreled through the house toward him, neon green bucket at the ready.

"I need a favor. Hopefully it won't take too much of your time. A member of our unit was in a car accident a few minutes ago. No injuries. I'd go myself, but the accident isn't too far from where you live—just off route ten. They're on their way home to Bourbon County, and don't know anyone in the area."

He envisioned Kylie's walk to the creek going up in smoke. *What kind of spin can I put on this disappointment?* "Sure. I'm at home now. I can be there in just a few minutes."

"Thanks. I owe you," Rick replied, as if Joe were the one doing him a huge favor.

He wanted to laugh at the absurdity.

"Never. I'll always be in your debt. Don't sweat it." If it hadn't been for Rick's nose for trouble and inability to stomach unanswered questions, Kate could have died. His cousin was more like a sister to him, and the thought of what could have happened to her without Trent's stubborn insistence on protection and Rick's intervention made him sick. He disconnected and looked down at his daughter. "You wanna go on an adventure? We're going to go rescue somebody."

"Yay!" With that, she was off, messy curls trailing in her wake.

Once he buckled her into her booster seat, they were off. Kylie happily sang along with the radio, kicking her legs in time to the music. A song and half later, they neared the stretch of road Rick described. He hoped like hell that Rick had been right and that this was a simple call. He was tired and still had to get Kylie settled.

Whether in uniform or plainclothes, each time he came up on a wreck, especially one where the car had gone off the road, a foreboding sense of déjà vu nauseated him. It'd been four years since he'd become a single father, but time hadn't helped his memories of that terrible day fade.

He slowed his truck as he came around a sharp curve. The area was heavily shaded, thanks to the rocky hills and thick woods along one side of the road. He came out at the curve's end and shock sucker-punched him.

Slender, bare legs ended somewhere under a very wet, very short, turquoise skirt. The woman bent over at the waist in the shallow ditch at the road's edge to look underneath the car's frontend.

Dwarfed by a baggy gray sweatshirt, she straightened, placed her hands on her hips, and looked down at the car before she turned at the sound of his truck. He waved as he slowed to a stop at the road's edge. The back window rolled down and, before he could form words to stop her, his daughter called out. "We'we here to wescue you and get ice cweam!"

He shook his head, and the woman smiled. He pulled his truck forward, past the car and off to the side a bit. He removed the keys and stepped out. Heading over to check out the mess, he looked for Rick's troubled team member. A petite strawberry blond greeted him with a shaky smile.

He extended his hand. "Hi. I'm Joe MacDonald, a friend of Rick's. I live nearby, so he called me to check on you. Are you with someone or out here on your own?" He'd expected one of Rick's soldier buddies and had no idea where the mix-up occurred.

"Hello, Cara Gregory. Nice to meet you. I got into this mess all on my own." Her slightly husky voice sounded a little deeper than

9

he would have expected. It was different, but far from unattractive. He felt the sultry melody deep inside, where it spread a golden glow, infecting him with hunger. Something about her pixie face, spattered with a few tiny freckles, and honeyed hazel eyes made him feel like a lumbering giant. She put her tiny hand in his and took hold with a tight grip that surprised him.

"I'm sorry about the trouble. When the storm rolled through, a branch fell from a tree and landed in front of my car and, well, you can see the result. I pulled the branch off the road and tried to get the car out myself, but the front wheel drive isn't helping any." She shrugged and pointed to the car behind her, with its front tires in the ditch, emergency blinkers flashing. She took a deep breath and straightened her slumped shoulders.

He looked back to the branch she'd pointed toward, which lay in the ditch by the road's edge. It had to have weighed as much a man. Her hands and sweatshirt were wet and soiled as if she'd been working, but the damn thing probably weighed more than she did. Yet she'd moved it herself? Maybe her tired, defeated vibe came from exhaustion.

Stubborn woman. It sounded like something his sister Leigh would have done, rather than being sensible and waiting for help in a dry car. He stayed silent and focused on the torn up grass and mud beneath the tires. Shaking his head, he replied, "I can pull your car out, no problem. Are you sure you're not hurt?" He focused on her red-rimmed eyes. Had she been crying?

"Other than feeling silly, I'm fine. I hate to be a bother. What can I do to help?" She placed her hands on her hips and turned to frown at the car, as if she were ready to move it herself.

"Not a thing. Why don't you sit in the truck with Kylie? I'll have you out in no time."

The outer corners of her pretty eyes crinkled, and she frowned at him. "No, really, I can help. If you have a tow strap I can—"

"Nope. Absolutely not." He took her trembling hand in his and pulled her up and onto the wet pavement. She trailed behind him. Even irritated, she was a pretty thing, all curvy, sexy lines and toned muscle. He opened the passenger door to help her inside. Her bunching skirt flashed him a peek of her smooth thighs as the damp material clung to her skin.

He forced his libido into submission, telling himself he had to get this mess sorted and get on with Kylie's evening. It didn't matter how delicious their damsel in distress was or how badly he ached to smooth his hand over her heart-shaped ass.

She set her foot in the floor of his truck, tried to climb in then stopped as if she didn't quite have the strength to pull herself up into his beast. Readjusting her foot, she prepared to try again.

"Still got the post-accident shakes, huh? It's okay. Let me help you." *Great. Now my voice is the low and husky one.* He grabbed her tiny waist and lifted her up and in.

Caught off guard, she put her hand on his shoulders to steady herself. "Um. Yeah. Thanks." She bit her bottom lip and the urge to lean in and suck it into his own mouth punched him in the gut.

I've been too long without female companionship.

"Are we gonna yank that sucker outta there, daddy?" Eager and excited, Kylie chimed in as he shut the door.

Scratch that. He'd been too long without *adult* female company.

Wishing he could be shocked, he stuck his head in the open window. "Kylie Jane, where'd you hear talk like that?" He never knew whether to laugh at or strangle his offspring.

The sweet scent of woman and summer rain washed over him. Thanks to his daughter's mouth, he'd stuck his head right into Cara's space. "That's what Mr. Cwark said when Gwampa and I helped him with his old twailer. It had fat tires and was stuck in the mud."

11

He thought for a moment and deciphered his daughter's speech. "Do you mean flat tires?"

"Yeah. That's what I said. Fat tires."

"It was awfully nice of you and your grandfather to help Mr. Clark. I'm Cara. It's nice to meet you." Cara nodded her head at him in a *get to work, while I distract the kiddo* gesture before she turned to his daughter. "How old are you?"

In a well-honed habit, he weighed the need to chastise his daughter against the need to move on to the next task—getting Cara's car out. The car won. He turned his back on the females making friendly chatter and went about hooking a tow strap to the back of her car.

***

"I'm six. How old are you?" The little imp in the car seat behind her spoke slowly as if she concentrated saying each word correctly.

"I'm thirty-two." Cara turned back a bit more and held out her hand.

"My name's Kylie. What kind of ice cweam do you like? I want vanilla with spwinkles." Kylie's small, slightly sticky hand gripped hers for a quick handshake.

"Chocolate is my favorite, but I like vanilla, too." Cara watched out the back window as Joe MacDonald opened a lid on the toolbox attached to the truck bed. A dark blue baseball cap shaded his eyes as he looked down, but the sight of the dark chocolate irises specked with golden flecks remained with her. Deep, warm, and far too observant. Hair a shade darker than his daughter's chestnut curls peeked out from beneath the hat, and she guessed he was a couple of weeks late on his haircut.

He dug around and pulled something out. Then, with long easy strides, he went back to her car. Tall and lean hipped, he walked across the uneven ground in an easy, effortless stride. Faded jeans and gym shoes had never looked so good on a man. When he bent over to hook the strap to the car and the faded denim of his jeans cupped his ass, her mouth watered. His sleeveless, navy blue t-shirt displayed muscled shoulders and defined, hard arms.

Kylie chattered on, telling her a story about a bird and a squirrel, and Cara nodded, all the while watching the little girl's father. He double-checked everything and returned to the truck and the front view stole her breath again. He walked with a seemingly unconscious, subtle swagger. Long-limbed and loose, each step he took made her think about things she'd long been without.

A physical relationship.

Okay, that was her being polite. She meant sex. Hot, sweaty, earth-shattering sex.

He came around to his door and climbed in.

"Are we ready, Daddy?" Cara pulled her gaze from Joe's hands on the gearshift and steering wheel to consider his adorable daughter. She imagined that, if Joe let Kylie out of her car seat, she'd be out there trying to pull the car out herself.

"We're ready, pickle." When he smiled and shook his head once in amusement, Cara decided she was done for. Joe MacDonald's smile short-circuited her brain. Both her head and her very interested body were telling her that he was the one.

Him. The. One.

What was she thinking? No. She was far too practical and levelheaded to fall in love, or even lust at first sight. Even as incredibly delicious as Joe was, he had a daughter and therefore likely a wife, or ex-wife. Not that there was anything wrong with that, but even if he wasn't married, he was likely attached. He probably had to fight the women off and bolt his doors at night.

The sound of a revving engine brought her out of her inner debate. *What in the world?* He winked at her, letting her know he was putting on a show for Kylie's sake.

"Let's do it!" She looked behind her just in time to see two little fists punch the air.

Cara couldn't help it; she laughed. Kylie was too precious.

Despite the excitement in the truck's cab, Joe eased on the gas and the truck crawled forward at a snail's pace. She watched the tow strap pull tight then, with a lurch, her car made a little hop back up onto the road. Joe stopped his truck and put it into park.

"Did you get it? I knew you would!" Kylie craned her neck this way and that, trying to see beyond her car seat's high back.

"We got it, pickle. Sit tight a few more minutes while we take a look, okay?"

"Then we'll get ice cweam?" Hope radiated in bright waves from her smile.

"Yes, then we'll get ice cream." He opened his door and stepped down with one long, muscled leg. The denim stretched tight over his thighs. *Was the material a little threadbare up near—* "Cara? Let's go take a look. Okay?" He wore a shit-eating grin that said he totally knew where she'd been looking.

"Sure. I'll take a look and let you know how your daddy did, okay, Kylie?" Grateful for the distraction, she looked to the little girl.

"Okay, but I know he did good. My daddy knows how to do everything, except make pwetty bwaids. He twies to make my hair pwetty, but his hands awe too big." She said this with the confident authority that only a secure and well-loved child could. The thought of a man who would even attempt to braid his daughter's hair did strange things to Cara's belly.

She smiled at Kylie and exited the truck. Joe waited for her at the car's bumper. When she was almost there, he crooked a finger at her.

"We have a problem." He pointed to the passenger side wheel well and pulled his phone from a clip at his waist.

Dismayed, without a single thought other than fixing the problem, she turned and bent over to get a closer look. Part of the fender had crumpled and pushed in against her tire. She leaned over a little more so she could grip the metal and pulled. It didn't budge. She hadn't really expected it to, but it didn't stop her from being disappointed.

She put her hands on her knees and looked again.

"Hey, Mike. How are you? I need a favor, if you're not too busy," Joe said from behind her.

A warm breeze ruffled her skirt, but the damp material stuck to her rear.

Shit. I'm wearing a skirt! A wet and transparent skirt! She rarely wore them anymore and had put it on only to make her mother happy.

She turned around to see Joe standing behind her with another of those devastating grins and zero shame as his eyes trailed over her from the bottom up.

"I'll go check on Kylie." She couldn't remember the last time she flounced, but she was pretty sure that's what she did on the way back to the truck. *Exactly how much of my backside did I show him?*

She thought back to when she'd dressed that morning and reviewed her clothing choices. Knowing she'd see her mother, she'd chosen simple, white boy shorts and a slip. For once, she was thankful for her mother's lectures. Maybe it had served as an added layer of protection. Then again, if it hadn't been for her mother, she'd likely be wearing cutoff jeans or nursing scrubs.

A good-looking man never made her lose her composure before. Maybe it was all the stress? Postponing the last semester of school had been a hard blow, but she hadn't been given a choice, had she? Her mother needed long-term care and refused to leave her home. Betty Gregory might be difficult and stubborn on her best days, but she would always be her momma.

Better yet, she could blame everything on the storm.

She opened the truck door and leaned in. "How are you doing, little bit?"

"Fine. How much wonger?" Kylie's enthusiasm had dimmed, and it looked as though she might be getting tired. She clutched a ragged stuffed frog in one hand, and her head rested on the side of the car seat.

"I'm not sure. We have a small problem. I dented my car, and it's not drivable."

"Daddy'll fix it. He's good at fixing people's pwoblems. He's a policeman." She sounded out the word *police* with extra care.

Something thumped in the truck bed, so she looked back to see Joe had shut the toolbox. He came around to her side of the truck. "Mike's a reliable tow truck driver. He's on his way. I'm afraid if I try and tow you, we'll do more damage than good. As soon as he gets here, we can be on our way." Close, he leaned against the side of the truck, crossing his arms over his chest.

"Our way? I can't ask you to take me home. You've already done too much, and you promised Kylie ice cream. I can ride with the tow truck driver."

"Nope. Rick said you're headed to Bourbon County, right? The body shop is back the way you came. They're in opposite directions. Mike'll take your car. Pickle and I'll take you."

Irritation washed over her. He'd decided everything and expected her to follow his lead. Sure, his solution made sense, but she hated being told what to do.

"It's getting late. I don't want Kylie to miss her treat. She's been so good." The little girl had. She might be full of energy, but she listened well.

"You're going with us." He turned around and walked back to her car, as if the matter were settled. *End of story.* She watched his ass for an appreciative moment then shook off her lust-fueled daze. She reminded herself that she hated bossy men.

***

For some reason, he couldn't resist prodding Cara. Normally he wasn't quite so pushy, but something about the petite redhead made it impossible for him to behave. Red? Blond? The pretty shade seemed to be a little of both. It fell to her shoulders in a straight, carefree, cut. She was a tiny thing, with curvy hips and smallish breasts.

When she bent over to inspect the damage to her car, he'd almost swallowed his tongue. Her skirt rose until he could see where the backs of her toned thighs met the sweet curves of her ass at very bottom edge of her white panties. Judging by her embarrassed blush when she faced him, he'd bet his last dollar it had been an accidental slip.

He parked the truck as Kylie squealed in delight. "Sprinkles!"

He'd been fooled by a pretty damsel in distress once before. He couldn't call the fumble a true mistake because, in addition to the misery she'd wrought, Michelle had also given him his greatest treasure. Not a single day since she'd been born had gone by where Kylie hadn't given him a reason to smile. Even on the days where he wanted to pull his hair out in frustration or give in to the fear that he couldn't be everything Kylie needed, he was humbled by the gift of fatherhood.

The little stinker was his everything, which was why, no matter how sexy and sweet Cara Gregory appeared to be, he couldn't take a chance on anything that might put Kylie's tender heart at risk.

No matter how lonely he'd become.

He got out and opened his daughter's door. Unbuckling her seatbelt, he smiled as she threw her arms up in the air so he could lift her up. Yes, she was getting a little big for their routine, but as long as she let him, he'd carry her or hold her hand. He suspected she'd outgrow their little habits before too long.

They met Cara at the sidewalk, and he set Kylie down. "My seat!" He heard the stomp-stomp-stomp of little boots as his daughter no doubt raced to her favorite outdoor table. He knew she'd be sitting under the faded umbrella swinging her feet, not caring in the least that her shorts were wet from the rain water puddled on the benches, but his eyes were locked on Cara's.

"What's your pleasure?" Her husky voice grabbed him by the throat with a silken, but unbreakable, grip. Heated desire crept through him until all he could think about was hearing her throaty cries as he ran his tongue up her neck. "Joe?"

He blinked.

"What flavor ice cream? My treat." She tilted her head at him and grinned.

"No. I got it. This is our ritual." He tried to tamp down his libido. As much practice as he had over the years, it had become easy. But now? He'd lost his willpower.

"Nope." She echoed his earlier denial. She faced him with her hands on her hips and a sassy tilt to her head. "You've got about ten seconds to make your choice or I'm going to surprise you."

"Strawberry." He told himself his craving had nothing to do with the blush he'd seen on her cheeks after she'd nearly flashed him her backside.

Without another word, she walked away, and that damned skirt swished in her wake, taunting him.

She returned a few minutes later, loaded down with ice cream. She presented Kylie a double scoop of vanilla in a cup, and she must have requested extra sprinkles. His daughter's eyes lit up at the sight. "Thank you!"

Cara handed him a cone piled high with strawberry. She met his gaze and he forgot what he'd been going to say. She sat beside Kylie beneath the umbrella then handed her a napkin. A trail of melting ice cream dripped down the side of Cara's cone and she tilted her head to run her tongue along the seam where the ice cream met the cone. Spellbound, he watched as she turned her cone to repeat the process on the other side.

"What kind did you get, Cara?" Kylie sounded out her new friend's name with concentration on each syllable, her voice breaking through his fascination with Cara's tongue.

When Cara raised a napkin to wipe her mouth, he barely resisted offering to take care of the matter himself. With his own tongue.

"I couldn't decide, so I went with one scoop of peanut butter cup and one scoop of chocolate. How's yours?" She looked at Kylie as if she really wanted to hear the answer.

"It's almost as good as cousin Katie's homemade banilla." Kylie scrunched up her nose and tried again. "Vanilla. She has a secret recipe."

Cara nodded at his daughter. "Secret recipes are the best." How's your strawberry?" Pretty hazel eyes met his, and he realized he'd barely tasted his treat. He'd been too fixated on her delectable mouth to notice his ice cream was melting as well.

Not thinking, he dipped his head to catch a trail of pink headed straight for his hand and swiped it with his tongue. Her desire softened

19

expression sent lust rushing through him. Her lips parted, and all he could think about was how they would taste.

Cool ice cream and the sweet warmth of a beautiful woman.

He shifted in his seat as his jeans grew uncomfortable.

Her smile began soft and shy before it turned amused. "Um, you have ice cream on your chin."

Chagrinned, he grabbed a napkin to wipe it off.

"Sometimes Daddy makes messes. He doesn't mean to; he just has big hands."

He turned to his daughter, who shoveled a bite of sprinkles with a pinch of ice cream for good measure into her mouth.

Cara leaned forward and pointed. "You missed a spot." She looked down to the table, but all the napkins were gone, most of them balled up in Kylie's fist. She paused for a beat then lifted her hand to sweep her thumb below the corner of his mouth.

Low and a little husky, her voice hummed over him. "Got it."

Feet kicking in happiness, Kylie giggled. "He needs a keeper. That's what Gramma says."

He shook his head. As usual, he didn't know whether to be amused or aggravated at his daughter, the parrot.

Cara laughed, and the sound gripped him by the balls. It was a damn shame he didn't have the time or space for a woman in his life.

Chapter Two

Three weeks later

"Come on in, man. We're waiting on one more member, and then we'll get down to business." As Joe entered Trent Dawson's house, a feeling of déjà vu knocked him the gut. The last time he'd been invited to an impromptu meeting at Trent's, they'd planned the rescue mission that brought Kate home.

Trent waved him in and they headed into the makeshift command center in the heart of his open, sprawling home. Once again, furniture had been rearranged and Trent's TV moved. Pete's computer had already been connected. "How's Kylie?"

"She's good, but summer boredom is setting in. Leigh's keeping her tonight. She'll probably come home with her fingernails polished in every shade of the rainbow. I'd like to bring her up this weekend, if you and Kate don't mind." Joe surveyed the room, but he didn't see his cousin.

Trent reclined on the couch, seemingly unbothered by having his home rearranged again. "Kate will be thrilled, but she's welcome anytime. Even if we're not here, Harlan and Sandy would love to have her up at the big house."

Joe shook his head in amusement. Trent's home might not be the "big house" on the Walker Farms property, but it was far from

21

little. The large, airy home appeared rustic, but whispered wealth in an understated, masculine way. "Is Kate around?" He grabbed one of the dining room chairs, spun it around and sat, crossing his arms across the back.

"No. Stubborn woman didn't want to wait on me. Someone contacted the rescue about an abandoned mother dog and her pups. She plans to take 'em out to the shelter." Trent ran a hand through his shaggy, dark blond hair then shook his head. The last time he'd talked to his cousin, she'd despaired of Trent ever letting her out of his sight. It seemed he might have loosened his hold, but wasn't happy about it.

Joe suspected Trent would happily house all Kate's critters, both personal pets and rescues, just to keep her close at all times. He couldn't say he blamed the man for his protective urges. They may not have seen eye to eye in the beginning, but when it came to keeping those they loved safe, nothing else mattered. They would always agree on that.

"Hey, Joe. I didn't expect to see you here. You're the last person I expected Rick to bring in on this op." Pete Taylor barely looked up as he spoke, instead staring at the glowing screen of a massive laptop from his usual spot at the table.

"Man, when are you going to learn how to control that mouth of yours?" James Holloway placed a chair at the table then loomed over Pete and pinned him with a dark glare. "What did Rick tell you?" When he didn't get an answer, James rolled his eyes and walked into the kitchen without sparing him another glance.

Suspicion tickled at the base of Joe's neck. Maybe he shouldn't have blindly offered his help.

After everything they'd done to keep Kate safe, he hadn't hesitated went Rick called him in, but what kind of op did they need him for? He'd never met a more competent crew.

He could read between the lines. Kate's rescue had been about family. They hadn't needed him, but they chose to include him.

He took in the room around him, looking at it with a more discerning eye. Noah Ramsey, the quiet giant in the corner, greeted him with a single nod. James Holloway returned to his chair at the table with a bag of chips. Their postures were relaxed, but he'd seen them move like silent wraiths in the dark. The night he'd been out on Kate's recue? They'd defined lethal grace as they'd worked together with flawless precision, each move they'd made coordinated as if they'd become one being.

Rick talked low on his cell while he paced in the kitchen. Disconnecting the call, he made his way to the living room. He took a seat at the head of the table and set his phone down. "Mayhem will be here in a few minutes. Family trouble. Joe, I'm glad you could make it."

"No sweat. I'm happy to help." *Time to cut through the bullshit.* "Why did you call me in? This isn't something I need to leave my badge behind for, is it?" He hadn't thought twice when he'd done it the last time. Kate's life had been on the line. But it wasn't something he would ever do lightly. Dark Horse needed to understand he couldn't simply lay it aside at their whim.

"Possibly, and I hate to put you in this position again, but hear me out. I had two reasons for calling you. First off, and probably the most important reason, is I think this is likely connected to Kate and her trouble with Bailey. Trent and I agreed that you should be given the option of joining the op. We'll lay it all out and let you decide." Rick picked up his phone as if to use it or check messages, but set it back down as if he remembered he'd just done that. Raking a hand through his black hair, he sighed.

"If it has anything to do with Bailey, then I'm in all the way." He barely restrained himself from asking if Kate was safe. He knew Trent wouldn't have let her off the Walker's horse farm if she'd been in the slightest bit of danger.

Trent walked over to stand beside the table, arms crossed over his chest. "We figured that would be your answer, but there's more. You need to know what we'd be asking of you if you decide to join. If you don't, we totally understand, but the fact of the matter is that having you on board would save us valuable time. On the other hand, it might put you at risk."

"The second reason we called you in is that we would like your help identifying someone, possibly one of your own." Rick's tone held all the seriousness of a funeral.

"My own what?" His prior sense of unease morphed into a scraping, biting dread.

"We got word through Detective Bowie with the state police that someone from Potter County Sheriff's Department is meeting one of Bailey's lackeys tonight."

Silence filled the room with an oppressive, smothering pressure.

Fuck. A punch to the gut would have been less painful. He'd sworn to do the right thing and always uphold the law, and he knew he wasn't responsible for his fellow deputies. That didn't make the thought of one of his coworkers crossing that line any easier to bear.

"Where do I come in?" He uncrossed his arms and fisted his hands on the chair back. *Doublefuck!* He'd promised himself that he'd only walk the line between what was within his duties as a deputy and what wasn't that one time. A member of his family had been in mortal danger. Talk about being caught between a rock and a hard place. He was torn between being thankful, even honored, that they trusted him enough to include him in something so volatile and wrecked because leaving his badge behind wasn't something he could ever do lightly.

"We want you to hang back and observe. Just see if you recognize anyone or if anything at all sets off your alarm bells. Mayhem and Holloway will handle the rest. They've already been briefed. We'll set you up outside to watch the bar's front door. Just watch for anyone familiar. If you see anyone from Potter County that shouldn't be there, alert me and we'll decide what to do from there. But tonight we observe only. If you don't want in, then we understand." Rick's all too serious eyes met his. There was no expectation, nor condemnation. He'd done exactly as he'd said. He'd laid it all out in black and white, leaving the decision to Joe.

"Count me in." Those three little words held a world of weight, but what else could he do? Turn his back because someone he knew, possibly trusted, might be involved in something illegal? *Hell no.* "Whatever you need from me, I'm there."

"That's what we figured you'd say. We're happy to have you on board." He turned to Holloway. "James, you and Mayhem follow. We'll go ahead and get into position."

"Sure thing. I'll update you when we head out."

***

"I'm late! Sorry. I had a mama drama, as silly as that sounds. I'll be ready in five." Cara flew through Trent's house, barely announcing her arrival before she slammed the bathroom door behind her. She dropped her duffle on the closed toilet and stripped out of her clothes. Folding the flowered skirt and pastel blouse, she wished she could toss them into the garbage can, but that would only cause her more grief in the long run.

She'd taken her mother to what was supposed to be a dinner out with Anne, her mother's friend from church. Not wanting to listen to her mother's harping, she'd dressed in one of her few mother-approved outfits. The formfitting blouse—one size too small—pulled tight across her shoulders. The top button barely closed just above her breasts. It seemed an odd pairing when worn with a simple, seemingly church-worthy skirt, which fell to just below her knees. Then again, her mother had picked out the skirt and given it to her for her last birthday. When the light hit it just right, it became nearly see-through. She'd worn a slip and hoped her mother hadn't noticed.

Cara feared her mother wouldn't rest until she "caught herself a doctor" or, like tonight, the widowed pastor of the county's largest church. Her mother had always expected her to dress in what Cara called sex kitten meets school teacher. As a result, she'd been uncomfortable all evening.

When her mother invited her to dinner, she should have known better. Her mother and Anne had conspired, trying to set her up with the pastor with the hopes that she'd be married, barefoot, and pregnant by the year's end.

According to her mother, that was a woman's lot in life. She'd assumed, when Cara had gone to nursing school, Cara would eventually catch, marry, and set up house with a doctor.

But that hadn't ever been Cara's life plan. Before that, when she'd joined the National Guard to help pay for her degree, her mother had flipped out.

In the beginning, she might have been guilty of letting her mother believe she would marry the first man to show her a ring, just so she could have some peace. Now, home and still husbandless, her earlier omission had come back to bite her on the ass.

Amused at herself, she thought it was funny that participating in a late night op appealed to her far more than a church dinner. But she didn't care. She hadn't seen her guys in forever, and the change in pace might help her leave the gray funk she'd been living in for the past few weeks behind.

None of them were familiar with the op's location, but their goal was to get a couple of people inside to blend in. All she and James had to do was observe. Noah was going in solo, so she and James decided to go on a date for their part. She'd toyed with the idea of going full on tramp, but after she'd been on display for her mother's scheme, she couldn't make herself do it. She pulled on her favorite jeans then put on a simple short-sleeved blouse that flattered her shape. She put on a soft, chocolate colored, leather belt and matching heeled boots. Refreshing her makeup, she used a heavier hand than usual.

She packed up her things and flew out the bathroom as quick as she'd come. James waited for her at the end of the hallway, looking down at his phone. When he heard her heels click on Trent's hardwood floor, he looked up. His mouth dropped open, but nothing came out.

"That bad or that good?" She smiled and placed a hand on her hip.

"That damn hot. My god, Mayhem, you clean up pretty. You don't need all that paint, but it looks good on you all the same. We won't have any trouble tonight, that's for sure. Every man in the bar will be struck stupid by the sight of you in those jeans."

"You've seen me in jeans before."

"True. Something's different though. Good different." He cocked his head as he put his phone in his pocket and looked her over.

"Thanks. I worried I might have gone a little overboard with the boots." She would not let nerves get the best of her. No way, no how. She had a job to do. She'd be more comfortable in scrubs or behind the wheel of a MRAP, but she could do this. She might be wearing heels but this job was no less important than her others.

"Sweetheart, you killed it. I have to say, that I drew the lucky straw tonight. Let's go." He held out his hand. It felt a little odd, putting her hand in his, but they'd been friends for years. He was a good man, maybe a little wild, but still one of the best she knew. It was a shame that she'd never really felt more than a passing attraction to him.

"What do you say we go spy on some lowlifes?" He nodded his head toward the door.

"Sounds fun." She gave him her best cheeky smile and they were off.

In no time, they arrived at the Thirsty Beaver on the outskirts of town. The bar had seen better days, but the parking lot was full. The moment James turned off his truck, she heard music blaring through the door as someone walked in.

"You ready?" James had his hand on the door handle, but waited for her answer. Was she ready? Yeah, she was. She wanted to put her skills to work. She'd always been observant. She thought fast on her feet. Why not put that to use doing something good?

"I'm ready." Not waiting for him to get her, she carefully climbed out. She took his hand in hers, and they walked across the lot. He dropped her hand, put his on the small of her back and leaned in, as if to draw her close. She froze, stopping him with a hand on his shoulder.

He stopped and looked down to check on her. "What's wrong?"

She nodded her head in the direction of the door. He hadn't seen what she had, because he'd been focused on her reaction. She knew the moment he recognized the problem. "Mother. Fucker." Her blood froze when his curse confirmed what she already feared but hoped to deny.

Memories assailed her. She could feel the hot breath in her face just as she had the day it had happened. His anger, the pain, her fear, rushed through her in a tidal wave.

The door opened and loud music filled the night as Boyd Campbell walked inside the bar, oblivious to the upset he left in his wake. A cool, humid breeze blew through and snapped her out of her panic. *No way. There is no way I'm going to bail on this.*

If anything, the slimy bastard's presence only solidified her determination to be a part of this op. She wouldn't let him get the better of her.

James turned as if speaking to her, although he spoke into the mic hidden in the collar of his shirt. "We'll call it off. Rick? Did you see—?"

"No. We're not backing out. Get me MacDonald. He's my new date." She knew exactly what she had to do. There was no way Boyd would believe she and James had hooked up. They'd been more like a brother and sister in Afghanistan. Plus, Noah was already inside, in position. He'd be sitting at a table drinking beer and watching the crowd or shooting pool. Seeing two members of their unit inside the same bar was a stretch, but three? No way he'd believe it. "Rick. I can do this. Send me MacDonald. He's the only one that will work. I'm good, I swear. Have him come in and play Casanova in fifteen minutes. I'm dumping James as we speak." She pushed James in the chest and called out. "You prick!" Then she stomped off toward the bar. And thanks to her heeled boots, she had no choice but to saunter with her ass swaying all the way.

She prayed she was right. The only thing she knew was that Rick and the boys had her back. No matter what happened, they'd be there. With that unshakable knowledge, she headed in.

***

"You prick!" A husky, feminine voice came through Joe's earpiece loud and clear. He watched the front of the lot and the bar's entrance but didn't see anyone out of place. Then he saw a familiar male form throw his hands in the air and turn his back on a small woman. The man stomped off toward the parked vehicles and recognition hit him. The tall, pissed off man was James Holloway. So that meant that...

His attention snapped back to where James had been standing. The spot was empty. He scanned the lot and his attention snagged and focused on the door. A curvy little woman with sexy legs and the finest ass he'd ever seen stepped inside the rowdy bar. The door closed behind her.

He knew those legs. He'd dreamed of having them wrapped around his waist. And that hair? He'd lay odds that it smelled like sunshine and flowers. And there was no way he'd wait fifteen minutes before going in after her.

He'd known she was a friend of Rick's. The Dark Horse founder had even referred to her as a team member, but he still hadn't put it all together. He had no doubt that she was an intelligent, capable woman, but he couldn't picture her as a war-hardened soldier. The Dark Horse crew had been in some nasty situations in Afghanistan.

She was too small.

But she was a nurse, right? Maybe she stayed on base or something and waited for the trauma to come to her? What were they doing putting her in a situation like this?

Talk about a mess. If Rick's information was correct and someone from Potter County showed, then they'd likely see and recognize him. They'd question his reasons for being at a dive like the Thirsty Beaver, but that couldn't be helped. He'd think of something.

He checked the time and cursed. She expected him to wait a full fifteen minutes? No way.

"Joe." Rick's voice sounded in his earpiece.

"Yeah. I'm going in." He reached for the handle of Trent's truck. He borrowed it because his beast stuck out like a sore thumb, and anyone from the Sheriff's department would recognize it.

"Wait. She'll be fine for a few. She can handle herself. Listen. Do you remember the images of Boyd Campbell from Kate's rescue? Remember what he looks like? He's lean, rangy looking, with brown hair." Even through the connection, he heard Rick's tension.

"Yeah, I do." He'd never felt such extreme anger for another person from just their picture before. Everyone suspected Boyd had kidnapped Kate and delivered her to Senator Bailey. He'd also framed Trent for murder. When that fell apart, he planted damning evidence in a way that placed all suspicion on Bailey. After all of it, he'd vanished like a cockroach in the light.

"He and Mayhem have a history, and it's not pretty. Years ago, when she refused his advances, things got ugly. He pinned her against a wall and crushed her throat, injuring her larynx. It's why her voice sounds the way it does. Afterward, he dropped off the grid."

She is so tiny. His anger burned hotter, brighter.

He felt his blood pressure rise and a sudden urge to choke Campbell came over him. He gripped the steering wheel and squeezed, reminding himself it wouldn't be cool to put his fist through Trent's window. He took a deep breath and let it out slowly. "What's wrong with her voice?" It sounded fine to him. The first time he heard it, the low, sexy tone had gone straight to his dick.

"Nothing really, it just never went back to the way it used to be."

"Is there anything else I need to know?" His hand itched to remove the pistol he'd left behind.

"Don't go right up to her. Wait five minutes then go in, but sit at the bar and have a beer. Watch her like you're attracted to her. Think about how the scene will look before you make your move. If you rush in and storm right up to her, it'll look suspect. You don't even have to make a move, just provide an extra set of eyes. Watch your back. Noah's inside, and he'll tell us if he smells trouble." Rick sounded resigned, as if trouble were inevitable. Joe prayed that wasn't the case.

Storm right up to her? He wasn't that big of an idiot.

A little voice somewhere in the back of his head laughed hysterically.

He sat back to watch the five minutes tick by. Hell, he could do this. He'd give her six.

His fingers fisted on the steering wheel until they turned white.

***

The heavy door closed behind her, and she casually scanned the room. On her first pass, she spotted Boyd sitting alone in a dim corner booth. She kept her face composed and walked to the bar. She stopped just shy of placing her hands on the grimy surface.

The bartender, who looked like he'd had his regular Saturday bath about ten Saturdays ago, turned to her with a grunt. His eyes widened and focused on her breasts. "What can I do you for?" He smirked and placed extra emphasis on the words *do you* making her want to retch.

Slimy bastard.

She just stopped herself from rolling her eyes at his lame joke. "Light beer, bottle."

His ragged gray beard twitched, and she got the impression it hid a leer. "How about we try a Cowboy Cocksucker, on me?"

Vomit!

"No, thanks. Light beer, bottle, unopened. I'd rather take care of matters myself." She smiled sweetly.

He reached under the counter where she heard a cooler open and close. He smacked the bottle on the bar. "Four-fifty."

Smiling, she laid a five beside it. "Keep the change." She twisted the top off her beer and slapped the cap on top of her payment. Turning her back on him, she made a seemingly casual perusal of the Thirsty Beaver's crowd. She'd thought she'd felt someone's gaze on her back and, when she turned and leaned against the bar, she saw why.

At least three men openly stared at her in various states of appreciation. Maybe she had gone overboard with the boots, but she loved them and didn't get to wear them often.

She found both Noah and Campbell. Noah stood by a pool table, watching his opponent line up their shot. A crack sounded as the cue ball smacked the eight ball. The black ball spun into a corner pocket with a thud. Noah shook his head as if he didn't believe his bad luck. He pulled a few crumpled bills out of his pocket and slapped them on the table.

She hid a smile and pitied the man who thought he'd found a sucker. She'd give Noah two more games before he couldn't control himself any longer. Then he'd clean house. Still deep in his role as a novice, he brushed his russet hair out of his eyes and glared at the white cue ball, as if casting all blame on it.

Campbell remained seated in his booth on the far side of the room. When his sweeping gaze met hers, any hope of remaining anonymous went up in smoke. Though his harsh face stayed passive, his dark eyes glittered with a tempest of emotion. Cold hatred bored into her as he raked her from head to toe with his slow sneer. A sinister smirk crawled across his lips.

She refused to show any of the fear or revulsion rioting in her belly, so she focused all of her energy on controlling her expression and body language.

A tall, gangly, kid dressed in a button down shirt, tapped her on the shoulder. "Hey there, darlin'. How about a dance?" She'd be surprised if he was a day past twenty-one, but he drew her attention with his hopeful proposition.

Turning, she smiled and shook her head. "Thanks, but—"

"Oh, come on. Please? I'll behave. My buddy over there bet me that I couldn't get the prettiest girl in here to dance with me. That's you. We'll split the take, and he'll never know." He'd mixed his plea with a dash of honesty and ingenuity. "Just one dance, and I'll leave you be. I'll be a perfect gentleman."

She laughed. "Okay. One dance." She placed her hand in his outstretched one and let him lead her to the dance floor. He rested his hands lightly on her hips and held her at an elbow's distance.

"So, what's a nice boy—?"

"So, what's a nice lady like—?" They laughed when they spoke at the same time.

"You first, ma'am." He smiled and nodded his head to her as they swayed to a tune about pretty girls and rusty pickups.

"Hey, now. I'm not that old. Don't be calling me ma'am unless you want me to call you junior or sonny-boy." She let herself relax and fall into her role. She couldn't forget she had a job to do, but what better way to blend in than to dance to an old jukebox tune with the first guy who asked her? He was sweet, even if he made her feel older than dirt at thirty-two years old.

"Yes, ma— uh. Okay." He blushed from the collar of his shirt to the roots of his hair.

"What are you boys doing in a place like the Thirsty Beaver? Are you even old enough to be in here?" It went without saying that it wasn't the type of establishment to check IDs at the door. She'd be surprised if they even checked them before serving alcohol.

"I'm twenty-two, promise. My friend, Jack, he turned twenty-one last month. We actually came here to look for his sister. She's not here though. Thank God." He took her hand in his, spun her around and drew her back to him. He nodded with a wink then returned his hands to her waist.

"Well, I hope you boys find her, and I want you to be careful. Even if you're legal, this bar is a rough place." If she slipped into her slightly bossy, but caring nurse mode for a moment it couldn't be helped.

"Yes—" He snapped his mouth shut because she gave him the look.

She laughed, and he spun her around one more time. As the room whirled, she saw that Boyd had left his seat. They slowed to a stop as the song ended. Her dance partner tipped his head. "Thank you."

She swore she saw him press his lips together to keep from calling her ma'am.

"It was my pleasure." She nodded her thanks.

Then she inwardly cursed. She'd left her beer at the bar, right in the bartender's reach, and would have to buy another. Surveying half the room, she turned. Boyd was no longer in his seat. Across the crowd, she met Noah's gaze for what was supposed to be a brief moment, but something dark and furious overtook his features. In one split second, the lovable, ginger teddy-bear vanished, and a fighting mad beast took his place. He smacked his cue on the table and moved.

Dread and fear coalesced, suffocating her.

Suspicion told her what she'd find behind her, and she braced. Before she could turn, a hand gripped her wrist and spun her with a brutal jerk. Her eyes met the muddy brown gaze of Boyd's. Her heart stopped.

"Cara, fancy meeting you here. Some coincidence, huh? Fate's funny that way." He squeezed harder and pulled her close. She remembered the smell of his hot breath in her face and the crushing, suffocating pain she'd suffered.

Not again. She would not be a victim.

"Sorry, man. This dance is mine." A familiar voice, one she heard in her dreams at night, sounded from her side. Without hesitation, Joe stepped in, chest to chest with Boyd. Hot, angry tension pulsed off him, beating at her.

Boyd's nostrils flared and his chest heaved. He dropped her wrist, only to fist his hands tight by his side. The people close to them noticed, grew silent and stepped back, riveted.

This was the last thing they needed. Joe looked ready to wipe the floor with Boyd, and Noah would be right beside him. She figured either one of them could get the job done on their own, but if they both laid into him here and now, then they would all be in for one hell of a mess.

They could all kiss this op goodbye. And wasn't Joe a deputy? This had nightmare written all over it and not one of the men seemed to care as heated, heavy anger filled the air.

Damn. It was up to her to get this under control. She wrapped her arms around Joe's waist and pressed her chest to his back. Standing on tiptoe, even in her boots, it was a struggle to reach her chin to his shoulder. She spoke directly into his ear, but loud enough for everyone to hear. "Finally! Sweetheart, I thought you'd forgotten our date."

"Never. Not in a million years." He refused to step back or even move his focus away from Boyd as he spoke. "I got held up on the farm, but I'd never let you down." His easy words seemed to take on deeper meaning in the tense situation.

"How about you buy me a beer, handsome? I lost my last one." She drew on every bit of her mother's "fifty ways to catch a man lessons" and pouted. Tangling her fingers in the ends of his hair, she tugged hard enough for it to bite, demanding he turn to her. His tense body wouldn't budge, but when he turned his head, she relaxed a millimeter.

"In a minute, baby." Even knowing his words were for show, the low and maybe even a bit affectionate tone weakened her knees. She held tight, noting the rock hard stiffness of his posture remained. She didn't think a lightning strike could make him move.

She adjusted her hold in his hair and did the only thing she could think of when faced with the sexiest mouth she'd ever seen on a man. She strained through the awkward position of their bodies and took his mouth with hers.

His breath left in a rush and, when his body softened, she grasped the opportunity and turned him to face her. His mouth parted, and she dove in as if she'd been starved for him.

And her act? It wasn't much of a show. This might not be the time or place, but her hunger was all too real. She would shamelessly use it to get them out of this mess.

Joe's arm wrapped around her waist and pulled her flat against his body.

"Fucking cock tease." Joe's body turned to heated steel as Boyd spat his ugly words at her. "You'll fucking get yours." His last words trailed off as he walked away midsentence.

She jumped, wrapped her legs around Joe's waist, holding on like a monkey. She poured everything she had into another kiss, fighting against the violent rage blasting off him. His big hands cupped her ass and squeezed with enough force she wondered if she'd have bruises in the morning. A small part of her wished someone like Joe—or even Joe, if she were honest with herself—hungered for her that intensely. But, no, that near painful grip wasn't hungry possessiveness, but blind anger.

"Mother. Fucker." She heard the tightly leashed fury in Noah's voice when he arrived at their sides, but she couldn't let anything distract her. Joe was ready to explode and, as much as she'd like to watch him wipe the floor with Boyd, she couldn't allow it. Bigger things were at play, and he knew it. Or at least he would when the haze of anger cleared.

She pulled her mouth from his and put it to his ear.

***

"Joe. Not here, not now. Remember the job? I know you'd like to kill him for what he did to Kate, but you can't. You have to remember the bigger picture." Her husky voice and soft breath blew through him, a cool, cleansing balm. He tightened his grip then realized his hands were squeezing her ass, a full on, crushing, palm grab. He forced his hands to relax and slid them down to her outer thighs. God, he hoped he hadn't hurt her in his fury.

But, Kate? She thought his anger had been over what Boyd had done to Kate? When he walked in the door and saw Boyd with his hand on Cara's wrist, some internal switch tripped and he'd become a berserker, ready to tear through walls to get to her, if need be. The only thing he'd known was that Boyd had hurt Cara and looked poised to do so again. Kate, the cousin who was more like a sister to him, never crossed his mind.

"I think our plans for the night just went south. Boyd's leaving." Noah's spoke at their sides and it took a moment before Joe realized that Noah was speaking to Rick, not them. The man did it so casually that anyone watching wouldn't have a clue.

In his earpiece, Joe heard Rick's muttered curse. "Op's dead. Everyone fallback."

Op's dead.

The words slapped him back to a very screwed up reality where the only good thing was the feel of Cara's body plastered against his. Then again, the sweet heat wrapped around him was a lie. She'd been the only one to keep a clear head. Who knew what kind of mess she'd prevented?

"I'm good, you can let me go." He spoke quietly into her ear and barely resisted the urge to pat her ass.

"Are you sure? I don't want to unleash a madman on the Thirsty Beaver." She relaxed her grip on his hair, her fingers trailing over his neck. Her honey gold gaze met his. He felt as though she looked deep inside, assessing far more than his anger.

"I'm sure. I'm good." In fact, too good. If she didn't let go of him, he'd likely embarrass them both. "You can let go."

A bright, amused smile lit her face. "I did. You're the one holding me. You'll have to put me down."

Well, hell. "Just testing you." He gave up the fight and patted her ass before setting her down and releasing her.

She shook her head and laughed at him, not fooled in the slightest.

"Rick's ready to explode. We need to get back to base and chill." Noah spoke low and serious, but he wore a friendly smile. He slapped Joe on the back as if they were old friends and not at all discussing what they would all consider a failure.

They exited into the humid night. Even with moist air, so thick and heavy, it smothered, he breathed easier, freed from the bar's crowded atmosphere. Noah waved and walked toward his vehicle. Joe returned the gesture with a single wave of farewell. He stopped where the cracked sidewalk ended and the gravel parking lot began. "Cara, since you dumped your first date, I guess you're riding with me?"

"Sure. Where's your ride?"

"I drove Trent's." He nodded in the direction he'd parked. We worried that mine would be too recognizable if anyone I know from Potter County showed up." Gravel crunched under their feet as they walked through a row of old pickups.

"Smart. But Rick always is." She tucked her small hand in his so casually he almost believed their pretend hookup was real. They came to Trent's truck and he stopped cold. He recognized the battered mustang pulling into a spot one row back and four spaces over.

"Shit. We're up again, babe. I suspect the guy you were looking for just rolled in." The mustang's crooked headlights turned off and the driver's door opened. He had nowhere to go. He grabbed Cara by the waist, sat her on the hood of Trent's truck. Not missing a beat, she wrapped a leg around his waist and pulled his hips into hers. He hid his face in her neck.

She twirled her fingers lazily in the ends of his hair. "Who is it?" Her whisper, barely audible, brushed again his cheek. She smelled of peaches with the slightest hint of beer making him grow thirsty and so very hungry. He ached to explore her softness with his hands and mouth, taste her tempting body.

Adrenaline—it had to be. Why else would he get a hardon when faced with a situation so fucked up, he didn't know how to define it?

Deep down, he'd known something wasn't right in his department, but he never would have guessed this. What was he going to do? Could it be a coincidence?

"Joe? What is it?" Sweet Cara—equal parts, sugar, brains and beauty. He knew women like her existed, since he was related to two of them. He'd never thought he'd meet another. "Do we need to call in backup?" Bless her for being so observant. Like she knew his world flipped upside down.

Gathering a few of his wits, he murmured into her ear and shirt collar. "No. Someone keep eyes on the guy getting out of the black mustang, four cars down. I can't let him see me." The seductive scent of woman and sin teased him. He trusted his team, pushed his shock aside and focused on the haven Cara's body offered. The silken skin beneath his cheek and the anchor of her leg around his waist spun a captivating web. For just a few moments, he'd allow himself the escape.

Her hands moved from his neck to his back, rubbing up and down in a gesture that was likely meant to comfort, not arouse. He willed his dick to obey. It bucked against his jeans to get at what it wanted.

Cara.

He didn't blame his body for responding, but it wasn't the time or place. His life was too busy and he couldn't indulge himself, no matter how much he wished differently.

She shifted a fraction, inadvertently increasing their physical contact, and whispered against the hollow of his throat. "The door is open, but no one's gotten out yet."

Holloway's voice spoke through his earpiece. "I can see the driver from my location. His face is in shadow, but I can see the dim light of something in his hand. My guess is he's checking text messages. He's putting his phone away."

"Mayhem, MacDonald, hold your position," Rick ordered.

"There's movement. I think he's getting out." Holloway reported and time slowed to crawl.

With a screeching creek, a car door shut nearby.

Virtually blind with his head tucked into Cara, Joe listened intently to Rick's updates. "He's headed your way. Hunker down, MacDonald."

Heavy footsteps in gravel neared, growing louder with each slow step until they passed. A cellphone chimed with an incoming message, and the footsteps stopped.

"He stopped about ten feet away and pulled his phone out. He's facing your direction, but looking down," Holloway said.

"So, Jack. I think I'm taking you home with me tonight. I've been lonely, and my husband's on the road for days at a time." Cara spoke, low, but loud enough that anyone nearby would hear. "You wicked man, if you want to do that; you'll have to buy me dinner first." Her husky, sexy as sin, laugh gripped him by the balls.

What was wrong with him?

She wrapped both legs around him, squeezed his hips and arched her back, all but throwing herself against the truck's hood and pulling him with her. His cock brushed against the junction of her thighs, and he saw stars.

"Mmmmmm. Yes." She purred against his neck and paused. "Are you really going to make me wait until we get home? Damn tease. One more kiss for the road?"

"He put his phone in his pocket." Holloway updated them as Joe heard footsteps on the move again. A car door shut nearby followed by the cough and roar of an engine coming to life. "He's leaving. Looks like our boy got stood up. Hang tight for just a few more moments."

Headlights swept across them as a car backed out and turned. He held his breath. Cara's body tensed beneath his. He shielded her as best he could, despite knowing he was the one who needed to stay hidden.

Holloway spoke again. "You're good. He's gone. I'll keep watch until you're out."

"Load up and get your asses back to base," Rick's tense voice commanded.

Joe lifted Cara and carried her to the passenger side. He told himself that it was for time's sake and hoped she wouldn't feel the trembling of his hands. He knew better.

He sat her inside, where she stopped him with a tender hand on his cheek. "Who was it?"

"Jimmy Hawkins. He's the Potter County Sheriff's cousin."

***

Cara walked into Trent's house, thankful she'd had time in the dark of the truck to get her hormones under control. She waved at her team and went to Trent's kitchen for water, giving herself a moment to get over her residual lust and nerves. Good lord, she'd never acted that way around a man in her life. To be fair, she'd been given a hell of a shock. One moment she'd been happy and laughing with the kid she'd danced with. Then Boyd showed his nasty hand, and she'd panicked. No, she hadn't run, but the terror had been stark and alive in her heart. She'd frozen and been useless to the guys, and she hated that more than anything else. She'd even had a moment to realize that they needed her to keep her cool and she'd blown it.

When she'd heard Joe's voice, she wanted to collapse, her relief was so bright. Then again, she'd been slammed with fear when the men had gone chest to chest in a full-on primal confrontation. The single thought in her head had been to stop Joe from killing Boyd, and she'd done the only thing she could think of.

She'd climbed him like a tree and plastered herself against him. She'd gone total hussy. Even her mother would have been appalled. She could hear her mother now. "Darlin' girl, you need to play hard to get, just a little. Make him work for you so when he finally gets you, he thinks he won the grand prize. Then, he'll move Heaven and Earth to keep you."

But, nope. She'd thrown herself at him, embarrassed herself and likely him as well. Who knew what her team thought of her now.

Time to face the music.

She went to the living room and found a seat next to Noah on the couch. Without hesitation, he wrapped his beefy arm around her shoulders and tugged her close in a rough, but affectionate hug. "Smart thinking, sweetheart. You did good. You okay?"

"That's what I want to know." Rick interrupted from his seat at the table they'd moved into the room. "We'll start at the top with the most important business and work our way down. No bullshit, how are you?"

God, I love them. She pulled her hair back then remembered she didn't have a scrunchie and let it go. She'd worn a totally different type of uniform tonight. Was that why they treated her differently now?

"I'm fine. I admit I had a bit of a shock and when Boyd grabbed me, and I was scared for a moment. To be honest, he terrified me, but it was knee-jerk. I'm good." She looked around at her team, assessing their moods and saw nothing but concern for her. There was not one hint of disgust, anger, or even disappointment that she hadn't done her job. She met Rick's steely gaze. "I promise."

"You kicked ass, Mayhem." Holloway, sitting at the table with Rick, nodded his head to her. "I didn't have eyes inside, but I can only imagine how charged the situation became. I wish I could have seen you diffuse all that anger without bloodshed."

"Uh, well. Literally throwing myself at Joe wasn't exactly textbook, but it was the only thing I could think of. Luckily it worked."

"It had nothing to do with luck. It was skill." Joe's quiet words entered the conversation. He sat at table's end, leaned back in his chair, as if he didn't have a care in the world. His eyes, on the other hand, glittered with a mix of emotions. "Will you be safe at home? What are the chances he'll let this insult go? Or will he come after you?"

"Mayhem, you're welcome to stay here. We have plenty of room. Kate would want you to stay." Trent's storm gray gaze met hers. "It might be the safest option." Trent wasn't boasting. The Walker's horse farm was a topnotch facility. His horses were cared for, like the most precious of treasures. After Kate's trouble, Trent had increased his already tight security measures.

"No, thank you. I'll be fine. I can take care of myself, and I've got Momma to take care of. We'll be fine." She loved her mother, but wouldn't dream of making anyone else put up with her theatrics.

Trent didn't reply, other than to frown as if he wasn't happy with her decision.

Rick spoke and everyone turned at the sound of command in his voice. "Cara, I agree that staying here at Trent's would be safest, but we can't force you. That being said." He pinned her in place with his will. "If at any point, you get the slightest feeling that you're being watched, I want you to pack your bags and get both yours and your mother's asses out here. No argument."

"Okay." She hoped it didn't come to that but, if it did, she wouldn't have any choice.

"Good, now that family is taken care of, onto business. MacDonald, Pete can probably pull up info from the license plate on that Mustang, but I want to hear it from you. Who are we dealing with?" Rick's thumb tapped a steady rhythm on the table, as if he were thinking.

Joe took a deep breath and straightened in his chair, sitting upright. He put his forearms on the table and looked around at the team. "I never saw him, but I'm guessing the driver was Jimmy Hawkins. Dale Hawkins' cousin."

"Why does that sound familiar?" Rick frowned as he thought.

"You probably saw campaign signs for Dale Hawkins the last time you drove through Potter County. He's up for re-election this fall for Sheriff. Years ago, Jimmy got into a little trouble as a juvenile and Dale took him in, supposedly to straighten him out. This makes me wonder if he had another motive. They've been close since then."

"Fuck a duck. I don't envy you, man." Pete stared, slack-jawed from his seat, parked behind his ever-present laptop. Then he shook his head and returned to typing. "I'm running a search on the car's license plate now. We'll have an answer in just a wee moment."

"Mustangs are a dime a dozen. Maybe it's not your guy." James pointed out what they were likely all thinking. What made Joe think that a common car outside a bar, one county over from his own, could be the same one he knew? Cara didn't doubt Joe, his instant alertness and frustration had been obvious.

"I recognized the junk heap as it turned to park. He'll tell you he's restoring it, but the only thing he's done is replace the driver side door. The paint doesn't match. It was Jimmy." Joe ran a hand through his hair and shook his head. "I hope I'm wrong, but I'm not. The car will come back as his. He would die before loaning it to someone else."

Noah returned to his seat beside her and opened a bag of chips. He pulled one out and offered the bag to her. "A better question is, what was he doing in Bourbon County, at a dive like the Thirsty Beaver? Did you see anyone else connected to Potter County?"

"No, I wish I had."

"What a mess. Too bad we can't chalk it up to coincidence. His Potter County connection paired with the fact the message he received could have been from Boyd canceling their meeting looks awfully damning," said James.

"Food's here. Keep talking. I'll be right back." Trent stuck his phone in his pocket and all but ran out the door.

"Bingo!" Pete called out as if he'd actually won a game. "Joe, my man, it looks like you're tonight's winner. The Potter County plate number James got off your Mustang is registered to one James A. Hawkins."

She looked to the group. "Now that we have confirmation of what we already suspected, what's next?" She handed the bag of chips back to Noah.

The front door opened and Kate MacDonald, carrying a white carryout bag, held it wide open for Trent. He carried in a stack of pizza boxes and the house filled with the mouthwatering smell of Pop's pizza. The couple set out the food, plates, and napkins together. They spent as much time touching as they did working. Light, casual touches, so comfortable in each other's presence that it was second nature to reach out to one another.

Cara was envious even as she was happy for them, Trent especially. She'd only met Kate briefly a few times, but she genuinely liked the other woman. And Trent deserved only the best. Love and happiness couldn't have landed on a more deserving man.

"Kate, love, I would've have ordered. You didn't have to." Rick rose and walked to kiss her lightly on the cheek.

She smiled brightly and gave him a friendly side hug. "I know. That's why I told Trent not to tell you. You take care of everyone. It's not a big deal." She lowered her voice. "No luck finding Mary?"

"None. She's a canny little brat." He sounded equal parts sad for and proud of the child he'd been trying to find for over a month.

"With both you and Leigh on the hunt, she doesn't have a chance. You'll have her safe and in a loving home in no time." Kate hugged him.

"She should be getting ready to go back to school. Not hiding out like some fugitive." He sounded so heartbroken that Cara barely squashed the urge to go give him a hug of her own. Sorrow and worry ravaged his features as he touched his forehead to Kate's temple.

Trent stood nearby, holding a slice of pizza, seemingly not bothered by their affection. "You'll figure out a plan. You know I'm on board. I don't want any of your bullshit 'asking for a favor' crap. You tell me where and when. I'm there. You get me? We'll track her, find her and do it without scaring her." Cara hadn't moved home yet when trouble found Kate, but from what little pieces she'd heard, both she and Trent had been through hell and only come out stronger and infinitely closer on the other side. Rick had seen them through it all.

She couldn't be happier for them.

Rick only allowed himself a brief moment to absorb Kate's care then looked to Trent. "I get you. That's the problem. I don't have a plan for this kind of situation. Who the fuck does? And she's not even mine."

"Mary is yours now. The law might say she's a runaway, but at heart, she's yours. That girl has no idea how lucky she is. You'll find her. I know it." Kate kissed Rick's cheek and he pulled away. Cara didn't miss that he left the kitchen without getting food for himself.

When Rick sat in front of his laptop, Pete left his and practically ran to the kitchen. "Food! Thanks, pretty Kate."

Trent scrunched his brow at Pete's use of his pet name for Kate then sighed as if giving up the fight.

"You're welcome. I know you guys started late this afternoon planning, stayed busy and likely didn't have time to grab a bite. It's not fancy, but it's—"

"Perfect. Thank you." Noah joined them and gave her an easy hug, kissed the top of her head and grabbed a plate from the stack on the counter. "So, where do we go for now? Situation smells worse than Pete's socks after PT but we don't have a lick of proof. I don't like it."

"Neither do I. As much as I wished differently, there's a damn good chance that Jimmy and Dale Hawkins are connected to Campbell. That's a can of worms I'm not looking forward to opening, but we don't have any choice. Anything connected to Campbell is highly suspect. I'll report what happened and what little we found to Bowie and update you all." Elbows on the table, Rick rubbed his face with his palms.

"I don't wanna be the bad guy, but I have a really bad feeling about this mess." Pete said what they were all likely thinking as he piled a mountain of pizza on his plate.

Chapter Three

"I'm hurting too badly today, baby girl. I don't think I can do it. I'll try again tomorrow." Her mother's grimace looked suspiciously more like a pout as she lay in bed watching her morning talk show.

"Momma, I'm sure it hurts you a great deal, but I promise if you follow the physical therapy orders, you'd have an easier time getting around. The exercises are meant to help you get stronger, not hurt you. No one wants you to be in pain." Cara repeated the exact same words she'd used twice already this week. And it was only Wednesday. "Everyone wants you to get better."

Stubbornness set in on her mother's features, hardening the pout. "Who expects a woman to walk so much after breaking a hip? Really. It's...archaic. I bet you don't see those doctors up and walking around after surgery. They're allowed to rest."

Where in the world did her mother get this crap? She felt as though she was trying to reason with a two-year-old rather than a fully-grown adult. When her mother set her up on the surprise date, she'd had little trouble getting around. Three days later, she acted as if she'd just come out of surgery.

"No, Momma, it's not archaic. It's proven medical science. Why would you think doctors get special treatment? After surgery, they're expected to follow the same guidelines as everyone else. Yes, it might hurt you some now, but it's worth it." Cara picked up her mother's shoes and put them under the bed, so she wouldn't trip over them if she ever got her up. It was funny how she could get up and make it to the bathroom and fix her hair and makeup without much trouble, but the moment Cara expected her to walk a little for recommended exercise, she turned into the worst patient ever.

"Hmpf." Her mother crossed her arms over her chest.

"Momma, you gave birth to me." She took a deep breath, hoped for an ounce more patience and continued. "I'm truly sorry it hurts, but I think you can tolerate the pain for a few minutes of exercise. You're a very strong woman and I believe in you. I mean, without pain meds, you squeezed a six-and-a-half-pound baby out of your—"

"Cara May! Don't you be vulgar in this house. I raised you to be a lady. I swear, I don't know where I went wrong. It had to have been all those filthy-mouthed soldiers you spent so much time with. Bad influences not fit for a lady's company. To this day, I don't understand why you left home for the Army. A woman's place is at home."

"Mother—" Her blood began to boil at her mother's hateful words.

"No, Cara May. Just because you got a piece of paper that says you're a nurse, doesn't mean you have the right to boss your own mother around." Her mother pinched her lips together in an ugly frown that Cara knew well. The look signaled the beginning of the silent treatment. It was just as well, as she'd never make headway in their fight, no matter how badly she wished differently.

But her mother carelessly threw out one insult she could not let go. "Mother, those filthy-mouthed soldiers are my friends. They're some of the best people I have ever met and I consider myself lucky to have served beside them. I postponed a program that means so much to me to come home and help you. Are you even aware of how badly you just insulted me and my friends? I'm ashamed of you." Not bothering to see if her words made an impact of any sort, she turned and shut the door carefully behind her. She would have rather slammed it hard enough to bust the frame.

She had more control than that, though. Barely, but still.

She'd walked out onto the porch to get her anger under control when her cell rang. She looked at the display and saw an unfamiliar local number. Grateful for the distraction she answered on the second ring. "Hello?"

"Hi, Cara? This is Leigh Ann MacDonald, Kate's cousin." A friendly, feminine voice greeted her.

"Um. Hi." She sat on the porch swing and wondered what she was supposed to say.

"Listen, I hated to call you out of the blue like this, but I'm out of options and Rick said you might have an hour or two to spare today. I need a favor, if you're able." The faintest trace of desperation in her voice bled through the phone.

Cara pushed back on the swing absently. She knew Rick wouldn't have volunteered her for something frivolous. "How can I help? I can leave for a few hours." Even though she might be upset with her, she wouldn't leave her mother for longer than that.

"This sounds odd, but I've got to make a delivery and I need an escort."

"Sure." An escort for Kate's cousin? It had to be better than arguing with her mother. "When and where do you want to meet?"

Leigh Ann gave her directions to the office where she worked. They'd meet and go together from there. *Wherever there was.* "And come armed. Rick said you could and that you know what you're doing. The menfolk think the little lady needs protection." Leigh's tone sounded like equal parts disgust and amusement before they disconnected.

Cara stared at her silent phone in bafflement.

Two minutes later, as she pulled out a looser shirt to conceal her gun if need be, her cell chimed with a text. *Leigh Ann is Joe's sister and Kate's cousin. You'll like her. Long story and she'll explain, but she's going into a situation that is most likely safe, but has a small chance that it might not be. We never allow her to go alone.*

Just do what you're good at and keep your eyes and ears open. And thanks. I owe you. This one is personal.

She changed and grabbed her Beretta and went to her mother's room. "I'm leaving and may be gone for a couple of hours. I'll have my phone on me, so call if you need anything. I love you."

Her mother made a face without looking away from her TV, but she replied. "Of course. It's not like I don't feel like getting out of bed. I could need any matter of things while you're out running around town."

She bit back an angry retort. "You can walk, even unassisted. The more you do, the better you'll feel. I'm not repeating this argument again. I'm headed out to do a favor for a friend." Not knowing what else she could say or do, she turned her back on her mother and left, hating that she felt guilty when she knew she had no reason to.

***

A startlingly beautiful, willowy brunette with emerald green eyes greeted her outside a bland office building in the heart of Riley Creek. She leaned against a newer sedan wearing a friendly smile. Despite her beauty, the smile seemed forced—like it was out of a sense of obligation and not true happiness. "Nice to meet you. I'm Leigh. I really appreciate you helping me at the last minute. If it weren't for Joe or Rick, I'd go by myself, but it's just not worth the very slight risk or their He-Man anger. It'll be a quick drop-off today. I won't keep you long."

Again Cara couldn't help but wonder what Rick had gotten her into. She smiled in return, not knowing what else to do. "Hi. What exactly are we doing? I don't mind, but I'd like to know what kind of situation we're walking into." Cara opened the passenger door when the other woman gestured for her to get inside.

"A sad one." Leigh's shoulders slumped, but she started the car and they headed out. "Earlier this summer, Rick and I stumbled across a runaway. Well, she's not really a runaway, because she lives at her home, but we can't seem to find or catch her there. Mary's father is in jail and will likely be headed to prison soon. Among other things, he was arrested for the manufacture, sale and trafficking of crystal meth. Now he's behind bars, where he rightfully belongs. His daughter, who we estimate to be about thirteen or fourteen, lives there alone. Rick and I alternate dropping off food and water for her. Someone is using the supplies we leave and has even left small gifts for us in thanks, but no matter what time we show, she's not there. We've never once encountered any trouble, but Joe is a bit overprotective and Rick is just as hardheaded."

Cara could only imagine. Protectiveness was part of Rick's DNA and, though she had only met Joe twice, she couldn't believe he would be any less so. She hadn't expected that things could be so bad she'd need a weapon, but after everything Rick and Trent had done for her in Afghanistan, she'd always be in their debt. They didn't see it that way, but she always would.

"No one knows who she is? You haven't seen her at all?" She didn't doubt Leigh's story, but it all seemed too impossible. How did a child of any age fall so far through the cracks?

"No one knows who she is. I've contacted the schools and no one from that address is attending school or listed as truant. Joe has looked through missing persons reports until his eyes crossed. Her father had horses at their place, likely so the manure would mask the chemical smell of cooking meth. When he was arrested, the last living horse went to Kate and her rescue. The girl showed up at Kate's one night looking for the horse. Rick, Joe and I are the only ones who saw her that night." Leigh wiped the corner of one eye as she drove.

"I can't imagine." Cara and her mother didn't always get along, but she'd had a decent home and everything she'd ever needed. She'd had friends and love. She'd had food and security. An aching pit opened inside her chest. "You're certain that she's living there and not just trespassing?" Cara suspected she knew what Leigh would say, but hoped she was wrong. Rick didn't make mistakes and Leigh seemed competent.

"The only things we found on our first visit were a few drawings in a ratty old notebook and a pitiful pallet on the bare floor. I don't think she has anywhere else to go. We figure she spends as much time in the wooded hollow behind the house as she does indoors." Leigh's voice was somber as she slowed the car and pulled off onto a weed-choked, gravel driveway.

The ache beneath Cara's heart grew as a small, pitiful house, little more than a shack, came into view.

"Damn him." Leigh shook her head as she shifted into park.

"What's wrong? And which him are you damning?" Cara got out and looked around.

"Most likely Rick, but it's possible I can lay this one on my brother. Someone's been out here and cut the grass. Rick has been slowly fixing things up. He's paid to have the electric and water turned on so I wouldn't put it past him to pay a lawn service to some out. But…" Leigh's speculation trailed off as she opened the trunk of her car and pulled out a couple of grocery bags.

"The more people you have coming by, the more you increase the chances she'll run and not come back." More out of habit, than necessity Cara snapped off her holster's thumb-break as they walked up the driveway.

"Yeah, and Rick would think the same way so that leaves my brother, the manicured lawn freak. By the way, this is the part where you're supposed to do your soldier thing and look for bad guys. We never find any, but you never know." Leigh shrugged her shoulders at the house's corner.

"Very true, and I already am. That soldier thing is not something we ever turn off. Once you learn it, if you live through the nightmare, the instinct becomes a part of you." Cara took in the details around them, paying extra attention to the windows of the house and shadows at the edge of the woods. "Do you usually go in the back door?"

"Yes. I think a stiff breeze might blow the front porch down. I guess you're supposed to go in first?" Leigh asked wryly and pointed to the back door. "They usually take out their gun and wave it around all macho-like."

"Yes, ma'am. I don't know about the macho part, but I think I can handle the rest." Cara looked at the peeling finish on the old wood and wondered how long ago it had been painted. When was the last time anyone had shown the house a little love? And the girl who likely lived inside it? She removed her handgun and held it down by her side, but ready.

She opened the door slowly, having no idea what might lay beyond, but all kinds of certain that it wouldn't be good.

"Mary?" Leigh called over Cara's shoulder. "It's me, Leigh, and I've brought a friend with me. Her name is Cara. She's taking Rick's place as my protector today." Silence and surprisingly cool air greeted them.

Cara looked around the barren house and her heart broke. Little more than exposed framework remained inside. In one corner sat a half-empty case of water and a couple of boxes of pre-packaged snacks.

Leigh carried the bags of groceries over and set them down beside the water. "I brought her some sports drinks, fruit and cookies this time. I try to change things up, but it's tricky finding things that don't require refrigeration and are even remotely healthy. And I can't help but include a treat each time."

Cara watched, speechless. She'd believed Leigh's story and seen Rick's heartache, but the situation smacked her in the face with a wretched sense of reality. Mary's existence wasn't a story and it wasn't Rick's heartache. Mary, the child, lived the reality.

She put her weapon away, looked up and fought back tears.

"Well, that answers one question at least. Joe must have been out here and not told me. She left him a gift as well. Here's mine." Leigh handed her a jaw-dropping sketch of a beautiful butterfly sitting atop a daisy. "No matter how many she's given me, they take my breath away."

"She drew this? It's gorgeous." The fine pencil lines and shadows making up the detailed wings stunned Cara.

"We believe so. She usually leaves something pretty for me . and something masculine for Rick, usually horses. Here's his newest gift. I'll leave it for him to pickup but I can't resist looking at them." Leigh handed her a sketch of a herd of running horses with a muscular stallion at the lead. "She calls me *lady* and Rick *Mister.* I wonder what she left for Joe or, as she calls him, *cop*?"

Cara looked down to watch Leigh lift up a sheet of paper that did indeed have the word *cop* written on it. "What in the world…oh no." Leigh's voice shook with despair.

"What is it?" She took the paper from Leigh's hand and braced herself.

Leigh's words tumbled out in a rapid tumble. "The little brat's trying to be an informant. I wish she were here so I could bust her ass into next week. I mean, I've never spanked a child in my life, and she's probably too old, and I don't even approve of spanking, but.... My god. What am I going to do? Maybe it's not real? Tell me it's not real."

Cara looked at the drawing, her heart in her throat. "We need to call Joe right away. Are you making the call or am I?"

"I..."

"I'll call. Are you finished for today?" Leigh appeared shaken, and Cara understood why, but this was a time for action. That, Cara could handle, no matter how badly her heart bled.

"Yeah. I just wanted to drop this off and see if she'd been here. You're holding the proof." Leigh nodded to the paper in Cara's hand.

"Okay. Let's go. You drive. I'll call Joe and then Rick. He'll want to be in on this as well." Cara took charge in her way. Completely, but with kindness. She hoped giving Leigh something else to focus on, even as simple as driving, would settle her nerves.

***

Relieved to be finished with court for the day, Joe stepped out into the sunlight. Although it might be a necessary evil that came with a job that he loved, he despised being trapped indoors, especially when it was due to someone else's stupidity. Starved, he started across the street, toward the diner, when his phone rang.

The caller ID read *Sis*. "Hey, brat. Everything okay?"

"Joe?" Though familiar, the voice sounded nothing like his sweet, but pain in the ass, sister. He recognized the caller by the way his body reacted to her sultry voice. Damn, he had it bad. She hadn't even identified herself yet. But why was she calling from Leigh's phone? Worry put the brakes on his lust.

"Cara? What's wrong? Leigh?" He stopped at the diner's door and readied to go back the way he came.

"She's fine. We're leaving Mary's house now. Have you been out here recently?" Cara sounded calm, all business. His tension eased, but his confusion remained.

Why does it matter if I've been out there?

"Yes. About a week ago I brought the tractor and mower out. I couldn't stand the thought of any kid with yard full of waist high grass. I didn't stay long. What's going on?" His appetite and patience long gone, he headed for the courthouse's parking lot. "Where are you two exactly?"

The sudden urge to do something filled him, only he didn't know what to do. Where was he supposed to direct his energy?

"We're almost back to Leigh's office now. I promise, we're fine. It was just easier to use Leigh's phone. I don't have your number." He'd change that quick. The thought of her needing help and not knowing how to get in contact chilled him. "Listen, have you seen the gifts, the drawings Mary leaves for Leigh and Rick?"

"Yes." She'd called him about drawings? Did they need to have Mary's house checked for carbon monoxide? "Probably not all of them, but a few. Why?"

"It looks like she left a drawing for you, but it's not a nice picture. She drew you a picture of a crime. Maybe. You need to see it. When are you free?"

"With a little time, I can free up my evening. Kylie is with Mom today. I'll have my parents keep her for the night. How about you and Leigh meet me at my place around five this evening?"

"Okay. I'll tell Leigh. See you then." She disconnected and the silence made him ache. He assured himself that the empty feeling in his gut came from his worry over Mary and her trouble. It had nothing to do with missing Cara.

***

After a few phone calls and a rushed shower, Joe answered his doorbell to find Cara waiting on his front porch. She raised her hand in a little wave and her smiled sucker punched him. Those bright eyes and jean-clad legs would be the death of him.

"Hey, come on in. The place looks like a bachelor pad meets a daycare. Just kick the mess aside and make yourself comfortable." He gestured for her to come inside. "Thanks for going with Leigh." When Rick said he'd handle it and make sure his sister was safe, Joe had thought he'd meant Rick would go or another Dark Horse member would escort her. Cara had never crossed his mind.

"I didn't mind. It was good to get out of the house for a little bit. Momma and I are getting on each other's last nerve. And your house is fine. Did Kylie stay with your parents?" Her voice rang with what sounded like genuine interest.

He picked his daughter's stuffed frog and snake up off the couch. "Yeah. They're always happy to keep her. Hell, I think they'd take her from me if I let them."

"But you wouldn't." There seemed to be a smile in her voice as she looked at their wall of memories. It had been Leigh's idea to cover the bare living room wall in framed photos. She assured him that if he put enough pictures on there, he wouldn't have to worry about making everything match. She'd been right. He and Kylie hadn't done too badly on the weekend project, if he did say so himself.

He tossed the animals in a toy box in the corner and walked over. Unable to resist, he laid a hand on the smooth skin of her bared shoulder. He just stopped himself from running his thumb under the strap of her tank top. "I can't say I haven't been tempted when faced with a tantrum but, no. She's my world. Thank you for going with Leigh. I didn't know Rick had you in mind, but I appreciate it all the same."

She turned to face him. "Does it bother you that he sent a woman to watch over your sister? I know you two are close." Her hazel gaze met his without judgment, only honest curiosity.

"I'll always worry about Leigh. She's my baby sister." When the urge to place his other hand on her opposite shoulder hit him, he forced himself to not only deny it, but release the first one.

"Nice evasion." She smiled crookedly and shook her head.

"What does that mean?" He didn't know what to make of her comment. Usually when his sister gave him the *it's a good thing you're cute, because you're a dumb man* look it amused him. When Cara gave him the same, he felt like he'd missed something important.

The front door opened and they turned to see Leigh walk in.

"Yay! It's about damn time. I'll have to knock from now on, won't I? Sorry I'm late." His sister wore a big smile as she breezed in and dropped her tote on his couch. She appeared to be anything but apologetic when she stopped and put her hands on her hips. "I won't stay long." Her grin only grew bigger.

Oh shit.

She thought he and Cara were a thing. He'd have to set her straight at the first opportunity. He gave her his best glare, which she ignored.

"Let's get to work so I can get out of here. I'm sure you two have better things to do." Leigh clapped her hands together once and sat. She pulled out a folder and laid it on the coffee table. Then all her excitement faded when she looked to Cara. "Did you tell Rick?"

"I did. He'll be back in town the moment he's free. And I suspect he'll move Heaven and Earth to make that happen yesterday. I told him we'd show Joe first, but we would keep him updated." Cara moved to the end of the couch and stood with her arms crossed under her breasts.

"What exactly did you two find? Was there anything other than the drawing to make you think she saw a crime?" He sat beside

Leigh and slid the folder close. Dread coiled in his belly. He knew his sister wasn't prone to theatrics and though he hadn't known Cara long, he didn't believe she would be either. But it was a child's drawing. How bad could it be?

Leigh pointed to the folder. "This is our only proof, but it's pretty convincing. You've seen the drawings she's left for us. She always lays a plain sheet of paper on top with a name written on it. Our usual gifts were waiting just like normal but lying on the floor beside them was a third. I'm no art expert but it looks like the same style and artist."

He picked up the seemingly innocent folder and opened it. Inside was the blank coversheet with the word *cop* written on it. "I had my badge on my hip the night of the fire at Kate's."

"Yeah. And I think Rick threatened to turn her over to you when she was fighting to get away from him. You were also at her place in uniform the day your department served the search warrant and found the lab."

Dreading what he'd find, he flipped to the next sheet. His blood turned to ice. He closed his eyes, hoping that when he reopened them he'd see something different.

"It's the old limestone quarry, isn't it?" Cara's voice was soft, gentle even, beside him. She must have moved closer when he wasn't looking.

"It is." He forced his eyes open. "I'd have to look at a map to be certain, but I think if you set out from Mary's backdoor and head deep into the hollow for a couple of miles you'd come up on the backside of it. "That fits the viewpoint this was sketched from."

Above the quarry, at a cliff's edge, a man faced the drop-off on his knees. His hands were tied behind his back, and Jimmy Hawkins pointed a gun at the back of his head. Dale watched from a mere few feet away.

"I'm sorry, Joe. I hated to share this with you, but…" Leigh's quiet words trailed off.

Grief and blistering anger choked his voice. "You did the right thing. I've had a bad feeling about the department for a while now and this only cements what we suspected the other night at the Thirsty Beaver." It killed something inside him to confirm that he'd been working for someone dirty for so long. How long had this been right under his nose? He'd been clueless.

"Will this be any good as evidence?" Doubt laced Cara's words as if her question was one born of futile hope and not curiosity. "What do we do with it?"

"*We* don't do anything with it. I want you two and Mary as far away from this mess as humanly possible. I'll take it to Bowie and show him. He already has his own suspicions. As far as evidence goes, it won't do much good. It's a drawing, not a photograph and even if the artist is willing to testify, she's a child whose father was arrested and taken away by the Potter County Sheriff's Department. To think that she could have been close to a possible murder…it makes me sick."

"Do you think they killed him? It would help if we could see his face, but the perspective is all wrong." Leigh leaned forward, placing her elbow on her knee and her chin in her palm. "Crazy girl. I'd ground her for the next ten years if she were mine." Worry and longing filled his sister's voice.

Making an easy decision he pulled out his cell and took a picture of the drawing. Joe had done his part and played by the rules. He would have given his life for his job. What had it gotten him? Nothing.

To think that these two assholes could be even remotely connected to the bastard who'd kidnapped his cousin enraged him.

He sent the photo to Rick, who likely waited to see what Cara and Leigh found. He'd dedicated his life to upholding the law, but what good were rules when the men who governed the laws pissed all over them?

He would put his trust in those who'd gone to wall for his family. *And speaking of my family...* He looked to his sister. "Leigh."

"Uh oh." Yeah, if anyone could read the meaning in his tone, his sister would.

"Be on your toes. As of right now, they don't have any reason to pay attention to you. Keep it that way, or I'll have you under lock and key in no time. No snooping and, for heaven's sake, do not go out to Mary's place alone. Promise me." He met her gaze with his.

"I promise. I can't stand the thought of her out there in danger. If they had seen her, she would have met the same fate, wouldn't she?" The glimmer of tears shone in her eyes.

"As much as it kills me to say it, yeah. Her body would be at the bottom of the quarry pond. There's no way Dale would let a witness walk away, no matter how innocent. He has too much to lose. I wish we knew exactly what he's up to."

His phone signaled a new message from Rick. It read a single word. *Fuck.* It echoed his exact thoughts.

"I need to go. It's getting late. Keep me updated, and I promise to behave. You have too much to worry about and I won't add to that." Leigh hugged him and then rose to leave. "Give pickle a kiss for me." He watched her go and trusted her words as the door shut behind her.

"Any idea where we go with this? I know you'd prefer to go through the proper channels, but I'm not sure we can go the legal route." Cara moved from where she leaned on the arm of the couch to sit beside him. She leaned over and looked at the photo. The barest trace of her scent tempted him.

"After the week I've had? I only have one option. There's no one I can trust except family. That's Dark Horse. They may not be related by DNA, but there's no one else I can depend on. It's too important. Too deadly." He closed the folder and leaned back.

"DNA doesn't have a damn thing to do with it." She continued, "You are a part of Rick's family now. He always goes to the wall and, if need be, further for those he's claimed. Bound by blood or not, the MacDonald clan became part of Dark Horse before Rick even knew he was going into business."

"I can't think of anyone else I'd want at my back in something this dangerous." He met her serious gaze.

"We'll help anyway we can, and I know Rick will back my words in a heartbeat. You know Trent will, too." Loyalty and quiet, absolute faith laced her words. It, and a seductive whiff of her fragrance, tempted him with things he couldn't have.

He stood and walked to the window. Where did they go from here? He remembered the taste of her mouth and the feel of her body in his hands, but it had all been for show. In all likelihood, not one moment of the desire he'd felt for her that night meant a single thing to her.

He reminded himself that she was so much more than a pretty face and focused elsewhere. "So. Mayhem, huh?"

"Ah." She said that one short, simple sound as if he answered some unspoken question. "Not who you expected, was I?"

"No you weren't. Don't get me wrong, it was a pleasant surprise, but no, you weren't anything like I expected when they referred to another badass named Mayhem." He shook his head and turned back around to face her.

She stood and walked back to Kylie's memory wall. "The guys have called me that for so long now, I don't even notice."

He couldn't help but ask the burning question. "So, how did you get the name? Were you a medic in the Guard?" Picturing her behind fortress walls, placing bandages on wounds and checking temperatures, he walked over to stand closer but held himself back.

He feared that if he caught that sweet scent, he'd be drawn in against his will.

"Nope. Transport. Put me behind the wheel of any vehicle, no matter how big, and I can drive it. There was a tiny little incident outside Bagram, and the guys have called me Mayhem since." There was something in the way she said the word *tiny* that made him pause. She faced him with a cheeky grin.

He imagined her bending over in her fatigues to tie a shoelace and an entire platoon of marching soldiers stumbling when the first row of men caught sight of the sexy view.

But, wait. Did she say Bagram? That was in Afghanistan. Maybe, thanks to her innocent looking face, she had been swarmed by orphans begging for food each time they went into town?

He crossed his arms. "Tiny incident? I have to hear this one." He smiled, waited for her story and prepared to laugh.

"A big part of what we did was PSD. Personal Security Detachment. We were escorting a General en route to Bagram. I drove the lead vehicle, a gun truck. We were just outside the city limits when a Toyota Hilux came barreling from around a crumbling building. The Toyota, it looks a lot like the Tacomas we have here in the states. Anyway, the terrorists had mounted a heavy machine gun in the bed. Crazy assholes loaded that pickup with ten men. Two of them stood in the bed, holding onto the roll bar for dear life, armed with rocket propelled grenades, and a third readied to fire the heavy machine gun. The moment the truck stopped, directly in front of our convoy, the three in back took aim and the truck doors opened. I didn't know what weapons the others had inside, but it couldn't have been good. I knew the moment their feet hit the sand, they'd take aim on us as well. I couldn't let them get those doors open or launch those grenades so I stomped on the gas and plowed into the truck."

Joe's smile fell from his face as her story continued. She wasn't boasting. She stood there talking about taking part in a war as if she were talking about going to work. Speechless, he waited for the rest of her tale.

"Holloway was in my truck, acting as my gunner. You should have heard him yelling at me. I still don't have a clue what he said. I can't tell you if he was cheering me on or cursing my name. Rick acted as our Tactical Commander and he'd been speechless, if you can imagine that. After it was over, Holloway said he didn't know whether to kill me or kiss me. Rick just shook his head and hugged me tight.

"The General was six vehicles back and heard all the noise, but couldn't see a thing. The coms were full of chatter. He asked what all the chaos was and someone said 'Never fear. Cara May handled it, sir.'

"All he heard was *May*. He bellowed that someone had better put an end to the mayhem, and someone else replied that Cara May handled the mayhem. So, I became Cara Mayhem, and then later just Mayhem." She cocked her head and looked at him with an odd expression. She shook her head wryly and with a single finger pushing up on his chin, she closed his open jaw. He hadn't realized he'd dropped it, but judging by the shock he felt, he was lucky it hadn't hit the floor.

"They were going to fire on you? Launch grenades at you?" He couldn't wrap his mind around it.

"Joe, we were in theater, at war. I was a soldier. I was fired at many times. Each day, when we left the base, we walked in danger. We'd travel south, clear the only road of IED's and later that day on our return, we had to clear that same path again. Nothing, not even a dead animal on the roadside could be taken for granted. Everything was filled with deadly potential. That was our job."

Holy hell. He could barely wrap his head around the idea. But for her it hadn't been an idea or a movie. It had been her reality. She lived it. Every instinct he had railed against the idea. Women were meant to be appreciated, even cosseted. They were mothers, sisters and daughters. Yes, they could be strong, independent as well, but damn it, they shouldn't ever have to go to fucking war. That was a man's job.

Yet, she'd volunteered and stood here amused at him for his bigotry.

Silence loomed heavy until a dark shadow replaced her amusement at him. "I appreciate you having my back when Boyd appeared. It caught me off guard. We have a very ugly history and for a moment I let him get the better of me. I guarantee it won't happen again."

She awed him. She'd seen the uglier faces of the world time and time again but remained a beautiful, kind soul. "Not a problem. I appreciate you not letting me annihilate him on the spot. I'm not sure I've ever lost my temper that quickly." Her stunning eyes trapped him. Her petal pink mouth made him hunger for one more taste.

"I apologize for climbing you like a tree. I threw myself at you like a total hussy. During the darkest times in the desert, I promised myself that I'd never play games and I'd always be honest about what I wanted. Whether we were in a dangerous situation or not, that didn't give me the right to go after you like a cat in heat." She tucked a strand of hair behind a perfect ear.

"Anytime." What had she done to him? He sounded like a bumbling thirteen-year old. "What I mean is, I wasn't just being nice when I said you handled the situation in the best possible way. In a split second, you assessed a dangerous situation and decided how to best handle it." He couldn't resist reaching out to see if her hair was as soft as he remembered. He allowed himself a moment to run the end of a lock through his fingers. Then he let it go. "Twice you came to my rescue. You impressed the hell out of me."

She took a single step closer and, if he wasn't mistaken, she looked to his mouth. "So…do you want to go out sometime? We could go out for a quiet dinner or we could do something fun and take Kylie. I'd be happy either way." She sucked on her bottom lip and stepped in even closer. He caught the scent that he craved but could not indulge in. She'd said the one word sure to throw cold water on his libido.

Kylie.

When her mother died he'd made a silent vow that his daughter must always come first.

"Ah. I can't. As tempting as the offer is, I can't fit a relationship, or even a date, into my life right now. So, thank you, but no."

He expected to see disappointment mar her pretty features. He was wrong. An utterly charming, crooked grin spread across her face and she leaned up to kiss his cheek. The simple sweetness of it nearly brought him to his knees. Then, clueless to her devastating impact on his senses, she stepped back. "Okay. The offer stands if you change your mind or find room in your chaotic life." She picked up her purse and then stopped with one hand on his doorknob. "Joe? I was impressed too, in more ways than one." Then she winked at him and walked out his door without looking back. All the while, he stood there dumbstruck and speechless.

***

"Momma? What do you say we walk over, and get lunch at the new coffee shop? I heard the desserts are to die for." Cara held the door to the doctor's office open and waited for her mother to walk out. "It's a pretty day. We should enjoy the sun before the stormy weather comes tomorrow." She held the door open even wider with her foot and put on her sunglasses.

"It's the wrong direction. You parked too far away. I'll never make it there and back." As soon as her mother stepped through the door she leaned harder on her cane. For her orthopedic doctor she'd been full of gracious smiles. The moment they'd exited the exam room, those had been replaced with the sour frown that seemed to be reserved for Cara alone.

"I think we both deserve a treat. It's only two doors down. If you want to go sit and eat, when we're finished I'll run and get the car to pick you up. Front door service." She'd tired of this game, but felt trapped in their routine.

"Hmph. I suppose, if you want to eat out so badly that you'd drag your crippled mother halfway across town for a piece of cake." She slung a purse the size of Texas over her shoulder and readjusted her cane. "You know, you really should watch your calories. If you're not careful, you'll have to buy a larger size wardrobe."

Cara released the door after her mother was clear. "Momma that wasn't nice. I was trying to treat you. I thought you might like something to eat other than my cooking." And if anything, Cara's shorts had felt a little loose when she'd put them on that morning. Their constant bickering killed her appetite.

She walked patiently beside her mother as she shuffled down the sidewalk with a pained gait. Cara swore her mother did it on purpose, but she had no idea why.

When they finally made the short distance, she held the door open. Her mother limped in and collapsed into the nearest chair with a huff. Not bothering to hide her frustration any longer, Cara shook her head and followed. She went to the counter and ordered for both of them.

"Anne wants to meet us for dinner after church tonight. I hope you'll wear something more appropriate than shorts." Her mother looked down her nose at Cara as if she'd gone out of the house in Daisy Dukes.

"There's nothing wrong with my shorts, Mother." She'd known she'd likely get an earful for the choice, but expecting the ninety-degree temperature combined with eighty percent humidity, she hadn't cared. And they were perfectly decent. The khaki shorts came past mid-thigh and she paired them with a light blouse and sandals.

"Well. I don't see how you ever expect to catch a man, if you insist on dressing like one." The server set their plates on the table and made a hasty departure. "I can't imagine you plan to work for the rest of your life."

"No, not forever. Eventually I'll probably want to retire. But that'll be a long time from now and has nothing to do with my relationship status. I like to stay busy. We've had this discussion." Yet again, her appetite disappeared.

"Your daddy would turn over in his grave if he knew. Why after all he gave to provide for us." Her mother took a dainty bite of her salad. How bad was it that she'd rather hike through the desert with her fifty-pound pack than listen to her mother's scorn? Some days Cara wondered if her mother started these conversations on purpose.

Cara decided to try the evasion tactic today. If only it worked as well on her mother as it had in Afghanistan. "I won't be able to make it to church or dinner tonight. I have plans."

Her mother set her fork down and sat up straighter. "Do these plans involve a man?"

Cara's words slipped out before she could stop them. "Yes. Several of them." She smiled innocently and took a bite of her sandwich which suddenly tasted delicious. They finished their lunch in silence, which suited Cara just fine.

"Take your time and finish. I'm going to walk back and get the car." Maybe a few minutes outside would help get her anger under control. Without another word, she left her mother at the table, taking her half-eaten cookie with her.

I will not feel guilty. I will not feel guilty.

She repeated the mantra as she passed the doctor's office on her way back.

Determined to get over the ugly emotion, she put the last bite of cookie in her mouth. The treat turned to sawdust in her mouth. The hair on the back her neck rose. It had been a long time since she'd felt such a strong sense of being watched.

She didn't like it one bit.

Purposely, she stumbled over a crack in the sidewalk and dropped her purse. She righted herself, straightened her hair and looked around in front of her. Nothing appeared out of place. She bent over to straighten her sandal, which in reality, was just fine and looked behind her.

There was something or someone not quite right across the street and two buildings down from the coffee shop. A man leaned back in the shade of an alcove, with his hands in his pockets as if waiting for someone or something. His pose appeared casual, but something struck her as out of place.

She straightened and continued on her way, reviewing the image in her mind. Something about the building nagged at her. He'd been standing in front of the old thrift store which had been out of business for several years. There were plenty of reasons for someone to stand in front of it. It could be nothing. Hell, it was likely nothing.

She decided that wasn't enough to take to Trent and Rick, but she'd stay on her toes, just the same. Even though on days like this one, she wanted to strangle her mother, she'd do anything to keep her safe.

Chapter Four

"Katie! Can we see the horses?" Joe followed his daughter across the grass at a slower pace. Pretty, feminine laughter greeted his ears as he neared Trent's home. The low, husky tones wrapped around him as he looked for the source. He walked around an enormous horse trailer attached to Trent's truck and stopped. There, in the yard, not far from the front door, Cara sat on the ground with a tangle of puppies in her lap. Furry little bodies wriggled and vied for her attention.

He couldn't say he blamed them. With sun-kissed cheeks and her hair shining in the bright evening light, she was temptation defined. He shaded his eyes against the intense setting sun and sighed.

Trouble. Pure trouble waits for me...

"Daddy! Look! Oh! I like that one. And that one. Can I have one?" Kylie's excited chatter bubbled and he couldn't help but smile as she all but shook with excitement.

Kate stood beside the Cara dogpile and smiled. "Are you sure you don't want one? How about two? They could keep each other company. I know you'd make a good fur-momma."

Cara shook her head in denial. "As much as I'd love to, I can't. My mother would have a conniption. I'm having enough trouble with her as it is. And as soon as she's finished recovering I'll have to go back to juggling school and work. It wouldn't be fair to any of the little babies." She held a black and white ball of fur up to her face and it licked her neck. "They are precious."

73

He walked over to the women. "Causing trouble as always, Kate?" He hugged his cousin close and reluctantly let her go. Not much more than a month had passed since she'd been kidnapped but sometimes it felt like the horror had only happened yesterday. He knew she understood and even loved him for his worry, but he promised to let Trent be the one to watch over her. Even though she was in the best of hands, he couldn't help but get anxious from time to time.

"Of course. It's the good kind of trouble today." She beamed up at him. "I guess, if I can't pawn one of these little guys off on Cara then I'd better get them back to the rescue. Unless..." Her smile changed from one of warmth to one of calculation. "Don't you think—" she nodded her head toward his daughter then finished, "is ready for a dog?"

"No. Hell no. Certainly not a puppy that has to be housebroken and obedience trained. Do not stick me with any of your rescues." He stepped back when she plucked a pup from the pile and held it up to him. She followed him step for step, stalking him until his back was against Trent's truck. The little ball of fluff licked his nose. "Can you imagine the chaos?" He heard Kylie's laughter mix with Cara's as he stared into a dopey puppy face. Something about the sound settled inside him and took hold.

"We just left the vet's office. They've had their second round of immunizations and will be spayed or neutered soon."

He took the puppy from her and held it against his chest. "No."

Kate batted her lashes at him and then put on her sad face.

"Your tricks won't work on me, Miss Kentucky. Take your critters elsewhere." The puppy in his arms licked his chin and whimpered. He held it out to her. Its soft body went limp and he could have sworn the thing gave her a conspiratorial grin that said, *don't worry. We'll wear him down.*

"I'll get you yet, Joe. Just you wait and see." He wouldn't be the least bit surprised when she did. He could imagine Kylie's delight if he surprised her with one. "Come on, boys and girls. It's time to go back to your momma. Kylie, I think your daddy has some boring work stuff to talk about. Do you wanna help me take these guys out to the rescue?" She took the one from his hands and picked up one more.

"I'll help you load them up." Cara began moving the pups in her lap to the grass, only to laugh when the first two crawled back when she moved the third and fourth away. "Let's go, you little stinkers." She extricated herself from the pile and stood. When she bent over to pick up a clumsy runaway he almost swallowed his tongue.

He'd seen her in a skirt, jeans and now khaki shorts. It seemed it didn't matter how dressy or simple her clothes were. That sexy figure was all Cara. When she carefully handed the puppy to Kylie and showed her how to hold it securely, he was reminded that, like Kate, she was so much more than a pretty face.

He put his hands in his pockets and went inside before he made a fool of himself.

***

Cara watched Kylie carefully walk with the puppy as she followed Kate to Trent's truck. Assured the little girl was being careful she let her gaze wonder to Joe. *Damn. She hadn't been crazy*. His long-legged stride was just as sexy as the first time she'd seen it.

"Maybe you should date my daddy. He's nice and you're nice too. He needs a giwlfwiend." Kylie pulled Cara's attention from Joe's ass as the man climbed up the porch steps.

"Um. Well." What should she say to that?

"Don't you like my daddy?" Kylie tilted her head as she looked up with a frown on her face.

"I like him just fine sweetheart. I—"

"Then you should date him. You'we not mawwied are you?" Suspicion darkened her face.

"No. Not at all. I—"

"Well, then why don't you—" The puppy wriggled in her arms and Kate stepped in to take it from her.

"Kylie. You're being nosy. Leave Cara be. She has work to do. Come on, let's take the puppies back to their momma." Kate took Kylie's hand in hers and opened the door to Trent's truck. She helped her cousin up to her safety seat. "Cara, Kylie's idea is not a bad one. Just saying. I may want to strangle him on a monthly basis, but he's one of the very best men I know." She waved and climbed in the driver seat. "Let me know if you change your mind about a puppy."

Well. What would you all say if I told you sexy as sin Joe MacDonald has no interest in dating me?

She went inside and found Rick, Joe and Trent gathered around the table. They had Mary's drawing and a large paper map spread out in the middle. On the TV screen someone had pulled up satellite images of the quarry.

She'd gone from puppies and laughter to grim-faced doom in the blink of an eye.

"I've tried to be patient. I wanted her to come to one of us for help. I worried that if we try to corner her that we'd do more harm than good." Rick stood with both palms braced flat on the table as he stared down at the sketch.

"You wanted to earn her trust." Trent frowned at the map on the table.

Joe leaned back in his chair and looked at the quarry image. "Things have changed. This is deadly. We have no idea if this was a one-time occurrence or God forbid, something worse, but we can't leave her there to stumble onto it again."

"Or worse, go looking for it. With this sketch, I think she's trying to turn them in." Rick's brow wrinkled as he concentrated, trying in vain to pull something useful from the piece of paper.

"When do we go after her?" All eyes looked to her as she stepped into the group.

"Mayhem, babe. This one's personal. It's not an official Dark Horse op but I can put you on the payroll. I'd welcome the extra help." Rick stood straight.

"Take your payroll and shove it. I can read between the lines. I know Mary has your heart clenched in her little fist." God, he could be such a dumbass at times. "You are the most loyal man I know, but has it ever occurred to you that others might feel the same toward you? That you might have earned it? This is a family op and I want in."

Trent remained silent, but he winked at her.

Joe looked at her like he expected her head to spin and expel pea soup. "Cara, we'll be going into some pretty rough terrain. It won't be a walk in the park. It'll likely be a sweaty, bug-infested hike. We may have to lie in the heat, waiting for hours."

"Uh oh. Joe?" Trent tried, bless his heart. He knew what was coming.

Rick straightened, crossed his arms and smiled, ready for the show.

"I know you have a soft spot a mile wide, but I'm really not sure you know what you're getting into. Maybe you can take Pete's place at the computer." *And his mouth kept going.*

She didn't know whether to laugh at the absurdity of his words or strangle him for the unintended slap. She knew that he'd die before he knowingly hurled an insult, but that's exactly what he'd just done.

Had he forgotten everything they'd discussed or had he not believed her?

She took a deep breath and told herself that he had an adorable daughter who thought he hung the moon. She couldn't hurt him too badly.

"Do you jog?" She kept her tone light, hiding her temper.

Trent snorted. She didn't dare look at Rick. She knew without looking that his grin had only spread wider.

"I do. I don't as often as I used to, but I do." Confusion slowed his response as if he didn't know what to make of her.

"Good. When can you go next?" *Oh, how she looked forward to this.*

"Kate would love to have Kylie stay the night this weekend." Trent helpfully volunteered a trusted babysitter. She pinned Joe in place with her smile, but she heard her friend's glee.

"The evening after next. I can be free by 6:30." Suspicion crept in as his brown eyes met her gaze.

She tilted her head to ask a question, but held Joe's gaze. "Trent? Can we use the Walker pond?"

"Sure. You know you're always welcome, but with everything that's gone on this summer, we're behind on the mowing. The grass is a little high."

"Perfect. Joe, I'll meet you here. Bring your running gear, but wear pants." Part of her hated to kick his ass in front of his daughter, but then again, he'd asked for it. And maybe the show would be good for Kylie.

"Now. When and how exactly are we planning to get Mary? I can't stand the thought of her being so near to danger any longer." She stuffed down her pride and focused on the most important thing—a child in need.

***

78

"Daddy, why awe you sad?" Kylie, fresh from her bath, snuggled into his side. He'd never know or understand why he'd been gifted with such a blessing, but he had. In addition to having enough energy for five children, she had his cousin's gift of empathy. He wrapped his arm around her and changed the channel from sports to animals.

"I had a rough day at work, but I'll be okay." He wouldn't outright lie to her, she was far too intuitive for that, but there was no way he was explaining to his six-year-old daughter that he'd had one of the worst days of his career. He prayed he'd never again have to notify another parent that their child had overdosed and was on the way to the hospital in an ambulance.

The girl's father probably outmatched him by three inches in height and fifty pounds of muscle. He'd had to catch the bear of a man and help his wife get him to the couch when his grief had been too heavy a burden to carry. Like Joe, their daughter, their only child, starred as the center of their universe.

Kylie released a heavy sigh. "Is it bad gwownup stuff?"

"Yeah. It was a bad day. Do you want a story for bed?" On nights like this, he'd be content to hold her to him until the sun rose, but bedtime waited. All too soon, she'd been in school again.

"Not tonight. Can I pway the fish game on your phone for a few minutes?" Normally he'd insist on the story, but he didn't have it in him to deny her anything.

"Ten minutes."

"Okay." He unlocked the passcode then handed her his phone. He kissed the top of her hair then lay his head on the back of the couch as an alligator slid from the swamp bank to the river on the TV. Or maybe or it was a crocodile? He didn't have a clue.

"Baby? Crocodile or alligator?"

She looked up from the phone's glow to the TV. "Gator. He's got a fat head and he's bwack. Cwocs have pointy heads and gween or gway skin." She delivered the information in a matter of fact tone, as if she viewed the animals every day. Her focus returned to the phone.

He didn't even have it in him to remind her to pronounce her words correctly. He held her close, savoring each second she was his. She shifted against him a bit and turned her head away.

How sad is it that the only shoulder I have to cry on is my six-year-old daughter's? He'd vowed to always put Kylie first, but he'd be lying if he said there weren't times that he longed for someone to share both the good days and the bad.

"Hello? Hi. Daddy had a bad day. He's sad and needs a fwiend." She faced him with a solemn little face. Big green eyes looked to him, all too serious. "Daddy, I'm going to bed. Hewe's Cawa. You can talk to her about the bad day. I love you." She carefully pronounced *love*. She handed him his phone and hopped off the couch. In the time it took his slow brain to process what she'd done, his daughter made it to her room and shut her door.

A hitch caught beneath his sternum and bucked.

He put the phone to his ear. "Hello." His voice broke on the word.

***

"Joe? Is everything okay? Let me get my keys, and I'll be right over." Cara shut the dishwasher then turned to look for her purse.

"No. Not necessary. I mean, yes, we're fine. I'm fine. Don't come over." His voice sounded strained through the phone.

"Are you sure? I'm not doing anything but dishes. Momma is set for the night." Heart racing, Cara stood in the middle of the kitchen, not sure what to do.

"I'm sure. My darling daughter is too smart, that's all. Never, ever underestimate the intelligence of a child." His voice evened out and strengthened, sounding more like the Joe she knew.

"No kidding." Kylie said he needed to talk, so she'd talk. About what, she didn't know, but she'd wing it. "I've had more than one child at the hospital shock their parents with words wise beyond their years." She went out the front door.

"You're going to school to be a nurse? Is that what I heard?"

"I am a nurse. I've had my RN license for a couple of years now. I'm one semester away from becoming a Nurse Practitioner. It's hard sometimes, but I love my job." She leaned against a post at the top of the steps and looked up at the night sky.

"Yeah." He sounded utterly defeated, making her heart ache. How bad must it be for Kylie to call for help?

"Joe, what happened today?" She picked a peeling fleck of paint on the porch railing.

A sigh whispered over the connection and his words sounded like he spoke more to himself than her. "Ah, why not?" His voice strengthened again. "I went out on a call. When it came through dispatch there was a lot of confusion and I happened to be close by. The call was all panicked crying with yells for help in the background. No one knew what to make of the situation. I arrived first at the scene and found two shell-shocked teens staring at a third on the floor having convulsions. The bedroom floor was covered in vomit."

Her throat tightened around her words. "Oh no. Overdose. How old?" After years of working weekends in the emergency room, the image sprang to life in her mind.

"She turned fifteen last month. Good student, rarely got into trouble. According to her friends this was the first time any of them had tried any drugs at all. Of all the horrible choices out there, they had to try smoking heroin. Why?" His grief-scraped voice cracked. "Her parents were devastated. Crushed."

Of course he'd shouldered that burden. She sat on the top porch step and leaned against the post. The sky was crystal clear and much too pretty for such a heartbreaking night. Tragedies happened, but the world kept spinning with cruel insensitivity.

"Did she make it?" Her words slipped out before she could pull them back. His pain was already too great and she dreaded his answer as much as she wanted to hear it.

"Last I heard she made it to the emergency room where they got her stabilized and she was being transferred out to a larger hospital."

"So there's hope. That's something." She looked at the half moon above and sent a wish into the dark sky for them all.

"Yeah. It's a slim chance, but yeah. There's hope." She liked to think the grief in his voice lessened, but she wouldn't bet on it. Maybe she could distract him? At least for a few moments?

"So are we still on for our run tomorrow? You're not going to wimp out on me, are you?" She didn't know if she could lighten the mood, but it was certainly worth a shot.

"We're on. You're going to make me eat my words aren't you? Will pulling my foot out of my mouth and taking back my words get me off the hook? What I said was stupid. It was a knee-jerk reaction, but still incredibly small-minded." His admission made her like him all the more.

"Absolutely not. I'm looking forward to kicking your ass, Mr. MacDonald."

"Shit. Well, at least watching you smoke me will come with a great view." She heard the wry smile in his voice and choked on her laughter.

Chapter Five

"I have ten on Mayhem. Who'll take that bet?" James Holloway announced as Cara bent over and stretched. And yes, she couldn't help herself. She made sure her backend faced Joe.

"No way. That's a sucker's bet. What about times?" Noah twisted the top off a bottle of beer and leaned over Trent's porch rail.

"Witch." Joe, who suddenly sounded closer than she'd originally thought muttered low enough that only she could hear. Then he chuckled and casually brushed against her in a way that no one could see and patted her ass. And considering she tried on two pair of track pants before settling on her old ACU pants she probably deserved the remark. Yes, they were camo and practical, but, they also cupped her curves nicely. She'd be a liar if she told herself that hadn't been the deciding factor.

They'd also protect her lower legs from scratches and bug bites when they ran through the tall grass surrounding the pond.

"Mayhem, what kind of course are you going to drag his sorry ass through? We need the details before we place our bets." Trent stood at his grill and opened the lid.

"Daddy, are you gonna let Cara beat you? You run fast too. You used to—"

Joe cut in suddenly and turned to Kylie, who sat in a chair on the porch beside Kate. "Pickle, I'll try my best, okay? It'll be a fun race. You can cheer me on from here."

Was something there in the odd look on Kylie's face? Likely, the little girl was only unflinchingly loyal to her father. Cara couldn't blame her. Everything about Kylie screamed daddy's girl. After losing her father at the age of four, she barely remembered her own and had always envied her friends' close relationships with their fathers. When she'd butted heads with her mother the emptiness had only doubled.

Leigh walked to the rail and looked down. Her voice was light, teasing even, but again… there was something in the way she met Joe's eyes briefly before she smiled at Cara. "Try not to hurt my brother too badly. I need him to help me move around some furniture this coming weekend."

"Okay. I thought we'd run down to the pond, around the far side and back up the hill. Twice." The Walkers had a large picnic shelter down where they held their annual family reunion. Years ago, when they all came back from Afghanistan, Sandy Walker adopted the entire unit. From the day that they stepped off the plane and onto American soil they'd all been welcome members of the family. Cara had been to more than one "cookout at the pond." The day long events usually included enough food to feed a small country and enough laughter to supply them all for the year. It had been something that they'd all needed.

Trent pointed his beer bottle in the direction of the pond. "It's about a quarter mile to the water, so you're looking at about a mile, maybe a little more of rough terrain. A lot of it is sloped or inclined, depending on your direction. It'll be tough jog."

"That's close to what I figured. Are you up to it, cop? Are you sure you didn't have too many donuts today?" She looked to Joe and smirked. She couldn't help it. She looked forward to this with a ridiculous amount of glee. Their conversation on the phone had lasted well over an hour the night before. How could she stay mad at a man who hurt so badly for someone else's grief?

"I think I can handle it. Like I said, the ass-whooping will be well worth the view." He stood with his hands on his hips in nothing but an old pair of sweats and beat up running shoes. The sweats hung a little low on his hips, giving her the slightest peek at the muscled V that pointed to what was likely even greater treasure below. She knew his skin tone, a golden tan, was most likely the result of time spent outdoors.

It was a crying shame that she wouldn't get a view of his backside to go with her run. He'd be eating her dust.

"Who's holding the money?" Pete moved to stand next to Leigh and looked around in all seriousness.

"I'm not going to bet. She's going to smoke his ass. I'll hold the money and set the timer." Noah set a tray of burger patties on the patio table.

"I'll be nice to Joe. I may want to put him on my payroll someday. I'll only give Mayhem a sixty second win." Rick handed his money to Noah and walked down the steps to stand next to them on the lawn.

"I'll take ninety seconds." Holloway placed his bet and handed a ten over to Noah.

"Ninety? Hell. I want three minutes. Pretty boy will be huffin' and puffin' before the second lap starts." Pete added his.

"Kate? You in? I'll take two minutes." Trent handed his money to Noah.

She looked to cousin from her chair and appeared to think. "It just seems wrong to bet against family. I'll sit this one out." The corner of her mouth twitched.

"I want in! Daddy's gonna win." Kylie spoke up, full of confidence in her father.

Joe sighed heavily and muttered. "Here's another punch on my bad-parent card." He walked to where his keys and wallet lay on the deck floor, under the bottom rail. He opened his wallet and handed his daughter two five-dollar bills. "Here, sweetheart. Give this to Noah." Then he winked at his daughter. An enormous smile lit her face, and she proudly handed her money over. She walked back to her father and he crooked his finger at her to come closer. "High-five." He held his hand up, and she smacked it for all she was worth.

Dear god. How could a woman not adore them?

"Leigh? How about you?" Rick pointed his bottled water from her to Noah.

"Nah. I don't want to listen to his whining. Next time I want to take Kylie for a girls' day out, he'll use it against me. I'm out." Then she looked to Kylie and winked.

Had she missed something? No. They were loyal to their family and putting Joe's pride first. All she could do was admire them for their close connection.

"All right then. Betting window is closed." Noah folded up the money and set it beneath his beer bottle.

Joe placed his hand lightly on her shoulder and turned her to face him. "What about you and I?"

She stared at his lips and slowly processed his words. There was something about the bottom one that she wanted to taste. She remembered the feel of his mouth against hers and the hard press of his body pinning her against the truck. She shook her lust-filled haze loose and concentrated. "You and I? You mean a bet?"

"Yeah. When you win, what do you want?" He smirked.

Oh, this was too good. She almost felt bad about this. *Almost.* She met his eyes. "Our date. You?"

"A kiss." If she wasn't mistaken, his gaze went to her mouth, which now watered at the thought that he might want that even half as much as she did.

"Only a kiss? Sure. You're on big boy." A grin stretched across her face, and she didn't bother to hide her happiness.

"Are you two finished making goofy faces at each other? We want our race." Noah stood at the porch rail and held up his phone where a stopwatch showed set at zero.

"We're ready." She smiled at Joe. "Do you want a head start, since you're not familiar with the path? We'll go down to that oak tree, around it and down to the pond. Go around the backside and up to the barn. Go around it and then back to the tree, pond and back here to finish." She pointed out her route.

"Nope. I'll play fair."

"Get ready." Noah announced, "Kylie, love, you do the honors."

"Go!" The little girl yelled, and they both took off. Cara threw herself into the run, eager to stretch her legs. She knew better than give it her all just yet. She'd need to conserve her energy for the final climb up the hill. It didn't look that steep, but she knew better. It was a bitch to climb.

***

Joe ran beside Cara, giving them both room to move freely. He'd looked forward to this all day. It had been a while since he'd had a good, challenging run, but he was no stranger to rough countryside. He'd spent his entire life in it.

He stayed even with Cara all the way down to the old tree. When they made the turn around the back of it he eased up and let her go first. He stayed behind her, just a few feet. And he hadn't lied. He did enjoy the view. He'd never in his life thought a woman in a plain white tank and camouflage pants would be so damn sexy, but she'd surprised him again. To her skirts, jeans, and shorts, she'd added fatigues and he still couldn't decide which he liked better.

They made it down to the pond in no time. Though the ground was uneven, the slope down was a fairly gentle one. He followed her around the backside where grass had grown near to mid-calf.

"Getting tired yet? You're not falling too far behind, are you?" She taunted over her shoulder.

"It's not too bad yet. I'm just admiring the view. It's a damn fine one. I could chase after it all day." He really could.

"Oh, yeah?" Her words came out a touch choppy as if she'd started to breathe heavier.

"Yeah. I only have one problem. I can't decide which I like best." She'd taunted him. He deserved his own shot.

"What's that, MacDonald?" she called out before she leapt over a downed log.

"I can't decide what I like better. I never expected to appreciate camouflage on a soldier so much, but apparently I do. But then those khaki shorts you had on the other day looked mighty fine." If he wasn't mistaken, her pace slowed a fraction. He matched it so he could stay in his place behind her.

They finished the pond section and ran up the incline to the old barn. He stayed quiet a while so they could conserve their oxygen. He savored the adrenaline flowing through his body as he hit his stride.

"I've always had a thing for faded jeans. I didn't think there was anything capable of flattering a woman's ass better." They rounded the barn and began to head back for the second lap. His lungs felt the beginnings of a good burn. "But I can't get the image of a pretty little woman in a turquoise skirt bent over, looking at her car out of my head. I think that skirt might be my favorite. You want to know why?"

The air filled with silence as they came to the pond once again. Halfway around the backside she finally responded. The breathiness in her voice dried his mouth and made him think of things far dirtier than running through the weeds. "Why, Joe?"

He waited until they made the last turn at the pond's end. When she straightened out and started the home stretch he suspected she might have realized she could be in trouble. Suspicion laced her words as she asked him again. "Joe, why do you like the skirt?"

Damn, he loved her voice.

"All I can think about is how easy it would be for me to bend you over the nearest piece of furniture, yank down those little white panties and sink myself in your hot little body." Halfway to the finish he cut loose, lengthened his stride and took off.

He heard her muttered curse as he passed her and smiled. He'd make sure the kiss was worth her while.

He ran up to the deck and scooped Kylie up in his arms. She threw her arms up and squealed. "You won! I knew you would!" She hugged him around his neck. "You're sweaty!"

"I am. Running's hard work." He kissed her cheek loudly.

"Well, hell. Mayhem? What was that?" Pete grumbled and he heard Cara's labored voice from the yard.

"He won. I don't know how, but he won." She plucked one of the icy cold water bottles off the rail that someone had set out for them and twisted the top off. He watched a bead of sweat slide down between her breasts.

"I thought you were some sort of track star, Mayhem. I know you smoked everyone in our unit at the base in Fort Campbell." James commented from his chair where he leaned back with his long legs stretched out in front.

"I ran track in high school. I placed second in the district cross country finals. I still jog almost daily." She took a sip of water. Then she put the lid on the bottle, picked up the other one and tossed it to him.

He caught it one-handed and looked to his sister who'd begun laughing. "Leigh?" He nodded his head to her and opened his water. His took his own drink, while Leigh answered for him.

"Joe went to state and placed second. He went to the university on a track scholarship." His sister's grin only grew brighter when Cara put her hands on her hips and shot him a dirty look.

"I told you I jogged." He smiled in return and looked up to his daughter, who had climbed up and around to sit on his shoulders. "Pickle? Do you know who else won today?" He gripped her ankles tightly, knowing what to expect.

"No. Who? What did they win?" She looked around the gathering for a clue.

"You did. You're the only person who said I would win."

"I did? Yay!" She threw her arms up in the air and arched as he held on tight.

Noah took the money from under the bottle and brought it over. "Here's your money, love." He held it up to her.

"I got the money?" Awe and confusion filled her voice.

"You did." Again, he gripped her ankles tightly. "It's yours."

"Yay!"

"Let's fix you a plate, sweetheart." Kate stood and held her arms up. When she squirmed to get down, he lifted her over his head and down to his cousin. After Kate fixed his daughter a plate, everyone else took their turn.

He hung back and waited.

So did Cara.

Her breathing had slowed a bit by now, but not completely. Her chest rose with each inhalation. Her sweat-dampened top had become sheer, displaying the pale blue sports bra beneath it.

He walked over to the rail and hopped over it to stand beside her.

She looked up with a wry smile. "So, MacDonald, when do you want your kiss?"

Now. And he feared one kiss wasn't going to be enough.

"On our date. When do you want to go?" He leaned in closer, unable to resist the pull of her golden eyes and flushed skin.

Her breath hitched and he didn't think it was due to their run. "Um…how about the night after tomorrow?" She bit her bottom lip, and he stifled a groan.

"I'll find a sitter for the night. Plan to be out late."

"Okay." She twisted the lid off her water but didn't remove it.

"And wear the skirt." He smiled and walked off to fix his own plate. He was suddenly very hungry.

Chapter Six

Just for a hint of spite, she didn't wear the skirt Joe requested. She figured it would have served him right if she was dressed in her old fatigues when he picked her up, but she didn't wear those either.

She wore her little black skirt and a shimmery halter top. She hoped she wasn't too overdressed, but even if she was, he'd be in for a treat. Or torture, depending on how their night went.

"Now, who exactly is this man you're going out with?" Her mother asked from behind her in the hallway beyond the open bathroom door.

"Your hip is feeling better today? You've been up and about more than usual," Cara commented sweetly as she leaned in toward the mirror to apply a hint of eyeliner. It wouldn't do any good to point out that she knew curiosity was the only reason her mother got out of her bed.

"Not really. Can't a mother make sure her daughter isn't making a fool of herself?" Cara knew the moment she chose her outfit that her mother would have something to say. She just hadn't known what to expect. It could have been anything from scorn to approval, though she doubted it would have been approval unless a doctor picked her up at the door. "That top leaves most of your back bare. Did you know that? What did you say your date does?"

Cara hadn't said. The omission had nothing to with Joe's salary and everything to do with her mother's attitude. "His name is Joe MacDonald. He's a Sheriff's Deputy and a very nice man. When he arrives I want you to be on your best behavior and keep your opinions to yourself." In the mirror, she met her mother's eyes. "I really like him, Momma. Please be nice."

Her mother blinked as if shocked by her words. The lines around her eyes softened. "I'll try, if he's as nice as you say. Is he smart?" She sounded doubtful. "Maybe he could become Sheriff or a police chief one day?" *And my real mother is back.*

She didn't bother telling her mother, again, that she liked supporting herself. She loved her job and would wither away and die without something that made her feel useful, needed. She'd be wasting her breath.

"You never know, Momma. He could." Maybe that possibility would be enough to skip the third degree when he arrived. She slicked on a clear lip gloss and called it good.

"Maybe you should put a little color on under the lip gloss. And maybe just a little more eye shadow. You didn't put much on." Her mother tilted her head in thought.

The doorbell rang and both she and her mother stood a little straighter. Her mother looked down the hallway to the door. "I'll get it." Cara caught the set of determination in her mother's jaw and inwardly swore.

Joe is a big boy. He can handle Betty Gregory.
Hopefully.

She closed her purse and followed her mother. She entered their small living room in time to hear Joe greet her mother, "Ma'am. It's nice to meet you." Cara couldn't see Joe, but judging by the way her mother's eyes widened and her mouth when slack, he'd impressed her in at least one way. Her mother might be in her late fifties, but she was still a woman. There wasn't a woman alive who wouldn't see the appeal in a man like Joe MacDonald.

"Well, hello. Come right in." Her mother pushed back her shoulders, opened the door wider and Cara got her first look at him.

94

She almost dropped her clutch. He'd dressed in a crisp white dress shirt with the sleeves rolled up to his forearms. His broad shoulders nearly filled the doorframe. Neat, dark blue dress jeans hugged his muscled legs.

"Cara, don't just stand there slack-jawed. He brought you flowers. Go get a vase and fix him a drink." Her mother looked at her as if she were speaking to a dimwit. Maybe she was.

"Actually, Mrs. Gregory. The flowers are for you. I figured if I stole your daughter for the evening, I should leave something half as beautiful in her place to keep you company."

Oh no. That is it. I'm done for.

The poor man had no idea what he'd just done. Her mother would have her married to Joe, barefoot, and pregnant by next Sunday if she had any say in the matter. And Betty Gregory always had her say.

But, despite the can of worms he'd just opened, how could she be mad a man who did something so kind? That simple gesture would have her mother on cloud nine for a week. Maybe a good dose of happy would help with her recovery.

She went into the kitchen to search for something large enough to hold the colorful bouquet. Finally, in the laundry room she found a dusty old vase. She washed it out and filled it with water. When she returned to the living room she found Joe in one of her mother's Queen Anne chairs and her mother sitting in her perfect Miss Manners pose on the flowered couch. Cara had no clue how she managed it with her "wretchedly painful" hip.

"That'll do, I guess. Set it on the table in the center. Where's his drink?"

Joe cut in before Cara could respond. "No thank you, ma'am. We need to leave soon or else we won't make our reservation." While her mother looked down on her terrible manners, Joe winked behind her back.

"You didn't tell me he owns a cattle farm." *Oh lord.* She'd left them alone for two minutes and her mother had gotten his full resume.

"I didn't know that." She'd had far more important things on her mind each time she'd seen him.

"It's only half of one. The other half will go to my sister, though she has no interest in running it. My father and I split the responsibility."

"You have a sister? What does she do?" Her mother's gaze swung back to Joe.

"Mom!" Cara counted to five in her head and took a deep breath. "Joe said we need to be going or we'll be late. Joe?"

He smiled and looked as though he was trying not to laugh. "Ma'am, it was a pleasure to meet you." He nodded to her mother and Cara could have sworn that her mother wobbled in her seat. "Cara? Time for our date." He wore a friendly, even innocent smile but his eyes simmered with dark promise.

She headed out the door and when his hand grazed over her bare back, she remembered his teasing words from the other evening.

***

When Betty Gregory opened the door wide and he saw Cara, it took every ounce of civility his own poor mother had beat into him over the years to keep from rushing in like some lusty beast. He'd wanted nothing more than to throw Cara over his shoulder and take her back to his cave where he could strip her bare and spend the next month making her his.

He'd loaded her into his truck and driven her out to Riley Creek. She'd seemed completely at ease making small talk or quietly watching the scenery pass by. She never asked where they were going.

He'd worried if when they arrived at their destination if she'd be disappointed. When he pulled into his driveway, he tensed, waiting for her reaction.

"Late for our reservations, huh?" She looked from the front door of his house to him.

Relieved to see her expression filled with bright amusement, he answered. "I didn't lie. I have steaks waiting in the secret MacDonald marinade. Perfect timing is essential for optimal flavor. It's a crime to ruin a good steak." He stepped down and walked around to help her down.

She opened the door and grinned. "Let's get inside, then. I wouldn't want to get arrested for breaking a beef law." He held her elbow as they walked to his door.

He unlocked and opened it wide then stiffened. Someone had been inside while he'd been away.

"What's wrong?" She stopped beside him and looked up in concern.

"My sister's been here. She must have snuck in and out while I was away." He shook his head and put his keys on the entryway table.

"How can you tell?" In that moment, when she stood right next to him, looking up with those gorgeous eyes, he discovered he had a new favorite smell. He breathed in the warm scent, slightly sweet and floral and his favorite dessert fell down a notch.

He put his hand on the bare skin of her back and tucked her closer. "I can smell her homemade peach cobbler. Let's go see what else she's added to tonight's menu." In the kitchen, on the counter, they found the cobbler and three more covered dishes.

"Oh my." She laughed and the husky sound slid right through him, teasing him in the best way. "There's enough food for an entire family, maybe two."

"Yep. Sis had help. That red pan likely holds my mother's hash brown casserole. Are you disappointed that you got all dressed up for an evening in? I admit, I misled you. I wanted to see you in a skirt again."

"A night in is perfect. As you can see, I didn't wear the blue one. Hope you don't mind."

"Blue has always been my favorite color, but black has suddenly come out on top." His hands settled on her hips. She looked up and he couldn't miss the way her gaze went to his mouth.

"So. It seems I owe you a kiss." She sucked on her bottom lip as if thinking about that exact thing.

"You do, and I expect payment." His hands wanted to explore her body and it took everything he had to deny them. But there'd been no promises of anything more than this one date. Would it be so bad if he enjoyed himself and took just a slice of heaven with him when he returned to the real world?

"If you insist." She raised up on tiptoe and tangled her fingers at the back of his neck. He met her halfway but paused, letting her make the final contact. A butterfly soft kiss lighted on his mouth and he closed his eyes. Letting her take the lead, he held her close and savored the moment as her mouth merged with his.

A low groan escaped and suddenly he could care less about their bet.

***

A growl rumbled deep in Joe's chest, and the sound did odd things to her body. Her breaths deepened, her head grew light and her breasts swelled. She wanted more with a hunger that surpassed any she'd ever known.

She might never get enough of Joe MacDonald.

The world around her jerked and then she was in his arms. Reflexively, as if they were meant to be there, her legs wrapped around his waist. A large, calloused palm cupped one ass cheek. His mouth broke away from hers. She opened her eyes to see nothing but dark, intense desire staring back at her.

"Jesus. It's bare. Are you naked under that skirt?" His heavy chest heaved beneath his shirt, and she decided it needed to go. *Like, yesterday.*

"Thong." Confident he'd hold her, she let go of his neck and started on the buttons of his shirt.

"Fuck me. Are you *trying* to kill me?" His hungry gaze rose from the deep V neckline of her top to meet hers.

"No. I like you too much for that. I just want you crazy for me." She smiled and tugged the tail of his shirt up from under her so she could get to the last two buttons. She unfastened them and spread open the material. Taking in the sight, she sucked in a deep breath. There was just so much male, muscly goodness.

"Color?" His other hand found its way to her other cheek. He licked a trail of fire up the column of her throat.

"Satin." He made his way to her earlobe and nipped it, making her gasp. "White satin. You seemed to have a thing for white panties. I thought I'd oblige you. I only had one problem."

"What's that?" He worked his way down her neck and kissed the flesh along the neckline of her top.

"I couldn't wear the matching bra under this top." She peeled his shirt back over his shoulders, baring more muscled flesh but the material caught at the top of his biceps. It wouldn't go any further as long as he held her up. She decided as long as he held her just like this, she'd make do with not having him completely shirtless. The heavy muscles in his upper arms would make an excellent secondary playground for the fingers that itched to explore.

His nose hit the top of her cleavage. "You're not wearing a bra, at all are you?"

"In a shirt like this? Are you crazy? With an outfit like this, a woman has to be very careful selecting her unmentionables." She ran a finger down the dip between his pectoral muscles.

He kept his chin nestled in the V of her top but he tilted his head up to meet her gaze. So serious, her Joe. "How do I take it off? I mean, it's only fair. You're stripping me out of my shirt. It's only right that I do the same for you."

She raised her hands to the knot tied at the back of her neck. She untied it and let the two pieces fall. The material slid down, pooling at her waist.

"You're right. It's only fair."

His eyes widened and his nostrils flared, making her feel like she'd magically become the most beautiful woman in the world. The house passed by in a blur and her back hit something soft. He pulled his shirt off and tossed it aside. He gripped one of her ankles and ran his thumb over the strap of her shoe. He tried to undo the tiny buckle but cursed. "Damn hands, always too big. Good thing I like the shoes on you. The heels do crazy things to your already fantastic legs."

He removed his clothing in no time, revealing acres of defined, masculine strength. Everything she saw defined male perfection. Power. "Now, about those panties." The low timbre of his voice slid through her in an erotic fog, blinding her to the outside world. Twice she'd been confident that she could handle Joe, and twice he'd proved her wrong. His laid back, easygoing appearance, hid depths of intense focus that shattered her composure.

When he aimed that single-minded concentration on her, she became helpless.

She reached behind her back and unzipped her skirt. The moment she brought her hands back to the front he tucked his fingers in the loose waistband and pulled it down her legs. She knew she was in excellent shape but sometimes, when her usual confidence faltered, a little demon whispered that maybe she was too fit. Maybe she wasn't feminine enough?

When his eyes glittering with fierce hunger swept her from head to toe, she found the power to kick that little doubt-spreading bastard to the curb. "Cara? Never seen anyone more lovely. Truly." She felt the truth of his words to the depths of her soul. "I want it all, every square inch of you. I guess it's a good thing I kidnapped you for the night. You're not going anywhere."

"When do I get my turn?" She wasn't kidding. She wanted to explore every hard ridge and dark, muscled, hollow of his body with her hands and then her mouth.

"If we can't fit it all in tonight, then we'll just have to schedule another round. Tonight's mine. I won the bet, remember?" He ran a finger along the waist of her panties. Then he tucked the same fingertip under the edge and repeated the process. "Deal?"

"Deal." The single word came out raspy on a weak, stuttered hitch.

"Fuck me. Even your voice gets me so worked up, I don't know which way is up." He knelt on the bed and kissed the material just above her mound. Air snagged in her chest and her spine arched.

"Cara." Demanding her attention, he paused, waiting until her gaze met his. Then with his eyes on hers, never blinking, he slid the scrap of material over her hips with slow deliberation. When at last, he pulled her panties over her heels, she braced both eager and unsure of what he'd do next.

He opened her legs, and braced them wide with his knees. She looked down her body just in time to see him take one breast in his hand and another into his mouth. The light scrape of his teeth over the hypersensitive nub set loose an unquenchable ache. Filled with glowing pleasure, she arched, pushing her breasts closer, a silent plea for more.

Never had she wanted anything, anyone this much.

When he answered her silent plea and drew more of her breast into his mouth, ecstasy swamped her. Tightening her legs, she urged him to take more and give everything. Yet he wouldn't be denied as he took his time. With his mouth and hands, he worshipped her.

Sure fingers parted her folds, testing her readiness. He needn't have bothered. She was drunk on her need for him, might die if he didn't fill her. How could she make him lose his mind? What would make him lose control?

Ever so lightly, she ran her fingers through his hair, scratching her nails over his scalp. She got as close to his ear as he'd allow and whispered. "Joe, damn it. Now. I need you inside me."

He raised his head, seeking more. She didn't get it, but he said he loved her voice, that it drove him wild. She wasn't above using it to get what she needed, especially if it got him inside her. She slid her hand down, scraping a trail over his muscled abdomen and gripped him in her fist. "This. You. I need you in me now."

"Damn you, wicked woman." He buried his head in her neck. "I'll get you for that."

"Now." She rubbed over his length, relishing the raw potency that waited for her.

"Condom first. Always." Something dark flashed through his features, but before she could analyze it, it was gone. He nipped her ear and pulled out of her hand, but when he opened the nightstand drawer, she forgave him the insult. Snatching the package from his hand, she smiled as he shifted back between her legs. With a little shake of his head, he grinned and then melted into her, swallowing her next demand with his kiss.

Whatever, she didn't need his mouth for what she wanted.

She ripped open the package and sucked his bottom lip. He expelled a harsh sigh and shuddered when she took him in hand, rolling the condom on.

Meeting her gaze, he cursed. "Even when we finish this, we are not done. Not by a longshot."

"I'm counting on that, cop."

***

A man could only take so much before he broke. After one delightfully heated taunt after another, he forgot why he wanted to prolong her pleasure. His focus shrank to a single thought that could be summed up in two words. *Take her.*

So he did. He slid home in one slow, sure plunge. Tight, heated ecstasy enveloped him. Her husky groan assured him that Cara was right there with him. It was all he needed. He pulled back against the grip of heaven, only to return. Her temptation pulled too strongly, and he couldn't resist the lure.

Her body met his, thrust for thrust and gasp for moan. Their pace quickened their hearts thundered.

Over and over he drove into her, knowing he'd never get his fill. The hazel light of her eyes met his and held him to her. He held her tighter, moved into her harder and deeper and let go. Her body clamped down on his as she arched, crying out his name.

He tucked her tighter against him, pulled her arms over her head and tangled his fingers with hers. Dazedly, her eyes met his. "Joe." And that was all it took to push him over the final, steep edge. With one last plunge, he followed her into bliss.

***

The pot gurgled to life and the scent of coffee filled his kitchen. A better and far more tempting sound followed. "Oh. Wow. This is good." Cara followed her words with a lusty moan.

He filled and carried two mugs to where she sat at his bar, wearing nothing but his shirt and a well-loved, satisfied glow. He took the fork from her hand for his own bite. Sweet with just a hint of savory to balance the toothache, the flavor melted on his tongue. "Enjoy it while it lasts. Sis refuses to share her secret ingredient with anyone, even Mom."

She took one of the mugs and hugged it close. "There must be enough for eight people in the pan."

"Looks that way, but it never lasts." He shook his head when she reached for her fork and dipped in to steal a kiss. He almost died right there on the spot. Everything that was Cara with a hint of peaches and cinnamon assaulted him, threatened to take him under and never let him up for air.

He didn't care. As her tongue tangled with his and her hands cupped his jaw, the world fell away. They'd forgotten last night's dinner and spent most the night feasting on each other. The night had been a whirlwind of tangled limbs, pleasured cries, and breathless ecstasy. They'd slept in and woken starving.

When his hand found the silken skin beneath his shirt, not even his favorite dessert could tempt him away from Cara. He moved between her legs and both hands went to her hips, gripping tight. Her hands fisted in the waistband of his sweats.

The front door banged open. "Dad! Daddy? Aunt Wee is gonna take me to the pway at the park! We're gonna meet Mickey and Bwee. I need my ball and fwog." The rapid stomp of little feet traveled through the house.

The fire in his blood froze, and he jumped back a mile, leaving Cara to straighten herself.

"Cara! Hi." His daughter stopped at the kitchen's entryway and looked up to smile at the woman who he'd been about twenty seconds away from taking right there in her chair.

"Hi, sweetheart. That sounds like fun. It's supposed to be a pretty day and not too hot." Cara smiled and acted as if it were perfectly natural for her to be sitting in their kitchen only half-dressed.

"That's what my aunt said. Dad? Can I have some milk?" Kylie walked to the fridge and opened it as if everything was normal.

He stood there speechless as his world quaked around him.

Leigh hurried in behind her niece and stopped, assessing the situation. "Sorry, guys. She insisted on getting a couple of things for our trip to the park. I didn't think. Let's go, squirt. We have snacks and drinks packed in the car. Your friends will be waiting." She gently took Kylie's hand in hers and waved on their way out. "We'll be gone most of the afternoon, and I promised her pizza afterward, so we won't be back until early evening."

A moment later, the front door opened and closed. His daughter left without her toys and, though she hadn't complained, his gut protested.

Cara smiled wryly and shook her head. "Wow. That was a close one."

How could she be so unruffled? So unmoved? His daughter had nearly caught them in the act. The day he'd found out he was going to be a father he'd vowed that his child would always, *always* come first his life.

He should have known this might happen. Kylie always forgot things. She was a six-year-old. They were messy and forgetful.

"I guess we should be thankful they showed up when they did." Cara took a sip of her coffee and followed it with a bite of cobbler.

"Thankful?" *What the hell does she mean by that?* There was nothing good about the situation. His daughter had almost walked him on him having sex!

"Yeah." She tilted her head and looked at him oddly. "If they'd walked through the door just a few minutes later, things would have been really awkward."

He shook his head at her. "My daughter almost caught me in the act. It doesn't get much worse than that."

"Joe. If she saw anything, which as fast as you moved I doubt, it was just two adults kissing. Her world won't end. I promise."

But she might have questions. Be confused. There'd be an entire line of new things he'd have to address as her only parent. He was her world. She looked up to him. He couldn't do a single thing to screw that up.

"I'm not so sure about that." He turned his back on her and went to shower.

Chapter Seven

A knock sounded at Cara's bedroom door as she pulled on a clean shirt. "Yes?"

"I fixed lunch. You better hurry, or it'll get cold." Her mother's words sounded more like an order than an offer.

She combed out her damp hair and debated. She wasn't hungry. She'd had a good sized helping of dessert for a late breakfast at Joe's. After the tense drive home, food was the last thing on her mind. First, she'd tried to reason with him about the situation. His mood had only grown surlier. She'd given up and tried to distract him with talk of the upcoming Dark Horse operation.

His cooperation had increased, but with such a sad subject, his mood hadn't improved.

"Cara May, all my work will go to waste if you don't get out here and eat."

Ugh. Next would be the, *I slaved over this meal on my bad hip for you* guilt trip. "I'll be right out." She wasn't born yesterday. She knew the only reason her mother fixed lunch was so she could give her the postdate third degree. The longer she waited, the more painful the experience would be.

She met her mother in the kitchen. "Smells good. You didn't have to, but thanks." She sat at the table, waiting for the first strike.

Her mother gave her a pointed look. "I figured you'd need a hearty meal after being out. All night."

"Mom. I'm thirty-two, not a teenager." She fought the urge to squirm in her seat. "We're both adults and—"

Her mother interrupted by setting a plate in front of Cara with a loud thunk. "Oh, shush. I know that. I had you when I was in my mid-twenties. I know what you were doing. I just wish you would've held out until you got a ring on your finger. Please tell me you at least left him wanting more? You can't let him get away, Cara May. You'll have gray hair before too long!"

Actually, she already had a few, but her mother didn't need to know that. "It's early. I like him, but it's complicated." She took a bite and waited, knowing she wouldn't let the subject die.

Her mother set her fork down. "How complicated can it be? You're both single. That's all that matters."

In for a penny, in for a pound. She sighed and looked across the table and out the window. "He has a daughter. She's his entire world, and I think he's worried about bringing anyone new into her life. I don't blame him for being cautious. He's a wonderful father."

"A little girl? How old is she?"

Cara looked to her mother. A new light entered her eyes.

She answered cautiously, not quite sure what her mother plotted. "She's six and cute as a bug. I really like her."

Her mother sat up straight and her eyes narrowed with determination. "Eat up, Cara May. We're going shopping."

***

Joe sat on Mark and Patricia Cline's front porch and waited for their oldest son to get home from his summer job at the movie theater. The Clines were a good family and had been nearly as shocked as the Grants over Haley's overdose. Mark had assured Joe that Brayden would be home immediately after work. In addition to whatever sentence the judge handed him, the sixteen-year old would receive counseling and likely be grounded until he entered the senior citizens' home.

Joe couldn't be any more thankful that everyone involved, parents and teens alike, had cooperated so far. But a piece of the puzzle remained elusive. The vague story they'd given on that terrible night didn't satisfy him.

Where had a couple of teenagers in Riley Creek found heroin?

The thought sickened him, but his feelings didn't matter. Only one thing did. Finding the source and doing everything in his power to ensure the kids in his town were safe. Maybe he was being idealistic, but he didn't give a damn. These were children playing with deadly things they had absolutely no business touching.

If it had been his child? He couldn't imagine the pain. Even thinking in the hypothetical was enough to make him want to put his fist through the bricks on the outside of the Clines' house. He thought back to a few days ago when the situation began. The horror of it all. Kylie. Cara.

The two of them had so much in common. They had such tough exteriors, almost to the point of brashness, but beneath the hard shell lay the softest of hearts. They were both smart and stubborn enough for three men.

Kylie had his mother, Leigh, and Kate as feminine role models, and he couldn't ask for better. But they weren't a part of her everyday life. He was the only adult that she saw every day. He knew he gave her his all, but often worried it wasn't enough. What if Kylie had a strong, caring, and beautiful influence like Cara in her life everyday?

He wanted to kick himself for hurting Cara. In no way was she at fault for his hang-ups. If anything, she deserved another damn medal for putting up with his sorry ass. It was likely too late, but she deserved an explanation and his apology. That is, if she wanted them.

If she didn't, he couldn't say he blamed her.

He'd been such an idiot.

A faded, red SUV pulled into the driveway and slowed to a crawl. It parked in the space between his patrol car and the family's minivan. When it shut off, the driver didn't immediately get out. Joe watched as Brayden sat with his hands on the steering wheel and his head bowed.

He stood and crossed his arms over his chest. It wasn't too long before Brayden's shoulders slumped. Another minute passed before they hitched and fell again. Finally, the kid opened the door and got out. For all of Brayden's excitement, one would have thought that Joe waited at the step to the gallows in a black hood.

"Hey, Mr. MacDonald. I mean...uh...? Officer? Yeah. Officer MacDonald. It's good to see you, sir." If Joe didn't feel so badly for the kid, he might have laughed at the absurdity of his words. Brayden was bone white beneath his freckles.

I'm not that intimidating, am I?

He dipped his head to the teen. "Brayden. How was work?"

"Um, it's okay. Everyone is asking about Hayley. Do you know how she is?" Worry and cautious hope laced his words.

If only hope were enough. The young girl had an entire town hoping and praying for her recovery. But wasn't that what Cara had said? As long as she lived, they had hope, and that was far better than the alternative.

"I spoke with her mother a little bit ago. She's still in ICU, but the doctors are trying to wean her off the ventilator."

"That's the breathing tube, right? So, that's a good thing?" Brayden rubbed the toe of one battered gym shoe against the sidewalk.

"Yeah. It's a small step, but it is in the right direction. Brayden, son, I know you don't want what happened to Hayley to happen to anyone else, especially not to any of your friends. The best way to prevent that from happening is to find the source. You're a smart young man. Why would you try smoking something like heroin? I'm not sure you guys could have picked a nastier drug. You can help me get the bottom of this. I need your help."

Brayden turned gray and chewed on his bottom lip. His hand shook and Joe worried the kid might vomit on his own shoes.

"Brayden? I really need this information. We don't want what happened to Hayley to happen again. You can help prevent that by telling me what you know." Joe wanted to be able to reach into the kid's head and pull out the information he needed, but something had a grip on his tongue.

The screen door banged open behind Joe. "Bubby! You're home!" Nicholas, the Cline's four-year-old, ran straight into his older brother's arms.

Patricia followed him out and held her arms out toward Brayden. "Nicky! I told you to wait on your brother in the kitchen. Come on. Let's go."

"I want bubby. I wanna show him the picture I colored." The little boy wrapped his arms around Brayden's neck and held on.

The teen hugged his little brother close, kissing the top of his head. "Go inside with Mom. I'm almost done, and then I'll come in. Go with Mom." He handed the boy over and watched them go inside. When the door closed, he stood straight and looked Joe in the eye. "I found it on the ground outside the movie theatre. It was all my idea. My fault. When I go back in front of the judge, I'll tell him everything." With his spine so brittle, a soft breeze might snap it in two, he walked past Joe and inside.

Joe watched through the screen door as Brayden picked up his brother and hugged him so tightly the little boy kicked and wriggled to get down.

***

The brief spell of pretty weather with tolerable temperatures and cool breezes had come and gone. The summer heat and humidity had reclaimed its territory in a fierce grip. Even as the evening shadows grew, sweat dripped down Cara's neck and caught in the damp collar of her shirt.

What an odd world she'd created for herself. Just yesterday she'd gone toe to toe with her mother, who'd insisted on buying her a new wardrobe. Cara had won. Barely. She'd shamelessly used her mother's recovery as a reason to at least postpone the trip.

Today, sweaty and likely headed toward stinky, she held her position in a tree and waited, surveying the green world around her. Thanks to their lighter weights and smaller statures, she and Pete had been charged with lookout duty. After two hours in the heat and six different trees, she'd struck out.

She whispered into her mic. "The woods are too thick. Everywhere I can see, I'm blocked by greenery." Frustrated, she wanted to scream out and release her anger. In a few months, the landscape would completely change, but they—and more importantly, Mary—didn't have time.

They pored over maps and satellite images until they were cross-eyed. Joe shared his local knowledge and even discreetly asked his father for info on the Caudill's hollow and the land backing up to the old quarry. Joe said his father assumed he'd asked for a Potter County work case and he hadn't bothered to correct the assumption.

In the desert, they'd learned to listen to the locals. Just because they were on their home turf didn't make that any less true.

They worked under the assumption that Mary had somewhere to go during the day and came home at night. They hung all their hopes on the only theory they had. It might not be much, but they were all willing to roll with it, even without hard intel.

In all the years she'd known Rick, this was the first time he'd ever gone into a situation without a concrete plan. It was more of a Hail Mary pass, and they all knew it.

Not one of them objected. Everyone had shown up to participate, even when they hadn't been invited. Noah, James and Pete offered their time and skills. Kate appeared dressed in old jeans and boots, ready to join. She'd gone toe to toe with Trent until he'd caved.

Sort of.

As a compromise, she manned the computer and satellite feed, since Pete and Rick were both in the field. Joe and Rick had agreed not to tell Leigh until they had more info. The moment they had anything remotely useful, Kate would call her in.

Rick's voice came through her earpiece. "Move to five." He sounded so cool and in control. She knew it for the lie it was. None of them were unaffected, but Rick shouldered the most guilt, even though it wasn't his to bear.

That stain belonged to Mary's father and no one else.

She climbed down her tree, checked her coordinates, and looked around. A worn path, a flash of color or even a piece of trash would reassure her they were close.

They'd sectioned off the search area into parcels. They'd covered four of the eight they'd outlined for today. If they didn't find anything today, everyone agreed to come back at the first opportunity.

Noah's voice came over the mic. "In position."

A moment later Holloway's followed. "In position."

She found her tree, jumped up to grab the lowest sturdy limb. She caught it one hand and with a little swing, grabbed hold with the other. The muscles in her shoulders ached, reminding her she needed to add some upper body training to her morning routine. Ignoring the roughness abrading her palms she adjusted her grip and readied to hoist herself up.

"In position." Rick checked in.

Then Trent and Pete did the same.

Dangling, like a monkey she took a deep breath and flexed.

Something rustled in the brush about thirty feet to her right.

Cara paused, listening. A moment later, a little farther out, something scrabbled against the ground. The tree trunk obscured her view and the sound could have been any number of animals. The woods were filled with deer, turkey, foxes, and even the occasional bobcat. Her gut told her something more watched her.

She released her hold and dropped down on the balls of her feet. She went with her intuition, gambled and gave herself away. "Mary? Sweetheart? We're here to help you. I promise." She stepped around the tree to get a better view of the area the sound came from.

She heard more movement before she saw a flash of sky blue fabric from behind a tree.

"Can they hear you? The men?" a small voice filled with shaky bravado asked.

Cautious hope flooded Cara as she stepped forward. "They're my friends, my best friends. They're here to help you. It's not safe out here. We only want to get you to a good place."

"I'm not leaving my home. Can they hear you now?" Silently, Mary stepped into view with an eerie sort of grace. A petite teen, with her long blond hair in a braid over her shoulder, stood a short distance away. She wore battered shoes, torn jeans and a newer looking blue shirt. An ancient, battered, camouflage hat covered her head and shaded her face.

"They can." Cara pointed to her mic. "We work as a team. Always."

"Are you police?" Suspicion flattened the girl's mouth.

"No. We used to be in the Army together. Now we work together to help people who don't have anyone else to lean on." She had no idea what they would do now that they had found her, but she hoped that if she gave them enough time the guys would come up with something that wouldn't terrify the girl.

Mary tilted her head as if considering Cara's words. "Turn off your headphone thing. I need to show you something. Only you."

"Mary, they're good men, I promise. We always work as a team." She kept her voice soft.

The girl cocked her head and made an odd face. Then she whispered a single word. "Mary?" She shook her head as if casting off an old memory. "No. Turn it off." She pointed to her ear and then crossed her arms, waiting.

"Okay." Cara turned the mic volume up, making sure the guys could hear everything. "You lead. I'll follow."

"They can't follow us. If they do, I'll know. My granddad was a Marine. He showed me how." She picked something off the ground beside her and hugged it. "And don't get too close."

When the girl turned around and walked away, Cara followed.

"And stop making so much noise. I know you can be quiet. I don't want them following us."

Well, damn. She stopped her regular walk and quieted her footsteps.

***

Joe listened to Cara and the girl through his headset. Cara came through clear and calm. Mary's voice came through distant and weak. Impatience urged him to run, catch up to the females, but that wasn't how they played this game. Rules had to be followed, especially with so much at risk.

Rick's order came over his headset. "MacDonald, Ramsey, you two are the closest. Follow, but stay back. Keep them in sight and let Mayhem do her thing. It's possible Mary singled her out because she felt more comfortable around a woman. We won't be far behind you." Joe agreed. Whether because she was a female or her smaller size, it was likely the girl felt safer with Cara.

He moved cautiously in the direction where he heard faint rustling.

Either way, he'd be there to make sure Cara had backup. On quiet feet, he followed, hyper-alert. He felt, rather than heard, Noah's large presence. For such a large man, he was spookily silent.

The girl's voice came over the headset, distant and flat. "And stop making so much noise. I know you can be quiet. I don't want them following us." Almost instantly the telltale sound stopped, leaving him with no trail to follow. *The girl is too smart for her own good.*

He doubled his pace and care, reigning in the urge to charge through the trees and brush. While he didn't think the girl was a threat to Cara, the back of his neck itched in a way that had nothing to do with the heat.

"Boss, I don't like this." Noah's hushed voice mirrored his own feelings.

"Nope. Something stinks and for once, it's not Pete's socks." Holloway stated what they all likely thought.

"MacDonald, Ramsey, stay on course. Get as close as you can without causing Mary to rabbit. Holloway, Taylor double your pace and take the left flank. I'll take the right. Mayhem, don't let her out of your sight, but be on your toes. We got your six."

He almost stumbled over a downed branch when a new voice spoke in his ear. Kate, uncertain but ready to help broke in. "Guys? On the TV screen, a gray truck just entered the quarry lot and is parking beside a large building. I think it's the old garage on the map. Two more vehicles are driving down the road to the quarry. One SUV and a black car."

Rick's voice, filled with urgency came through his earpiece. "Mayhem, pull her back. Even if you have to tackle her to the ground, kicking and screaming, stop her."

"I can barely keep up." He got the impression Cara chose her words carefully. "Honey, slow down. I can't keep up. You may know them well, but I'm a stranger to these woods."

"You need to see. Come on! We have to hurry before the men find us."

"Mary, wait!" Cara called out but he couldn't hear any response from the girl. Then Cara spoke in a quiet, but rushed voice. "Damn it, she's running. I'm following."

Her words struck a painful, artic chill deep into his bones.

Kate's next update was no better. "Um, on the laptop monitor, Cara's dot is moving toward the garage. She's almost to the clearing. Somebody stop her." He wished like hell he could do exactly as Kate demanded in a near-panicked voice.

He broke into a full sprint, no longer giving a damn if he sounded like an elephant in the forest.

"Sweetheart, we're on her tail. I promise we won't leave her hanging. You're doing a fine job. Keep it up. We'll get her. Love you." Trent sounded rushed as he reassured Kate.

"Mary! It's not safe! Please stop," Cara tried again.

Kate broke in with another rushed update. "Cara's at the edge of the clearing."

Then he heard a single shot, a short pause and more gunfire.

"Mayhem, report!" Rick shouted.

A sapling branch slapped Joe in the face as he came to the clearing and forced himself to stop. His hand went to his gun, ready. He had to keep his head together, or he'd be of no use. He reminded himself he had Kylie to think about as well. But all he wanted was to grab Cara and Mary, get them somewhere safe and then paddle their asses.

With his back to a tree, weapon at the ready, he spun to assess the scene. He saw Cara on the ground twenty yards away.

He saw red.

***

"Mayhem, report!" Rick barked in her ear. She pinned a struggling Mary beneath her right arm and took aim with her left. Her position, her everything, was beyond awkward, but she couldn't split her focus anymore.

As much as she'd like to, she didn't actually have to hit anyone. All she had to do was get close enough to keep them off her and Mary until the guys arrived and provided cover. Her knee stung and throbbed like a bitch, but she ignored the pain.

Mary squirmed beneath her.

"Hold still. My team will be here any moment. They'll get us out of this." Cara prayed her words sank in and the teen would listen. Then she saw movement and didn't hesitate. She'd been fired on once. A child's life was in danger. This was no time for doubt. She fired in the direction where she'd seen a shadow of movement, hoping it was enough to make the asshole think twice about shooting at a child.

If there was a miracle and she hit him with her left hand, she'd feel absolutely zero remorse. She held her position, took a breath and answered Rick. "We're okay, but I need cover, ASAP. Mary and I are pinned under fire."

Noah responded first. "Under fire? No shit, Mayhem. Sounds like a warzone."

"Nah. That's her norm, remember? She excels under fire. My girl's got this." Holloway's words spoke of confidence, but she heard the underlying thread of worry.

Pete checked in—as always, raring to go. "I'm in position. Let's get these fuckers."

Rick spoke next, his words so much more than an order. "Call'em out as you fall in. I'm at your nine o'clock, Mayhem. We got you."

"I know." She couldn't let the soft reassurance go without acknowledgement.

"I got your three o'clock," Trent drawled.

"I'm at your seven. We got you." Noah, her gruff bear, offered his support.

Holloway spoke softly, but she saw the hard line of his jaw clench in her mind. "I'm at your four o'clock. I dare those motherfuckers to blink in your direction."

"Cara, I got your six." Joe added his support. "Get your ass out of there."

"Mayhem, you're covered. Grab Mary and run for it." Rick gave the final command.

Cara wrapped her right arm around the girl's chest and spoke close to her ear. "My team's here. This is our chance. We're going to run for that big oak tree. They'll protect us. No matter what happens, stick close to me and we'll be fine." She lifted the girl then released her only long enough to grab her hand in a brutal grip. She wasn't taking any chances.

She stayed low and raced for the shadowed safety of the woods.

A warning shot fired out from her left. The girl flinched, but stayed close to Cara's side. Another immediately followed from her right. She had no fear. The guys would die before they let any harm come to her.

Time blurred and seconds felt like days as they ran across the short distance until finally she entered the cover of the forest and pushed Mary behind the large trunk.

Rick jerked his head toward the direction they'd come in. "Take her back to the rendezvous point. MacDonald, go with them. We'll take care of this and meet you there."

"Copy. Let's get you somewhere safe, sweetheart." She tucked the girl under her arm.

"Where are we going?" It didn't escape her that, even though he gave them a little space and stayed quiet, the girl tried to stay as far away from Joe as Cara's reach allowed.

"Back to our safe point. It'll be a good meeting place and it's out of harm's way. Getting you somewhere safe is our priority. We'll be there in a few minutes." Cara listened but her mic had gone silent. She wondered what the guys were up to. She suspected Rick chose Joe to go with her because of his position in the Sheriff's Department. "We'll figure out what to do, where you'll go from there."

"I don't need to go anywhere. You can't make me." The girl's blue eyes took on a stubborn edge.

"Mary, honey, we want what's best for you. I promise we'll get you to a good place. I swear it."

The girl cocked her head again. Her words took on a hard, resolute edge. "My name's not Mary. It's Addie. I'm not leaving my home. You can't make me go to one of those stupid group homes for bad kids. I'm not bad." Her volume rose with each word, until she nearly yelled. "No!"

Like a cornered wild animal, she lashed out, tripping Cara. When her bad knee hit the ground, she cried out and fell, the side of her head hitting a rock. Her vision dimmed and pain spliced through her skull.

"Fuck." Joe appeared at her side, cradling her head. "Cara, babe?"

"I'm fine. I think. She got away, didn't she?" She turned her head back and forth, testing for pain. The forest spun around her, and she grabbed her ears, trying to stop the spinning.

"Yes. It's my fault. You fell and I blinked and hesitated. Then she vanished. I fucked up." Sorrow marked his features.

This was going to kill Rick. She hated to break the news, but the sooner the better. There was a miniscule chance that they might run across her on their way back in. "Kate? Break in and tell Rick that Mary, or Addie, is loose. She ran from us."

"Oh no. Will do."

"He sent me with you two because of my badge, didn't he?" He gently cupped her face in his hands and looked at the injured side.

"Probably. Don't be offended if he leaves pieces of what happened out. He's trying to protect you, not shut you out." She winced when he pulled a flap of torn fabric off her abraded knee.

"I figured as much. You know, I almost had a heart attack when I heard the gunfire and then saw you on the ground. Even after I realized you had it under control, it took a minute for me to get my pulse to slow."

"Sorry, but there was no time for me to do anything other than act. That's just the way combat is."

He ran a hand over his hair and smiled wryly. "Mayhem, my ass. You are one rock-solid warrior, aren't you?"

She smiled back. Not a compliment she was used to, but she was more touched than if he'd called her the most beautiful woman in the world. "Shh. It's my secret. Don't tell the guys."

"Can you walk?"

"Hey. I'm a badass soldier. I can't let a little tumble ruin my reputation." Her brave words didn't stop her from groaning aloud as she tried to stand. Mid-crouch, he put his hands under her arms and gently hoisted her the rest of the way. For the briefest of moments, she gave him her weight and savored the sensation of having someone to lean on.

"Shit, Cara. I should have chased after her. Not one of us will be able to sleep tonight for worrying about her." Joe took her hand in his as they walked back to the rendezvous point.

"I doubt you would have found her. She grew up here and knows the territory like the back of her hand."

"My brain knows that, but my heart doesn't care."

"I know. I think, short of tying her up, she would have found a way to escape."

Late evening turned to night as shadows overtook the landscape, matching their moods.

Chapter Eight

Cara watched Trent's home come into view through Joe's windshield. At the end of the long, curving driveway he stopped his truck. Low on energy and spirits, no one seemed to notice the tension between her and Joe.

Holloway and Trent hopped out of the extra cab behind them and grabbed their gear from the bed. Everyone had been subdued on the way back for their routine post-op meeting. As always, Rick insisted that everyone attend while the details were fresh in their minds. Nothing short of hospitalization excused an absence. Thankfully, Kate didn't mind having a houseful of soldiers from time to time.

"Stay put. Let me come around and help you down." Her hand paused on the door handle at Joe's order.

"I can get down, really. I think it's just skinned and bruised." When she saw his face, she decided it might be best to obey. She waited, watching his long-legged stride eat up the ground. Her mouth watered. His natural, unconscious swagger spoke of earned confidence.

Why did he have to be so damn sexy?

Here she was battered, bruised, sweaty, and stinky while he looked like a hero on book cover. He opened her door, revealing fatigues, boots and sweat mussed hair. It was so unfair. Feeling all sorts of awkward, she held out an arm, planning to use his shoulder to brace herself for the climb down.

He shook his head and used both hands to grab her waist, but instead of setting her feet down on the ground, he gently pulled her to the edge of the seat and moved in between her legs. His arms flexed in the glow of the truck's interior light. Thick veins displayed against a backdrop of muscle stole her focus.

"Babe?"

"Uh?" She looked up dazedly. Maybe she'd hit her head harder than she'd thought.

He smirked and she almost swallowed her tongue. "I owe you an apology. I was an ass the other morning, and you deserved better."

His apology caused something warm to blossom deep inside her. Then again, she'd be lying if she said his forearms didn't contribute to her case of warm and fuzzies. "It's okay. It was bad timing. No big deal."

"My sister's timing had nothing to do with me being rude to you. That's all on me. I hadn't planned on things going that far, that fast. I panicked and I used Kylie's appearance as an excuse to lash out and retreat." His shoulders slumped and as if defeated, he touched his forehead to hers. "I have no idea what I'm doing."

She cupped his face. "It's okay. There aren't any rules. We'll figure it out as we go."

He closed his eyes then hugged her to him in a tight, yet gentle hold. She worried that she might actually need him to carry her to Trent's house, not because of her injuries, but because he'd turned her bones to jelly. Engulfed in his solid, comforting warmth, she wasn't sure there could be a safer haven.

Nearby, a door on Rick's new, monstrous SUV slammed.

Pete called, as he headed to the front door, "Let's go, lovebirds! I want to get home to my own honeybee sometime before dawn."

"Man, one day somebody's going to shut that mouth with their fist." Noah grumbled and went inside.

124

She felt Joe's heavy sigh a pat on her side. "We better go. The peanut gallery's waiting." He helped her down and offered to take the weight off her bad knee.

"I'm good. I promise." His narrowed eyes said he didn't quite believe her, so she gave him another way to help. "Will you carry my gear for me?" It cost her to ask him to do that much. She always carried her pack.

"Absolutely. But don't think I don't know what you're doing, stubborn woman." He kissed her temple and unknowingly soothed the sting.

She couldn't help it. She flashed him a big cheesy grin.

***

"You stupid motherfucker! What were you thinking? You just announced our presence to half the county." Boyd watched as Dale Hawkins spat in the face of Jimmy, the idiot cousin who'd started a Wild West shootout with Dark Horse.

He huddled in the garage corner and sniveled, making excuses. Jimmy had likely fried the majority of his brain cells with each and every cheap high he'd crossed paths with in the past ten years.

He'd like nothing more than to dropkick both of them over the quarry pond's cliff. Unfortunately, he needed them, especially Dale. They were short on time and manpower. It wasn't like he could go down to the local bar and recruit a new lowlife every time the Sheriff lost his temper.

"What have you been into? You swore that, if I brought you in on this, you'd keep your nose clean." Dale's volume grew, making Jimmy's tremors worse. Boyd hoped the pitiful excuse for a lackey had enough brain cells remaining to understand that silence was his best friend. They didn't have time for family drama.

"Just a little something from my girlfriend's brother. Just a sample is all." Jimmy wiped his nose on the back of his hand.

Smack!

Dale backhanded Jimmy hard enough to bust his lip, splattering droplets of blood on the dusty wall behind him. "Family ties will get you only so far, boy. You get your shit together, or you'll end up at the bottom of the pond like Smith.

Boyd stepped in. "We need to get out of here. I doubt anyone will show tonight, but I still don't like it."

"Let's get out of here and regroup, let the dust settle." Dale picked his phone and keys up off the long table. "Who was that crazy chic? Never seen anything like it."

"I suspect she's had some military training. I'll see what I can dig up through my contacts." He wasn't showing Hawkins all his cards yet. Pawns had to earn their entrance into his world and the good Sheriff didn't have the control to cut it. Too much rode on this, and he wasn't giving anything away to a man whose bottom line was greed.

Money might be important, but it wasn't the only motivator.

Dale looked at him through narrowed eyes. "You've mentioned these mysterious contacts of yours more than once. You better not be doing anything shady behind my back. Don't you forget who owns this county. You're a guest in Potter County, nothing more."

Boyd stifled the urge to deck Hawkins. He'd love nothing more than to be far away from po-dunk Riley Creek. He bit his tongue and reminded himself of his end-goal. "Let's roll out before anyone shows, or we'll all be up shit creek."

***

Cara eased down to sit on the couch beside Noah. Straightening her leg out in front of her, she held back a wince of pain. She mentally crossed her fingers and hoped she'd be able to stand after the debriefing was over.

She didn't have to remind herself that the minor sacrifice had been well worth the pain. Every time she closed her eyes, the memory replayed in a horrifying loop. Her stomach dropped to her knees, and she shuddered when she remembered the moment the girl broke through the woods and into the clearing surrounding the quarry. Thinking back on it, the only thing she could figure was that maybe the girl thought to show Cara her find, and then split before they guys caught up with them.

She heard that first gunshot and stopped dead in her tracks. There'd been the slightest pause before someone down in the old garage had shouted. "You fucking idiot!" The familiarity in that voice kick-started her heart. As if the first gunshot wasn't warning enough, Boyd Campbell's voice plunged her into action.

Whatever the girl found had to be a hundred kinds of dangerous.

Mary—or Addie, as she'd called herself—stood frozen in place, an easy target. A second shot fired, and Cara sprang into motion. She'd drawn her weapon, tackled the girl, and flipped the safety off. She fired two shots for the single hope of buying them time.

It worked.

The guys provided the cover they needed to make it out safely.

The only downside? They'd opened an enormous, ugly can of worms. When at the rendezvous point she'd relayed her suspicions about Boyd's presence she'd braced herself for disbelief.

There'd been none. Not a single drop.

Noah had shaken his head and muttered a single word. "Figures."

With a sharp head snap, James had looked straight to her and pointed. "You better watch your six. You get the slightest itch, you call me, call us in. I can't wait to take this bastard down."

Now in the comfort of Trent's home they focused on her again.

"Maybe it's time you and your mother moved in with Trent or the Walkers." Rick opened the lid of his laptop and leaned back in his customary chair at Trent's table.

"I'm all for that suggestion. Hell, Rick, make it an order." Trent leaned back and slid his arm around Kate's waist when she moved to stand with him.

Brimming with warmth and concern, the gorgeous brunette added her support. "Seriously, Cara, you're both welcome, wanted even. We'd sleep better knowing you're safe."

"I will be, and I promise to call if I notice the slightest thing out of the ordinary." She met their gazes squarely, letting them see the truth of her words.

"I'm disappointed, Mayhem. Seriously, I thought better of you." Pete shook his head as if disappointed by a child.

"What did I do?" She looked to her friend, completely lost as to how she'd let him down.

He looked at her, one hundred percent serious. "I thought you bled blue. Now I know differently after all these years. I'm ashamed. I mean, seriously, how many UK games have we watched together? You've screamed yourself hoarse for the Cats. Now I see you covered in red. I just don't know if we can be friends any longer." His words were totally ridiculous, but the emotion in his eyes was anything but.

A lump formed in her throat. "Sorry, Pete."

"Yeah, well, you better be. If anything happens to you, who else am I going to get to throw popcorn at the TV with when the Cats play Louisville?" He pointed his finger at her then looked down to his laptop, moving onto the next topic. *Work.*

God, they hadn't watched a game together in years. She'd have to fix that this winter, even if they met at the arena or if she had to make the long drive home.

Home. She'd forgotten how much she'd left behind when she'd moved away for school years ago and then got caught up in the work race.

Rick stood and turned his back to the group as he stared at a map. "Pete? We need a list. Put Mary at the top."

Pete looked from Rick to the computer and at the mess of wires spread across the table.

"I'll make the list." Kate touched her hand to Trent's shoulder and went to the kitchen. She returned with a legal pad and pen from one of the drawers. "Go ahead."

Cara rose her hand in a signal for attention. "When I called her Mary, she looked at me in an odd way and said her name was Addie. Might want to look into that."

"Got it," Kate said.

Rick looked to Joe. "I made a couple of phone calls on the way here. Last chance to back out. Concerning Potter County Sheriff's Department, this the point of no return."

She watched as Joe met Rick's gaze dead on, without hesitation. "I'm in, no matter what happens or who's involved. There's something dirty brewing in my hometown, I don't care what it takes, I want whoever is responsible held accountable. Kids have access to drugs. A young girl was nearly killed by flying bullets. The choice is easy."

Rick nodded as if he hadn't expected anything different. "Okay. Are they loaded, Pete?"

"We have enough to start. The others are downloading as we speak." The TV screen blinked to life.

"Make sure you send copies to Bowie and the Kentucky State Police. We waited and watched after Cara and Joe left with the girl. We got pictures as they fled the scene. There were no real surprises, and we did get confirmation of what we suspected. Kate? Next on the list, I want this plate run again. We take nothing for granted." A photo of a gangly, greasy-haired, male standing next to the open door of a battered Mustang filled the monitor. His face was slightly blurred by motion, but Cara thought he might have a split lip.

"Got it."

"Next." The next photo showed an SUV driving out of the open bay door of the garage. The words Potter County sprawled across the side.

Joe spoke, his voice flat, utterly devoid of emotion. "That's Dale Hawkins' new county issued ride."

"We've already run another search, but add him to the list," Rick said. The last picture appeared on screen, catching Boyd Campbell as he stepped into a gray truck. "And last, but not least, we have our confirmation. The snake is back."

***

"Joe." Dale Hawkins nodded to an empty chair in front of his desk.

He'd been waiting for this. He might not have known exactly when it would come, but he knew one way or another that he'd be singled out and warned off.

"Sheriff." He couldn't help it. He didn't take the seat he was directed to. He stood beside it and faced Dale.

"I received a call from Mark Cline. He said you've been harassing his boy, Brayden." The man wouldn't meet his eyes. He sifted through paperwork on his desk, as if Joe were beneath his notice.

130

He knew better. Dale Hawkins couldn't meet his gaze because he was a lying sack of shit. Someone was watching the Clines. "I went out there once to talk to Brayden, and Mark gave me his permission. He'd said that they were eager to help." He'd seen the conviction in Mark's eyes.

"Good. Then your job is done. There's no need for you to go back out there and bother the Clines any more. They're good people."

"They are." That's why they'd been willing to help. "I'd like to know where a couple of good kids in Riley Creek found heroin. Wouldn't you?" He gambled and watched the Sheriff's response carefully.

"Leave it be, MacDonald. The judge will sort the kids out, and that will be the end of it. I suspect some drifter left it behind accidently. If you know what's best, you'll leave it at that." Hawkins pushed his shoulders back and raised his head to finally met Joe eye to eye. "Are we clear?"

"We are." He probably should have tucked his tail and played the part but he couldn't. He didn't back down. With a disgusted sneer, he turned on his heel and left the office. Looking at his watch he saw that it was almost time to clock out. He had the sudden need to take his daughter out for dinner and ice cream. He messaged his mother to let her know he'd pick Kylie up. When the urge to include someone else in their dinner date hit, he didn't resist. He picked up the phone and called Cara.

Chapter Nine

"Mom, I'm fine. Quit fussing over me." She tried to usher her mother out of the laundry room. "I'll get that. I'm perfectly capable of washing my own laundry."

Her mother flapped her hands at Cara, literally shooing her away. "Your knee is swelling again. Go watch TV or something. Go on."

She was glad that her mother suddenly felt better and had been cooperating with her physical therapy orders. The day after she'd hurt herself, her mother caught her limping. Since then, her mother had gone from patient to caretaker. If anything, Cara worried that she might do too much as she moved a load of Cara's laundry from the washer to the dryer. She stood in the laundry room doorway watching her mother and debated on whether this latest fight was worth the headache.

She also smelled a rat. But should she let it go or confront her mother?

"I don't know what possessed you to play softball with those boys. I don't know how many times I've told you that you'd get hurt if you didn't leave well enough alone. Look what happened. Your knee might scar! They might be a little on the short side, but your legs have always been one of your better features. Now you've gone and ruined one of them!"

She turned her back on her mother hoping she would wind down in a few minutes. She'd hated lying to her mother, but judging by her current fit, she could only imagine what kind of tailspin her mother would fly into if she told her she gashed it on a rock when she'd tackled a teenager who'd been running through gunfire.

Head spinning, pea soup spitting kids had nothing on her mother in a full-blown meltdown.

She sat down on the couch and picked up her computer. The screen had barely flashed on before she heard her mother call out from the laundry room. "I still think you should go and at least get an x-ray or something. Did you put that ice pack back on?" Her voice grew stronger as she came through the kitchen, likely on her way to check on Cara. *Again.*

She grabbed the cool ice pack and placed it on her knee just before her mother entered the room. "I don't need x-rays. It's feeling much better. I promise." And it did.

Her mother stood before her with her hands on her hips, staring down at the leg Cara had propped up on the coffee table and a pillow. "Is it still cold? It doesn't look cold. Give it here. I'll change it out." Before Cara could move, she'd snatched it off her leg and stormed back to the kitchen for a fresh pack. When she didn't come straight back but instead went into the bathroom next, Cara dropped her head to the back of the couch. She knew what was coming.

Sure enough a minute later her mother reappeared. "Here put this on first." Her mother held vitamin E oil in one hand and the fresh ice pack in the other.

Without a word, she took them both, applied them and then tried to focus on her computer.

Her mother had returned to her prior position, staring down at her with a frown, and she asked, "What are you doing?"

"I'm looking for nursing jobs in Borneo." She stared at her email until her eyes hurt, but nothing registered. She didn't know how much longer she could tolerate her mother fussing over her.

"Hmph." Her mother finally turned around and went back to her room. Cara figured, if she was lucky, she might have twenty minutes before she returned. She slid the icepack off and hoped the icy numbness had time to wear off before she had to put it back. At this rate, her knee could end up with frostbite.

She'd been giving her mother a hard time when she'd mentioned the job search, but since she didn't have anything better to do, she started a more realistic one. She wasn't finished with her program yet, but it never hurt to keep an eye on the market. Her hometown might be a little too close to her mother, but then she wondered.

What about Potter County? She'd be closer to home and her mother without actually being too close. With a larger hospital, there might also be more opportunities. She'd be closer to Dark Horse, if she wanted to work with them more often.

Her phone rang. She looked at the caller ID and smiled.

And I'd be closer to Joe. It was far too early to take their relationship into her career considerations, but still.

"Hello?"

"Hey. How are you?" She loved the sound of his deep voice.

"A little stir crazy, but good. What's up?"

"Kylie and I are going out for dinner and dessert. We wondered if you'd like to go with us?"

"Yes. When?" Her words came out rushed and maybe even a little desperate. She didn't care. She could think of no better reason to get out of the house and away from her mother than a dinner out.

His laughter came over the phone.

"Okay. Good. I didn't expect that kind of response, but we'll take it. We can pick you up in about thirty minutes. There's no need to dress up. I just picked her up from my parents and neither one of us has changed."

"That sounds perfect. And I didn't mean to scare you off by sounding so desperate. I've been cooped up with Momma for three days, and she's driving me batty. I need out. Please?"

"We'll be there in thirty."

"Thanks," she whispered into the phone.

Twenty-eight minutes later, his truck pulled up in front of the house while her mother peeked out the window. "Is she in there? I can't see her."

"Mom. Would you stop? They'll see you." She grabbed her purse and counted to ten.

After one more good peek, her mother dropped the curtain and stepped back. "You said she was cute. I want to meet her. Are you sure you shouldn't have put on a little makeup? Maybe a nicer top with your shorts?" She wrung her hands together.

"We're taking Kylie. I'd look foolish dressed up when they're in jeans and shorts." They both turned and looked to the door when they heard heavy footsteps on the porch. "Mom. Please behave, okay?"

"Okay." The hand wringing continued.

Cara softened. "Do you want me to bring you something back?"

"No. I'm fine. I just want you to have a good time."

A light, barely audible knock sounded at the door and her mother reached for it then stopped herself. She stepped back and looked to Cara.

"Go ahead, Mom. You can open the door. I just don't want you drawing up a marriage license or adoption papers, okay?"

Then something so out of the ordinary happened, it stole Cara's speech. Her mother laughed. Cara couldn't remember the last time she'd heard her laughter. Then she opened the door and revealed Kylie with her hand poised, ready to knock again.

"Hi. Is this Cara's house?" Kylie, with her hair in a single messy braid over her shoulder, looked up to her mom and smiled.

"It is. I'm Betty, Cara's mom. You must be Kylie. It's nice to meet you." Her mother beamed at Kylie in a full on, sun breaking through rainy skies, smile.

"Yes. Nice to meet you too. We're here to take Cara to dinner. Can she go with us?" Kylie seemed to take extra care with her words, making sure to pronounce each one correctly.

"Absolutely. You guys have a good time." Her mother nodded and reached out a hand as if to straighten the little girl's hair, but she pulled it back before making actual contact.

"Okay."

Cara stepped forward and smiled at Kylie. "Hi, sweetheart. It's good to see you again."

"Hi! Let's go eat!" She jumped up, as if she couldn't contain her energy any longer.

Joe nodded his head to her mother in farewell, and took Kylie's hand in his. When he took hers in his other her chest filled with warm and fuzzies.

"Is pizza and a movie okay? Kylie's been desperate to see the new cartoon movie."

"Please, Cara? It's supposed to be so funny. There's this one part where the bear does this thing with the dog and everybody laughs. It's your date though, so Dad said we should ask if it's okay with you." She looked up to Cara with huge, bright eyes that gave any puppy a run for its money.

"That sounds perfect." And it did. She let Joe help her up into the truck. He patted her thigh and shut the door.

As she buckled the seatbelt, the hair at her nape stood, and chills raced down her spine.

He watched the cop help Cara into his truck and then lift his daughter into her car seat. *The perfect little family.* Completely clueless that he watched them, they wore smiles as if it was the greatest day ever.

Cara. The little bitch tease. It is all her fault. All of it. He'd almost gotten free of this shithole corner of Kentucky when Sutton had pulled him back in. It figured that two of the biggest threats to his plan hooked up.

Running his fingers over the scars her fingernails had left on his forearm, he remembered the feel of her throat convulsing within his hands. He could still clearly see the panic flashing in her eyes when she realized she couldn't fight him off.

He'd ripped her shirt and watched her chest heave as she struggled to breathe. He'd only needed one more minute to finish the job. He would have preferred to draw her terror out, to make her experience what she'd made him feel. She deserved it and more, after all she'd done to him.

He'd just wanted was a little companionship, but Cara made a fool of him.

When he tried to take what she waved at him, she played the victim. Then she'd cried out and those assholes had shown and interrupted.

He'd been the bad guy.

The instant Holloway pulled him off her, he'd known his days in their unit were over. Those six had stuck together like some sort of merry band of do-gooders. When Cara started wheezing for air and coughing, Holloway looked her direction, worried. The brief distraction was all he needed. He broke Holloway's hold and vanished into the congested, dark heart of Sharana. He'd made his way to a contact of his in the Afghan National Police. For a price, they'd hidden him until he'd found a way to get out of the country.

It had taken him four months and a deal with the devil, but eventually he'd gotten out of one hell and into another. He'd needed confidentiality, a new identity and a way out of the country. Through one of his uncle's contacts, he'd gotten all of it, but in addition to money, he owed Marcus Sutton a favor.

Marcus Sutton was the type of guy no one wanted to owe.

He'd known his time in Kentucky was limited, but he'd needed the money from his uncle. He'd known better. He should have left Bailey hanging when'd he'd felt the itch to move on. But he hadn't. He'd been greedy, and now he had to deal with the stupid sheriff, another idiot who thought his shit didn't stink and that, because he wore a badge, he stood above the law and the land.

Boyd wasn't sure that any amount of money he might make from their current operation was worth the risk to his neck. He'd rather be poor than behind bars.

The blue truck rumbled to life and drove away; it's occupants clueless that they were being watched.

He'd nearly finished off them off once before. He could do it again. He'd given a group of Chechen jihadis the details of a scheduled escort run. He'd put the Dark Horse crew right into their hands. It should have been like taking candy from a baby.

But somehow they'd screwed it up. Instead of taking the Dark Horse crew down, they'd ended up looking like heroes. He watched from the shadows as they'd driven right into an ambush. They'd been against enough firepower to arm a small country and Dark Horse still come out alive and shinning like fucking heroes.

He'd have to take care of the situation himself. It was the only way to be sure a plan worked. He would take care of things in Riley

Creek, right under Sheriff Hawkins' watch. That would give him one more failsafe.

And if he took out Dark Horse's diva? Well, then, the others would be crippled by their grief. That included the do-gooder deputy. It would buy him enough time to finish the job for Sutton and get the hell out of Dodge.

Chapter Ten

"I just want to look in the little girl's department. Give me two minutes, that's all I need." Betty Gregory pointed as she walked off, leaving Cara in her dust.

"Mom. We are not buying Kylie any clothes. I don't think Joe would appreciate us butting into his life that way. We don't even know what size she wears." Cara knew the effort was wasted before her mother even opened her mouth to reply.

"She's a little bit of a thing. I'd say she still wears a five or six. It doesn't matter. I'm only going to look at the sales. I'm sure she'll need clothes for school. I'll just be a moment. You never know when you'll find a bargain." A woman on a mission, her mother headed straight for the dress rack.

"Mom. No." She caught up to her miraculously healed mother and put her hand over hers as she reached for a dress. "I know you mean well, but I don't think Kylie likes frilly clothes and, though I adore her, I don't want to do anything that might scare Joe off." She shamelessly used the only thing she could think of that might make her mother listen. "He's a little gun-shy, especially concerning Kylie. If we show up with a new wardrobe, he might think I'm going too fast. You have to be patient." Though in reality, she would never use such a play on Joe or any man, she used it now on her mother.

Her mother pursed her lips and tilted her head as she looked at the dresses. "I suppose you're right. Maybe we need to get you a new dress, something for a nice date out. Let's go look." They'd come to, of all places, Riley Creek to get the new gym shoes her mother decided she needed for physical therapy. Never mind that there were more stores closer to home.

"Mom. I have everything I need. And Joe likes what I wear just fine. I promise." Memories of him stripping her clothes off the last time they'd been together played through her mind. "He's a good guy, but he has simple tastes. Besides, I don't want you on your feet much longer. I know your hip is doing much better, but I'm not sure going from zero to sixty is such a good idea. It's time for a break."

This time she got a frown in response. "Fine. If you insist." Her mother trailed a finger over a length of lavender ribbon trim. "When are you seeing him again?"

She took the shoebox tucked under mother's left arm and herded her toward the payment counter. "I don't know yet. We didn't set up our next date."

"Well, you should have. You never said how the other evening went. Good, I hope?" Her mother asked it as if making sure Cara had been on her best behavior.

"I had fun. It wasn't a typical date. We just saw a family movie and had dinner and ice cream." It was an altogether different type of experience than her first date with Joe, but she'd enjoyed it equally. She hadn't laughed that much in ages. The evening had been more about Kylie than them and she found that came with a different type of satisfaction.

At the evening's end, he'd dropped her off at her front door. He hadn't kissed her, but as he trailed his fingers down her cheek in a tender farewell, she'd seen his desire to do just that. He'd wanted to as much as she'd hungered for a taste.

So, no. They didn't have a date scheduled, but she didn't think it'd be long before they saw each other again. And she looked forward to it.

She set the shoebox on the counter and smiled at the saleswoman, a very familiar, slightly older looking lady with deep brown eyes. The rat she'd smelled earlier suddenly stank to high heaven. She greeted them with a warm smile. "Did you find everything okay?"

"Yes. Thank you," Cara answered, before her mother could, in an attempt to head her off. She needn't have bothered because there was no stopping Betty Gregory when she was on a mission.

"Are you Louise MacDonald? I'm Betty Gregory." Her mother introduced herself as if the woman she suspected might be Joe's mother should know her.

"I am. It's nice to meet you, Betty." Confusion dimmed her smile.

"This is my daughter, Cara May Gregory." Her mother set her enormous purse on the counter and dug for her checkbook.

"Um, it's nice to meet you, too." Louise smiled again and rang up the shoes.

Cara couldn't stand it any longer and blurted, "I'm a friend of Joe and Kate's. I moved in with my mother temporarily and met them recently through a mutual friend." If it hadn't been for her mother's recent surgery she might have hip-checked her into next week.

"Oh. That's lovely." When she looked down to bag the shoes, Cara gave her mother the death glare.

Her mother frowned and pulled out her debit card. Miracle of miracles, she finished her purchase without any more snooping. Cara bit her tongue until they were out the door. Then she let loose. "Mom! Really! Why? Why was that necessary?"

"Why what?" Her mother put on her best innocent expression.

Beyond exasperated, she shook her head. "I knew something was up when you insisted on coming here. How did you know she worked here?"

"I asked him." She tilted her head as if Cara was the one who'd lost a screw.

"Mom! When I dug out the vase? I left you alone with him for less than three minutes. Why do you do these things?" She wanted to pull her hair out as she growled, literally growled, at her meddling mother. She stepped down off the curb, turned and looked back.

"Well, you're my only child. Your father isn't alive to do the whole opening the door with a loaded shotgun bit. I can only do so much, Cara May." She stood with her hands on her hips, explaining the simplest of concepts to her dimwitted child.

Cara didn't know whether to be touched or supremely ticked off. She mirrored her mother's pose then growled again. Then giving up, she threw her hands up in the air. Deciding it was in her best interest to let it go, she reached for the bag. "Come on, Mom. Did you even really want these shoes?"

Her mother raised her hand to her mouth as if caught with her hand in the cookie jar and accidentally dropped the bag. Cara bent over to pick it up. Then she heard a familiar sound that jolted her into action. The distinct sound of a high-powered rifle firing. She tackled her mother to the ground before the report's final echo.

"What in the world?" Her mother's anxious question served as reassurance that at least she was okay.

"We have to get out of sight. Can you make it back into the store? Stay low. I'll be right behind you." By right behind, she meant on top of.

She nodded beneath Cara's chin.

Cara closed eyes, took a deep breath and opened them. "Let's go! Go!" She hauled her mother to her feet, put her hand on her head to keep her low and all but threw her the short distance to the door. Reaching over her she yanked the door open and sent her mother in.

Seeing she was in, she ducked even lower, just before another deafening crack rent the air with a thunderous boom. The glass door shattered, sending tiny fragments of glass everywhere. She shouted as her ears rang. "Go. Get out of sight." She bent double as she crossed the threshold and heard a loud ping hit the door's metal frame where her head would have been, followed by the echo of a third shot.

Dear God, the shooter means business. She saw that Louise MacDonald had pulled her mother behind the counter with her and she had a phone pressed to her ear. Cara kneeled behind a display of folded jeans and hoped the authorities came quickly. They were no longer in plain view, but if the shooter was desperate enough to come inside, they would be sitting ducks. Her hand itched for her weapon. She had taken her mother shoe shopping! It was the last place she'd expect to need a gun.

She heard faint sirens in the distance. Thankfully, someone must have been nearby.

"Mom! Stay put until the police get here. Are you okay?" *Fuck!* She'd tackled her mother who had a hip fracture and surgery. But there was nothing else she could have done.

"I'm okay." Her voice trembled a bit, but otherwise she sounded just like her mom.

"Your hip? I'm sorry I knocked you down, but I didn't have any choice." She talked to her mother across the aisle.

"It's fine, I think. Cara, my God! You were like...like...a warrior princess! Like a real soldier! You saved us." She shifted as if trying to get comfortable on the hard floor and Cara's throat clenched.

"Mom. I *am* a soldier." She met her mother's gaze.

"You are." The quiet awe in her mother's words were nearly her undoing. She wanted to pull her into a gentle hug and hold her close, but she couldn't reach her.

"Joe?" Letting the store phone dangle over the counter, Mrs. MacDonald held a cell phone to her ear. "I'm fine; we're fine. Your friend Cara May is here with her mother, and she told us not to move.

145

I'm sitting on the floor behind the sales counter with her mother. No, I don't think anyone was hit."

Joe!

She interrupted, saying "Mrs. MacDonald? Tell Joe there were three shots fired, possibly from long range. No casualties."

Louise MacDonald repeated the information into her cell phone then looked up to Cara. "He said to tell you he's five minutes out, but that an officer is pulling into the lot now. He also says that Caleb is cool." Her face scrunched on the last sentence as if she didn't understand why anyone would need assurance about one of Joe's fellow deputies. "He said that no matter who else shows, to stick with Caleb until he gets here, and that he's calling your friend Rick."

Cara got his meaning and sighed with relief. Then as her adrenaline wore off and the waiting game set in, so did realization.

Someone tried to kill her. Her mother and Joe's had been caught in the crossfire and could have been killed. This was no accident and no coincidence.

Boyd.

This had his name written all over it. He'd always envisioned himself as some sort of elite sniper. And attacking from long distance, from a safe vantage point with little risk to his own neck was totally his M.O.

God, I would love to wrap my hands around his throat and squeeze until he can't breathe.

A deputy dressed in black fatigue pants, gray T-shirt, and bulletproof vest appeared in the shattered doorway. "Ladies? I'm Caleb. We think it's clear, so you can move about, but we'd like you to stay inside and away from the door for the time being."

"Thank you." Cara stood and went to help her mother and then Mrs. MacDonald up.

"I can't imagine what's going on or why. I mean, this is Riley Creek. Nothing ever happens here." Joe's mother placed her hand over her chest.

"It was all so dramatic!" Her mother's eyes were bright with excitement as she fanned her face.

They all turned their heads when another siren grew in volume until it cut off with a sudden, startling silence.

Joe rushed through the door and straight to his mother, crushing her in a tight hug. "Mom?"

"I'm fine, Joe." Louise put her hand on his cheek, and the sight warmed Cara.

She also noticed that Joe made a damn fine picture in his uniform. He wore the same basic black fatigues and T-shirt as Caleb but filled them out in an entirely different way.

Then he met her gaze with an unreadable expression. "Cara *May*, what a surprise to find you in the midst of all this mayhem."

"Uh, yeah. About that. I can explain. Sort of." God, what did she say without offending her mother too badly? She needed to tell him everything, but they had a rapt audience.

He let go of his mother and came straight toward her. "My Mayhem. Don't worry about it. I'm just glad everyone is okay."

"Mayhem? Joe, you should have seen her! She was a stone-cold, soldier. Why, I don't think I've ever been prouder." Someone could have knocked Cara over with a feather. When Joe came over and gave her a hug of her own, she couldn't resist melting into his solid heat.

Sheriff Dale Hawkins appeared in the doorway, feet crunching on broken glass, and interrupted. "Hello, ladies. It's all clear outside. If you'll come with me, we have a few brief questions." Tall, with salt and pepper hair and a slight paunch, he smiled.

"Sir, I'd rather keep them inside until we're certain that the scene is safe. We haven't had time to—"

"I just came in from outside, MacDonald. It's fine. I'm sure it was just an accident." Hawkins smiled and talked down to Joe as if speaking to a child.

His body turned to steel beneath her hands. "No, I'm not sending my mother outside to a scene where shots were fired less than ten minutes ago."

"Son, I know she's your mother, and I can see that you're attached to the little lady. Maybe you're a little too close to this case. You can sit this one out. Caleb and I can handle it."

Tightening her hold around his waist, she waded in before Joe lost his temper.

"We'll wait in here. My mother has recently had hip surgery and shouldn't stand on concrete for extended periods of time. I've been around live gunfire before. I know—"

"I appreciate your input, ma'am, but we've got this under control." He smiled again, but it didn't reach his eyes. Something dark flickered in their depths as he looked to her.

Her mother stepped forward and her words caught Cara completely off guard. "My daughter is a soldier, and she knows what's she's talking about. She served in Afghanistan. Did you? Have you ever seen combat—?"

Oh. Shit. The last thing she needed was her mother broadcasting her past with Sheriff Hawkins. She let go of Joe and slapped her hand over her mother's mouth to stop her information vomit. "Mom. It's fine. I'm sure the good Sheriff knows what he's talking about. You're fine. I'm fine. No one was hurt." Damn, did it cost her to say the next part. "He's probably right."

Joe looked as though he wanted to flatten Dale with his fist, and she didn't blame him. But what could they do?

Rely on Dark Horse.

Chapter Eleven

She answered her phone as she shut the front door behind her. The caller spoke before she could get out a greeting. "Get your mother packed and then pack for yourself. That's an order." Rick's terse voice barked.

"Rick, I—"

"No. Hell, no. No buts. Get. Your. Asses. Packed."

"You know, I was going to call as soon as I got in and took a quick look at Momma's incision. I think she's fine, but I'll feel better after I check it." She dropped her keys on the table and frowned. Taking a deep breath, she told herself he worried about her safety and should be touched that he worried about her mother as well.

His tone softened a touch. "Are we having the meeting at Trent's or your place? We'll come after you, if you want."

"We'll come out to the Walkers'." In her room, she began to throw clothes into her suitcase, hoping her stay wouldn't last more than a few days. She knew she wouldn't be that lucky.

"I'm not sure I want you two on the road alone. I'll come meet you."

"I won't be surprised if Joe shows up here as soon as he makes sure his mother is settled safely at home." Her stomach still churned each time she thought about the danger that had almost come to Louise and her own mother.

They needed to talk, but she wasn't sure how they'd find the time.

"If he's able, I'll have him follow us in. If for some reason he can't, then I promise to call you. Right now, they're likely regrouping and planning their next move. Let me check on Momma and get us packed, okay?" She went in the bathroom and gathered her toiletries. "Rick?"

"Okay. I don't like this." He sounded quiet, subdued.

"I don't either. I had to tackle my own mother to the concrete sidewalk to avoid gunfire. As much as I hate to inconvenience anyone, I promise you, I'm not taking any more chances."

"We'll be waiting."

"I know. Thanks." She hung up and got out her weapons case. She checked over her pistol. She wanted it loaded and ready. Then she braced herself for an altogether different sort of battle.

She had to find a way to explain this all to her mother without causing a meltdown.

She found her on the phone with her friend Anne. "You should have seen it! Bullets were flying everywhere, like a real movie. Cara knocked me out of the way, like a stunt man."

"Momma, we need to talk," she tried to interrupt.

"That jackass Sheriff acted like it was no big deal. Idiot. Do I look like I was born yesterday? And then—"

Cara pulled the phone away from her mother in mid-sentence.

"Anne, I'm so sorry. I have to talk to Momma. I'll have her call you later tonight or first thing in the morning. Bye, sweetie." She hung up without waiting for a reply.

Her mother crossed her arms over her chest. "Why, Cara May! I raised you better than that. Hmph."

Oh boy. Here we go…

***

"Is your mother set?" After driving Cara and Betty Gregory up to Harlan and Sandy Walker's house, Joe looked down at Cara. Hours had passed since they'd been shot at, and his emotions still bounced from terror to blazing hot anger.

Moonlight made her hair shine and her eyes glitter as she leaned back against the tail end of his truck and smiled weakly. "Yeah, I think so. She'll love staying up at the Walker's house, and they'll treat her like royalty. I just hope she's not too big a terror. They're good people." *Good people?* No, the Walkers were the best kind of people.

Cara ran her hands up and down her arms as if chilled, but the night was far too warm for her to be cold.

He couldn't wait a single moment longer. He pulled her into his arms and crushed her to his chest. Her head dropped against his shoulder, and he felt her expel a heavy breath. She wrapped her arms tight around his waist and leaned against him, as if she couldn't carry her own weight any longer.

They'd both been busy since the shooting and hadn't had time for even a real hug, let alone time to talk. He tucked her head beneath his chin and savored the feel of her in his arms. When he'd heard dispatch say there'd been a shooting right outside the doors to where his mother worked, his heart stopped. He'd been fifteen minutes away, so he flipped on his lights, made the sharpest U-turn of his life, and put the pedal to the floor. The moment his hands were free, he'd called his mom only to her have her tell him that his "new friend Cara May and her mother were outside when the shots were fired." His pulse skyrocketed until he heard the rapid beat in his ears.

His mother and his…his Cara were part of a crime scene.

Then he realized who the target had most likely been and why. Half a day had passed and his blood still boiled when he thought about it. He squeezed her tighter instead of kicking his truck.

"I'm sorry. You must be so angry with me. I would have never set foot within Riley Creek if I had a clue that your mother worked in town or that there was a hint of danger to her. Momma insisted on shopping there today and I went along with her. I suspected she wanted to snoop but I thought it was just a general look through town, never where your mother worked! I knew better than to underestimate her meddling skills. When we walked up to the counter and I saw your smile and brown eyes looking back at me from the cashier's face, I wanted to strangle her. Louise was so nice, then Momma and I went outside and everything went to shit." Hands fisted in the back of his shirt, and she shuddered against him again.

Leave it to Cara to feel guilt when a jackass like Boyd put others in harm's way. He took her chin and tilted her head up. His heart clutched when he saw the stark guilt on her sweet face. When her legs trembled as if she were ready to run out of strength he picked her up with one arm and with the other, he unlatched the tailgate. He set her ass on it and needing her full attention, he moved between her legs.

"Look at me." He cupped her face in both hands and held her damp gaze to his. "You have no reason whatsoever to be sorry. None of this is your fault. I had only two thoughts today. One, light speed couldn't have gotten me there soon enough. Two, I wanted—no, I still want—Boyd's blood on my hands." He watched a single tear well, and his gut cramped. "I'm thankful you were there and in control."

"But if I hadn't been there, it wouldn't have happened. He had to have followed me and took the opportunity when he saw it. Being in Riley Creek probably made it that much more appealing. There he has Hawkins at his back. How could I have been so stupid?"

The tear slid from the corner of her eye and made a silver trail down to her cheek. He kissed the droplet, wishing that he could take her pain away just as easily. His little soldier had a marshmallow heart.

He rubbed his thumb over her jaw and took her mouth in a kiss meant to show her the tenderness she deserved. Her tongue touched his, sparking off a warm glow of arousal. The slow burn grew brighter with each brush of his mouth against hers. Merging, trusting, starving, their mouths communicated a growing passion. Her hands fisted around his belt and when her fingers grazed over the bare skin of his abdomen, the simmer boiled over. The heated potion filled him with rabid hunger.

She whimpered into his mouth and her grip tightened, pulling him closer. He slid his hand down her back and stopped at her waist. He pulled his mouth from hers, bent his head and met her forehead to forehead. There was only one thing he wanted more than the gift of her surrender.

He wanted Boyd and Hawkins behind bars. If that didn't work? He'd settle for their heads.

"Let's go. The guys are waiting on us. Are you staying with Trent and Kate or at my place? Kylie is already with my parents."

She bit her bottom lip and took a deep breath. Trailing her fingertips over his cheek, she gave him the answer he expected, the smart choice. "Here. I couldn't live with myself if I brought more trouble around you or your family. I suspect Trent's going to make Kate stay on the farm, and he'll tighten security even more. It's the best place for me to be." He didn't miss her unspoken meaning. She meant that it was safest for everyone else. Her own safety didn't factor into her choice. As badly as he wanted her with him, he'd accept her decision.

Of course, the right decisions were often the hardest. He'd accept it, but he sure as hell, didn't have to like it.

153

***

"Did you get it out of the fridge or the oven? It's not cold enough. Go on and get. I've got important matters to attend to." Boyd watched as Hawkins looked at the can of beer in his hand, barely sparing his pale, wraith of a wife a glance. Head down, she made a silent exit from their garage.

Boyd had come from their operations base at the old quarry. Each time he drove out there to check on Dale, his neck itched. It wouldn't be long until Dark Horse or the feds showed. They needed to pack up, hunker down and bide their time for at least a few months.

But they didn't have a few months. Ironclad deals had been made and they had a schedule to keep. If they couldn't supply their buyers, they wouldn't have a business.

Sutton would be back to breathing down his neck.

He heard the front door close and Hawkins set his beer on the workbench. "This mess stinks. It has cluster-fuck written all over it. What are you going to do about it? You screwed the pooch today. I can't continue to cover up your mistakes."

Boyd bit his tongue. Hawkins had left everything, even most of the decisions, up to him. Yet he wanted to play man in charge. "We need to get Dark Horse out of the way when our associates come to town. I think we should repackage somewhere else then have the meet where we planned. The buyer won't be pleased if it appears we don't have our shit together. This first deal is too damn important."

"MacDonald has to go, but if he shows up dead it'll be too suspicious. A dead deputy will bring to much attention to Riley Creek at the worst possible time." Hawkins leaned back against the workbench and frowned.

Boyd waited to see if the Sheriff would come up with anything worth contributing. When their paths first crossed, he'd thought that he might have found an ally worth his weight. He'd been wrong. So far all he'd done was wave his dirty badge around and point out the obvious.

A little over a month ago, he'd been out in the county with the local white trash, leaving a cockfight. What better place to find scum looking to make a quick buck? Not thinking, he'd pulled his truck out onto the road and had an open beer in the cup holder, in plain view.

He'd also had a dead light bulb in his driver side taillight. Hawkins pulled him over and Boyd had seen the same thing in the Sheriff's face as he saw in his own every time he looked in the mirror. *A total disregard for the law.*

When he'd pulled out his fake license, he'd also "accidently" pulled out a couple of hundred dollar bills. He'd handed his license over for inspection. After a brief moment Dale handed it back without the bills and sent him on his way.

He'd found his way in. He needed additional manpower, and who better to have on his side than the local law?

Now he wasn't so sure. Hawkins could be more liability than help.

"Any thoughts on how to get MacDonald and Dark Horse out of the picture on the day of the exchange?" He didn't expect much of an answer, but asked just to play the game.

"Yeah. I do." And when Hawkins outlined his plan, Boyd realized exactly how stupid the man was.

There was no way he'd sign on for that.

But it does give me a better idea. One that might actually work.

***

155

"Hmmm. Now that right there's not a bad sight." Cara turned from where she stood at the corral gate, watching the sunset. Kate spoke from beside her with her arms crossed on the top rail, wearing an appreciative grin. She followed the other woman's gaze to find that Trent was bent over, with Scarlet's hoof in one hand and a frown on his face. Kate's eyes locked on Trent, and Cara silently admitted that he did have an ass worth appreciating.

But the man standing beside her friend held Cara's attention. She didn't think she'd ever tire of seeing those long, muscled legs encased in faded denim. His flat belly and broad shoulders that stretched his T-shirt tight made her mouth water. Joe looked up and met her gaze. Heat flickered in his chocolate and gold eyes.

Kylie stood beside the men, but worry scrunched in her brow. "Will Scarlet be okay?" She leaned over beside Trent, trying to get a look at the old horse's hoof.

"She'll be fine, but I think our lesson is done for today. Storm clouds are rolling in." Trent released the horse and gestured for a nearby stable hand to care for her. "I thought Kate and I might take you to see Bonnie and the other foals before we go up to the big house. Are you ready?"

"Yes!" Kylie jumped up.

"That's my cue." Kate smiled brightly as she left Cara at the rail and went with her little cousin and Trent.

Joe ambled up to her with a lazy grin. His expression filled with dark promise and a hint of something else.

The good kind of trouble.

"Are you gloating Mr. MacDonald?" She tilted her head and raised an eyebrow.

His smirk only grew wider. "Absolutely not." He took her hand in his and steered her toward his truck. Behind her back, he'd arranged for her to essentially trade places with Kylie for the night.

Kylie would stay the night at Walker Farms and Cara would stay with Joe.

"Joe?"

Thunder, low and barely audible, rumbled in the distance.

He stopped and faced her, but she forgot what she'd been ready to say.

He tucked a lock of hair behind her ear, the side of his thumb brushing over her cheek. "I haven't been able to stop thinking about you."

A sticky, humid breeze blew through. "Joe, I…" She still had no idea what she'd planned to tell him.

With a whirlwind of emotions in his eyes, he murmured, "Come on. I owe you a steak. It's been almost a week since you've been off the farm. Even as pretty as it is, I'm sure you're ready for a change in scenery."

"Yes. It's the best possible prison imaginable, but I don't do well cooped up. I need to stay active or I get twitchy. If I get any more restless, I'll be climbing the walls."

"Let's get you out of here, then. I'm sorry about being late. I had to work over a bit." He helped her into his truck and buckled her in. He trailed his hand across her abdomen then shut door as if he hadn't stolen her breath.

She waited until he started the truck to continue their conversation. She'd spent more than a fair amount of time in the past week worrying about him and the Sheriff. "How is work? I can't imagine working under Hawkins and acting like everything is normal."

"I try to stay out of his way as much as I can. It's frustrating, but until we get this mess figured out, I can't really do anything."

"Is anything being done to investigate him? Surely he hasn't gotten away with so much without raising a red flag or two?" They came to the end of the long driveway and passed the Walker Farms sign.

He took her hand in his and rubbed a thumb over the back of it. "Unfortunately, he's smart. Along with his connection to Boyd, there is an increased chance that whatever they have planned could be bigger in scope than we first thought. I don't like any of it."

"What happened today?"

"Someone broke into Griffith's pharmacy last night. The place was a disaster, the area behind the counter littered with pill bottles. At first glance it looks more like vandalism than theft." His brow scrunched in thought.

"You think there's more, don't you?"

"Yeah. I do. All the evidence points to vandalism and, with Hawkins on the scene—hovering over every question, every line on the report—it stinks. For someone to bypass a security system, then take the time to open and dump out a half of the bottles in there? All the pills, the lids, bottles, everything was scattered on the floor."

"So, Hawkins says vandalism?" She watched his jaw tighten at her question and wished she could kiss his tension away.

"Yeah. Whenever I opened my mouth to ask Ned a question, Dale spoke over me. I had to leave or else they would have hauled me away for assaulting an officer." He shook his head but kept his eyes on the road.

She ached for him.

"I waited until my shift was over and then went back to talk to Ned on my own time."

"Was he able to tell you anything more?"

"Not really, but I felt a little better for trying, and he seemed to appreciate that someone took him seriously. He didn't believe that kids would break into a pharmacy to cause mischief either. Ned never came out and accused Hawkins, but he did make a comment about his close relationship with Jimmy, who's a known drug user."

"It sounds like Ned is wondering if he's covering for someone." She pursed her lips in thought. "Doesn't he realize that, even if he doesn't get caught, if he steps on enough toes, he won't get re-elected?"

"When I watch him now? I think he believes that he owns the badge and therefore the county. Even if I had the proof and could take him down now, I'd likely sacrifice the opportunity to find out what he and Boyd have in the works."

"Whatever it is, it's likely big and ugly." Dark, heavy clouds loomed in the distance. She rested her forehead against the window and closed her eyes.

He placed his palm on her thigh. "Yeah. I think there's little doubt of that."

They rode in silence until they arrived at his house. He ushered her inside and straight to the kitchen. He pointed to the barstool. "Sit. I'll be right back." He went out the back door for a moment then returned.

"Sit? When did you get so bossy? I figured you for a more modern man, Joe." Even full of sass, she did as told, making him smile.

"I have no problem with strong, confident women. I'm not a caveman, but you need a break and tonight, I'm going to give it to you." He poured a glass of wine and set it in front of her. "Drink. No more talk of impending gloom and doom. Unfortunately, I think it will find us soon enough."

"I wish I could disagree with you." She took a sip and watched him put a couple of monstrous potatoes in the microwave.

"I'm afraid you'll have to make do without the Thanksgiving style spread we had last time. I didn't tell anyone about our plans except Kate and Trent."

"We're alone?" She smiled into her wine.

"We are alone. We have the entire night to ourselves." He pulled a platter out from the fridge with two of the largest steaks she'd ever seen.

"That's enough meat to feed an entire family. I hope you don't expect me to eat that much. I won't be able to walk."

"Sweetheart? For what I have planned, you're going to need the calories, but walking is optional." He set condiments out and picked up the platter. "Come with me?"

"Sure." She followed him out and leaned against the deck rail. Taking a sip of wine, she watched the horizon. Dread coiled in her belly. A masterpiece of green fields, towering trees, and blue skies lay before her. A dark gray line hugged the horizon.

Please, not tonight. She sent a wish into the air, hoping that they could enjoy the evening without some sort of catastrophe. Joe seemed set on pampering her, and the last thing she wanted was to ruin his plans.

She turned away from the view and sat in a chair with her back to the sky.

***

Something wasn't quite right, but he couldn't put his finger on it. As he finished their dinner, she said all the right things and smiled at the appropriate times. When he'd suggested that they eat outside, she'd agreed but her unease had grown. Then he'd offered a lame excuse about not wanting the bugs to get the steaks and she'd jumped at the chance to go inside. She complimented him on the food, telling him it was the best she'd ever had, but she ate mechanically.

She was so not Cara, nothing like the Mayhem he'd come to know. He got up to clear their plates and offer her dessert when it hit him.

A storm had loomed all evening and finally decided to make its appearance. Lightning flickered outside, and she flinched. She tried to halt it, but the subtle twitch gave her away. She closed her eyes briefly, and her shoulders rose and fell. He saw her brace for the thunder. Still a good distance away when it came in, it rolled through the house slow and lazy. When silence followed, the tension in her shoulders eased.

Damn. His badass, tough as nails warrior princess was scared of storms. A fist squeezed his heart. He thought back to the day that he'd met her. A nasty little storm had just rolled through. Her eyes had been red-rimmed and he'd wondered if she'd been crying. She'd been shaky and trying to hide it. He'd thought she'd been a fragile thing upset by the accident.

He went to the living room and closed the curtains before going back to her. "Hey? How about we watch a movie, relax for a bit?" Not waiting for an answer, he took her hand in his. He drew her with him into the living room and tucked her into his side. He turned on the TV and raised the volume.

"Not fond of storms, huh? We'll just wait this one out." He hoped the forecast had been wrong. They'd predicted that this system would move through slowly, drenching the area. The skies would likely rumble through most of the night.

She stiffened beside him, staring blankly at the TV. "No. They terrify me. I hate it, but have no control over it. I'm sorry. I'll try to keep it together."

He hated that she didn't feel comfortable enough to meet his gaze. "Don't worry about it. If I survived Kylie's terrible twos and the tantrum filled threes, I can handle anything."

No response.

"Even when she's acting like the devil's own spawn, she's still my favorite person in the world."

161

She tilted her head to look up at him. "But she's so good."

"Now? Yeah, she is." He felt a small surge of pride in that. "We went through a dark patch about three or four years ago. Michelle, her mother, was killed in a car wreck and we'd been having trouble before that. We tried to keep the anger and frustration between the two of us, but toward the end, I discovered Michelle wasn't the woman I thought she was. As bad as things were, there was no telling what Kylie overheard."

Lightning flashed dimly behind the curtains, making her tense. "It's hard to hide things from children."

"Yeah. Between all the relationship turmoil and the trauma of her mother's death, she became a terror." He ran his hand up and down her arm.

"I don't blame her. You two had to have been her entire world and she watched it crumble around her."

"Exactly, for nearly a year, all it took was the slightest upset to send her into a full-blown meltdown."

"You saw her through it all. No wonder you're her hero."

Relaxed, comfortable, he'd let his guard down and his words slipped out before he could stop them. "Hero? More like the villain."

Cara started and then craned her neck to look up at him. "What do you mean? You're her rock."

Something nasty coiled in his gut. Thunder rumbled shorter, a little louder and he witnessed the panic in her eyes. She flinched, but fought the anxiety, focused on him. He never told anyone what happened that night. He'd carried the weight of his responsibility like a ball and chain for three years.

And he loved the way Cara looked to him, trusted him. He dreaded the sight of watching that light in her eyes dim. But, if he didn't share, he'd be no better than a liar.

A brighter flash strobed outside his window, only partially dimmed by the curtains. She put her hands on his chest, fingers gripping his shirt.

"We dated briefly in high school but didn't stick. I went away to college. When I came home after graduation, she came on strong. Really strong. We were sexually active, and she swore to me that she was on the pill. I cared about her a great deal, but there was just something almost desperate about her when we had sex. I always wore a condom. At least I thought I did." He paused and stared at the TV, not really seeing what was playing.

"What did she do?" When Cara tucked her chin into this shoulder and looked up to him with faith in those gorgeous honeyed eyes, he wanted to dig a hole and bury himself. He wasn't worthy.

"Got me drunk. As usual, we were like bunnies. Either I didn't wear one, or she tampered with it. I'll never know. Ultimately, I have to take responsibility for my actions. She may have taken advantage of my intoxication, but she didn't pour the alcohol down my throat. I did that. Doesn't really matter in the grand scheme of things."

"That night gave you Kylie."

"It did. She's my silver lining."

She flattened the hand on his chest, and he felt the press of her palm against his heart. "What happened, Joe?"

He released a heavy breath. "The day of the wreck, I came home early and overheard her on the phone with her best friend. We'd had a particularly rough week. I asked Mom to keep Kylie for the weekend, and I thought we'd go away for a couple of days. It'd be a chance for us to talk things out. I stood there, in the doorway to our bedroom, while she stood with her back to me, venting to her friend about our troubles. It was all fine until she went into great detail about how hard she worked to win me, and how she didn't think it was worth it any longer. Before I could step in, she admitted to her friend how

163

she planned her pregnancy and trapped me with it. I found out that she'd pursued me with the sole purpose of getting my ring on her finger."

"Oh, Joe." She cupped his jaw in her small hand, and he melted.

Rubbing the back of his neck, he pulled back and looked up to the ceiling. "Speechless, I stood there listening and waiting. It was like watching a train wreck and having no power to stop it. She finally turned around and saw me. She ended the call with a terse, *he's home* and immediately got mad at me. I lost my temper, her anger erupted, and we ended up in another shouting match. She grabbed her keys and ran out. I let her go and heard the sound of squealing tires as she sped off around the curve. I should have stopped her."

"No, that's all on her. She shouldn't have played games like that and, when she got caught, she should have owned up to it. Running? That's all on her."

"She ran from me. I figured she'd cool down after she got some space. Heaven knows I needed to get my temper under control. It's usually hard to provoke, but when I hit my boiling point, it's not pretty." He smiled wryly.

"I know." She smiled but he didn't get her meaning.

"You know?" He tilted his head in confusion.

"Yes," she said slowly. Then she moved and straddled his lap, so she faced him. "Boyd. At the Thirsty Beaver." Lightning flashed brighter, making her flinch.

He met her gaze and murmured, "Stay with me. What about the Thirsty Beaver?"

"When Boyd grabbed me. You were there, and I thought you were going to kill him." Thunder rolled in and through the house and her breaths came in short, rapid pants.

It was his turn to cup her face. He held her, willed her to focus on him. On them. "I wanted to, but I probably would have stopped before he quit breathing."

She frowned and told him with her eyes what she thought. "That's not funny."

"Nope. It's not. It's real. What he did to you was real. Given the opportunity, I think he would have done it again. I won't let that happen, no matter what."

"I had to climb you like a tree."

"Whatever. It worked." He leaned in close, just a breath away from her mouth. "Besides, any time you get the urge to monkey around with me, feel free." Unable to resist any longer, he took her mouth with his. Soft, sweet, giving, she let him in.

Lightning flashed. Thunder immediately followed, and rain crashed down in a roar. She tore her mouth away and buried her head into his neck. "I'm so sorry. I can't while it's storming. I'm a basket case."

"No you're not. There's nothing to apologize for. Has it always been this way?"

"No." Another loud blast of thunder signaled the storm's arrival. "It's been eight years." There was something in her words as she tried to pull away from him. She tried to straighten her legs to get up, but he held her in place.

"What happened?" He took her chin in his hand and tipped her face until he had her attention.

She closed her eyes and inhaled deeply. As if ripping off a bandage, she spoke quickly but quietly. "We were on a security detail. We'd already been through earlier that day and were on our way back to base. In that quiet, peaceful little speck on the map we'd never had any trouble. One moment everything was fine, and the next the world around us erupted. Justin went down, and I...God, I can still hear his cries of pain. I didn't think and ran to him. James grabbed me around the waist and pulled me back seconds before another explosion rocked the world." She took a deep, stuttered breath. Her hands fisted in his shirt.

"Justin's screams stopped cold, and the silence terrified me more than the noise had. It's not the storms so much as the pressure in the air and anticipation of the thunder that gets me. Logically, I know there's a huge difference between Mother Nature and man-made terror, but I can't always shake the fear." Another bolt struck close, too close, making her flinch again. When the loud boom followed a second later, his heart broke.

"We were only fifty yards or so apart, but it felt like two miles. The second blast, a rocket-propelled grenade, landed between Justin and me. It knocked him unconscious and, if it hadn't been for James, I wouldn't be here. I would have been in pieces all over the dessert. They got Justin out, stabilized and eventually home. When he made it back, we thought that he would be okay, but eventually he succumbed to his injuries. The Walkers were devastated."

The interior light flickered as the power threatened to go out, and he took the back of her head in his palm and pressed it to his chest. "Were you two involved?"

She shook her head against him. "No. We were good friends. He was friends with everyone, just a really good guy that everyone liked. When it thunders, I sometimes hear his screams then the following silence is even more terrifying. I try to stay in the present, but sometimes the fear pulls me back in."

Aching, wishing he could do something to take the pain away; he rubbed her back and cursed the storm. He'd always liked them, but from this point on he'd always view them through different eyes. His shirt grew damp beneath Cara's face, and he inwardly cursed.

"Come on, let's get more comfortable." Without waiting for a reply, he picked her up and carried her to his room. He stripped her down to her shirt and underwear and tucked her beneath the blanket. He stripped down to his boxers and joined her. Yeah, he'd planned on them spending the night together in his bed, but it hadn't been with her tears on his chest.

He'd take them, anyway.

Chapter Twelve

The storm would arrive soon, so she should hurry, but she also wanted to see what the bad men were doing. She worried they might be dealing drugs or something, and if she knew anything at all, she knew drugs were trouble.

Her father and his drugs destroyed her entire family. She didn't want the stuff anywhere near her. These woods were her home; they were *hers*. She wouldn't just watch them move in and take over. Her grampa would have run them off with his shotgun.

Addie crept through the darkness across the empty quarry lot. She just needed to get a quick look inside the window, so she could make a picture of the new guy and leave it for the cop. It had been almost a week since the pretty lady had been by with food. Addie figured that she only had another day or two at the most before she came back.

She came up on the big old building where the men all visited and slid along the wall like they did in the movies. She kept her back to the wall with her hands pressed flat beside her. She should have worn all black, but she hadn't planned on playing spy when she'd left the house.

Also, the lady who kept bringing her stuff usually brought her pretty things in girl colors—totally worthless for hiding in the woods.

She wasn't going to waste time wishing she lived in a world where she could worry about things like whether her clothes were nice or if they even matched. No, she wasn't meant for that world.

Addie, love, you were meant for bigger and better things than this old hollow. Don't you ever forget it. Every once in while her mother's voice whispered through the past and spoke to her. She loved hearing her voice, even if she no longer believed the words.

A loud noise crashed inside. "Damn it, Jimmy. I warned you. I swear, one more fuckup, and your body will be at the bottom of the lake." The voice sounded like the dirty cop. He acted like he was in charge, but the other two guys never really listened to him.

She worried more about the quiet one. He stood around and watched everyone in a real creepy way she didn't like. He was tall, with his blond hair buzzed real short. She'd seen him from the side twice, but she wanted to draw his face from the front. That's what police artists did, and she could draw just as good as they could. She remembered seeing one in an old movie she'd watched with her grampa long ago.

Her hands were getting sweaty, but it wasn't hot. The storm was chasing in a cool breeze.

She stood up, turned and looked inside the window. All four of them were inside. The dirty cop, the skinny one who was always in trouble, the guy with brown hair who always told the dirty cop what to do, and the new guy, all stood around a big table piled with black packages.

The cop waved his arms around and pointed to the skinny one. The brown-haired guy looked tired and serious. He paid more attention to the packages on the table than anything else. The new guy? He watched the first two with a scary look in his eyes.

It was the kind of look that at the same time made her want freeze in fear and run away. The brown-haired guy looked up to the first two, shook his head and went back to work but the blond guy, he never moved.

Until he did.

She hadn't made a sound. She knew that. She never did.

Somehow, he knew she was there, because his dark eyes swept from the two men straight to her. Turned to stone, she almost peed her pants.

Then he moved, and he moved fast. When the door banged on the other side of the building, it broke the spell and she ran. She ran faster than she'd ever ran in her life. The wind ripped through her hair as her legs pumped hard. Air burned her lungs as she panted in big heaving gulps. The night blurred around her.

And then it didn't. He'd caught her, and she jerked to a stop. He pulled her back tight against his chest. Hot breath hissed over her ear. "What's a pretty girl like you doing wondering the woods at night?" The hard hand on her belly rose higher on her body, to her ribs making puke rise in her throat. Her body froze again and she didn't know how to break the ice.

A hard jolt slammed into them, and the arms holding her released as the big guy fell to the ground. She fell hard to her knees. "Fuck. Sorry man." It was the brown-haired man.

She ran.

"I tripped over a rock. Shit." She recognized his voice as she fled into the woods, running until she couldn't run anymore. She'd wanted to spend the night in her house, dry away from the storm, but there was no way she'd go there tonight. She'd have to go to her secret place and spend another night alone in the dark.

It was her place in the world.

***

Cara woke immersed in the comfort of Joe's arms and wanted to cry all over again. She'd been a wreck, and he'd been…perfect. He'd held her throughout the storm, comforting her and never losing his patience.

171

The man deserved an award, but he'd have to make do with breakfast in bed. Then maybe afterward, she'd give him an entirely different type of treat. She carefully extricated herself from beneath his heavy arm. Inch by inch, she moved across the bed and away from his heat. She hadn't even set foot on the floor, and she missed his warmth.

With light steps, she went to Joe's bathroom and tended to her needs. When finished, she carefully opened the door and walked across his room to the corner where he'd put her overnight bag. She bent over to look for a pair of shorts.

"C'mere." A heavy arm wrapped around her belly and pulled her up into the heat of his body. "You can't sneak away." Sleep rough and growly, his voice whispered into her ear.

"I almost made it out." She couldn't say she was sorry he'd caught her when his palm splayed flat on her belly beneath her shirt. From her nape to her heels, she felt him against her back.

"No you didn't. I have what Kylie calls *dad ears*. I can hear a pin drop and go from dead asleep to wide awake in less than a second. It's a skill you learn when you have a kid who is too curious and very active. You can't get by me."

"Hmph." She crossed her arms over his. He tangled his fingers with hers and something inside her went soft and gooey. "I was going to fix breakfast to thank you for last night."

"No need." He kissed a trail across the curve of her shoulder.

"You fixed dinner and then dealt with my drama. I know that's not how you planned to spend your evening." She stared ahead at his closed closet door, hiding her vulnerability. As always, he saw through her.

He picked her up and carried her back to bed. Prowling up her body, he maneuvered her onto her back. He only wore in a pair of navy boxers; and she knew his body was enough to tempt a nun to sin, yet all she saw was his eyes. The chocolate and caramel depths trapped her in a whirlpool of emotion.

"No, it wasn't, but that didn't make it any less pleasurable." He swept a tender graze over her cheek with his thumb.

She laughed outright, a short, harsh sound devoid of humor. "I thought you were a good man, MacDonald. I know your momma taught you not to lie."

"There are far worse ways to spend a long summer night than with a beautiful woman in my arms. Truly." His face softened. "I'm glad I was there."

The corners of her eyes grew damp, and she tried to make him turn away. Of course he refused. His mouth met hers and then moved right on in. Slow, deep and seductive, his kiss burned her in the best way possible.

When he broke away, he said, "No more tears. I have a better idea." He moved between her legs, and she felt his hard length beneath the material of his boxers, pointing at what it wanted.

"Oh, yeah? What exactly is this idea of yours? I'm barely dressed."

"Wrong, sweetheart. You're overdressed, but don't you worry. I'll fix that." As if to put words to action, he pulled her shirt over her head. He slid her panties down her legs, his fingertips gliding against her skin along the way.

"Wait a minute. Now you're overdressed." She ran a finger from his chin, down his neck, chest and belly. She hooked it in the waistband of his underwear. "These gotta go."

"Yes, ma'am." The moment he finished stripping, she took the opportunity to pounce. She pushed all of her weight into one shoulder and shoved. Smiling, he let her have her way. She wasn't fooled in the slightest when he fell onto his back, but she wasn't going let her pride get the better of her. She'd be a moron to waste an opportunity to explore the body beneath her.

Acres of roped muscle stretched out before her. Starting at his shoulders, she trailed her fingertips down over his chest and grazed over his dark nipples. When the hard abdomen beneath her pussy twitched in response, she smiled.

"Bingo."

"Bingo?" He tilted his head in question.

"I believe I've found one of your weaknesses, Mr. MacDonald."

His eyes flickered. "Nope. Try again."

"Really?" She rubbed her thumbs in slow circles. His belly dipped and rose again. Shameless, she lowered her upper half onto his, making full contact with the heat of his skin against her core. She met his eyes with hers and swirled her tongue around one nipple.

"Yeah, really." His abdomen hitched.

"You know, each time I do this…" She tasted the other nipple. "I can feel your abs quake beneath my pussy. It's making me wet. Can you feel it?"

"Minx." He ran a hand down her spine and cupped her ass. He applied pressure and flexed his muscles. Then he used his hand to rock her hips, rubbing her body against his. "Yeah, I do feel it. What about you? Isn't this one of your weaknesses?" With his other hand, he grazed the barest of touches with the back of his hand over her nipple.

Powerless, she groaned.

"What about harder?" He cupped her breast and closed his thumb and forefinger over the hard peak in a firm, not quite painful grip. Sharp, erotic pleasure arced from where his hand held her to deep inside her core. "Turnabout is fair play." He gripped her waist, lifted her higher until his mouth had access to her breasts.

She tangled her fingers into his thick hair and held on as he took one in his mouth. She gasped and gave up the game. For the life of her, she couldn't find a reason why any game could be more important than the pleasure they brought each other. Letting him have his way, she melted as he rolled until she was beneath him, her new favorite place.

Home. Her inner voice whispered and sighed.

Running her hands over the taught muscles of his shoulders, she reveled in his attention. Wet, yearning, her body demanded he take her. Exploring further, she scraped her fingernails until she found his nipples. She grazed them, teasing him as mercilessly as he pleasured her.

She slid a palm downward and took him in hand. Rock solid and hot, his cock defined male prowess. Touching, kissing, relentlessly, they gave and took from each other in a wicked dance of indulgence.

Aching with bliss, her body cried out for his. "Please, Joe. I want you inside me when I come." Stripped bare of all pretense, she couldn't hide her vulnerability from him, but why should she? He'd seen her at her weakest, knew her darkest secret, and still hungered for her.

As if Joe understood that her need went far beyond the physical, he reached in the nightstand and took the briefest moment to protect them both. Testing her readiness, he found her damp and slick. "You're a gorgeous, silken dream." When he rasped a touch over her clit, sparks of brilliant pleasure shot through her.

"Please, don't make me—"

"Never." He entered her in a single, hard thrust, rocking her. Slowly withdrawing, he stopped just before leaving her entirely. Arching into his hold, she grasped his shoulders, readying for the next move.

Then he came back, filling her. Each powerful thrust filled her with white-hot pleasure and a need that threatened to consume her.

Taking his jaw in her hands, she pulled him close. She met his lips with hers, tangled her tongue with his.

Growling into her mouth, he increased his pace. Her body tightened, intensifying the friction and making her deliciously full as the head of his cock rasped over her most sensitive tissues. He wrapped an arm under one of her thighs, lifted and twined it around his waist. Driving even deeper with short, brutal thrusts, he pounded into her again and again.

Bliss ripped through her in a bright, blinding flash of ecstasy. She buried her head in his neck and held on as he carried her into a violent storm of erotic joy.

He rolled her again, collapsing on his back. She lay there on his chest, with his heart thundering in her ears.

"My gorgeous warrior princess, you're pint-sized. I love it." His heavy breaths heaved in and out of his chest. "I can put you right where I want you. Now, Mayhem, what was it you said about breakfast?"

Chapter Thirteen

Joe looked at the caller ID on his phone. The number was local but unfamiliar. He stopped outside the door to the station and answered, "Hello?"

"Is this Joe MacDonald?" A timid female voice asked.

"It is."

"This is Susan Grant, Haley's mother. I wanted to say thank you." He softened toward the woman who'd been through a living nightmare.

"Thank you? Mrs. Grant, I haven't done anything. How is your daughter?" He waved to Cindy, a dispatcher headed in to start her evening shift.

"Much better. She may be grounded for the rest of her life, and she's going to counseling and treatment. We thought that would be best, despite what..." Her words trailed off and hung, heavy in the silence.

"I think you're doing the right thing." As worthless as it was, he offered his support.

"You're wrong, you know. You did do something. You listened."

"That's my job, Mrs. Grant." He nodded to Caleb as the other deputy got out of his personal ride.

Her voice gained strength. "Well, then, you're one of the few still doing their job in this town." Then her voice weakened and trailed off again. "Is there anyway Haley and I could talk to you for a few minutes? It's about what happened the night of…"

"Sure. Do you want me to drive by your home? When would be a good time?"

"No." Her answer came quick and hard. He didn't blame her. The last time he'd come by, he'd delivered the horrible news of Haley's overdose. "Can we meet tomorrow? My husband will be home, and we can meet you somewhere. I'd like him there."

"That's fine." He got his keys out and started across the lot. Looking up at the sky and seeing heavy clouds, he thought about Cara, hoping for clear weather, despite the storm-riddled forecast.

He had to concentrate on her last words, as her voice became a whisper. "Haley wants to talk to you, but we don't want to come into the station." Something dark and angry twisted in his gut when she hung up without saying goodbye.

She knew something. What, he didn't know, but he'd find out. Her not wanting to come by the station was another giant red arrow pointing to Hawkins. Maybe they had something they could use as evidence against him. He could only hope.

Just as he put his phone away, it rang again. It was his mother. He greeted her warmly, "Hey, what's pickle into today?"

His mother's words made his blood chill. "I…Joe, I can't find her. We went by the park like usual. One minute she was swinging in her usual spot and then the next, she was just gone. I swear, I only looked away for a moment. I've looked everywhere for her. I went back and asked Andrew Jenkins—he was on the swing next to her—and he said…" His mother took a ragged breath. When she sobbed, he had to brace himself with one hand against the roof of his cruiser. His closed his eyes to shield himself from the wavering world around him. "He said he saw a man carry her off. My grandbaby. I should have asked him first instead of walking all over the park. I messed up. What do I do?" Her voice broke on a ripping sob. "I—I'll call the police. I'll call you right back. I need to call the sheriff."

"No!" Her last word snapped him out of his terror-fueled fog, and he barked at his own mother. His heartbroken, grieving mother had just discovered her only grandchild had been kidnapped, and he'd yelled at her.

"But what do I do?" Bless her, she didn't even stutter at his shout. There was no way in fucking hell that he was calling Hawkins in on this. Not even if he were the last man on the planet.

"Mom." He softened his voice and tried to pull his shit together. "I *am* the police. This is what I do, remember? I'll be right there. Don't leave. I'm coming to you. Okay?" He turned away from his cruiser and headed for his truck. "I'll be right there. Keep Andrew with you, so I can ask him some questions." Without waiting for a response, he hung up on his mother. His own fucking mother who'd just had her grandchild kidnapped out from under her fucking nose.

Son. Of. A. Bitch.

He opened the door to his truck and found a rolled up piece of paper. Wrapped around it was his daughter's hair scrunchie. He recognized it as the one he'd twisted around her single braid that very morning. Torn between wanting to snatch it up and examine it for clues right that very instant and fearing what it would say, he reached for the letter and dialed Rick's number.

Those fucking assholes had just declared war. He'd tear the fucking town apart with his bare hands if need be. Nothing, absolutely nothing, was going to stop him from getting his little girl back.

***

"I'm on it. I'll call in everyone. We'll pull every atom of intel imaginable and head out yesterday. MacDonald, don't go out there…fuck me. He hung up. If we don't get him contained he's gonna burn Riley Creek to the ground. What are those bastards thinking?"

Cara stood on Trent's porch and stopped her hand right before she knocked. Something had Rick on the verge of losing his cool, and he never lost his temper. She'd seen his SUV coming up driveway and decided to take a break from her mother. Something big and nasty was brewing, and Joe was a part of it.

She put her hand on the screen door handle when Trent spoke. "You call in the guys. Kate and I'll go up to the big house and tell Cara together."

"I—" Rick spoke but Trent cut him off before he managed more than a single word.

"No. Don't go playing protective overlord. I don't care what the night brings. You leave her out, and she'll never forgive you. I don't care if you're willing to sacrifice that for her safety or whatever excuse you've cooked up. One of us is telling her. Decide which." It was nearly as rare to hear such a hard edge to Trent's voice, making it only more alarming for its rarity.

She'd had enough and didn't want to wait around to see what Rick would decide. He might not like it, but ultimately he'd listen to Trent. She opened the door and stepped in. "What's going on?"

A stiff breeze tried to pull the screen door from her hand. She felt the humid air at her nape and remembered the forecast. A menacing line of storms was expected to roar through the region later in the evening. That might be a problem for her, but it certainly wasn't enough to make Joe want to "burn Riley Creek to the ground" as Rick had said.

Both men looked to her with faces darker and more somber than she'd ever seen them.

Rick's shoulders slumped, and he pinched the bridge of his nose. "Fuck me."

Trent turned to answer, "Bad shit, really bad shit's gone down. We were getting ready to call in the team and tell you."

She crossed her arms and tilted her head. He knew he hadn't fooled her, but he kept going. "A few minutes ago, Joe received a panicked call from his mother." Cara's throat tightened. Louise MacDonald hadn't seemed the type to panic when shots had been fired right outside her work. "She said another child at the park witnessed a man carrying Kylie away. She called Joe, understandably extremely upset. Joe is likely racing to the Oak Knob Mine as we speak."

"Why isn't he going to the park? We need a description. Oh God. This is connected." A two-ton weight sank in her belly. "They're dead. If Joe doesn't get to them first, I'll kill them." White hot rage screamed through her in a fiery storm of anger. Righteous and hate-filled, she wanted to commit murder. Happily, gleefully, she would rip them limb from limb. "It has to be Boyd and Hawkins. Let's go. What are you waiting for? Call the boys. Bring everybody and everything in. The mines? We'll need gear. I'm going to change and grab my…my everything."

Then it hit her. She stopped in her tracks. Nausea clawed at her throat.

"Why exactly is Joe going to the mines?" She needed to know just as badly as she needed the answer.

"The reason Joe isn't going to the park is because a note was left in his truck. It gave him the location where they hid Kylie. We're certain that Boyd or Hawkins left it."

She wanted to lash out and punch something.

"Joe is calling a friend he trusts to go and meet with his mother and talk to the kids in the area Kylie was taken. Trent? Why don't you drive her up to change while I grab our gear and make the calls? Pete's the only one who's out of town." Without waiting for an answer, Rick dialed a number and turned.

"Let's go, babygirl."

God, no one had called her that since well before the Mayhem incident.

They hurried outside and to his truck, but he stopped her before she got in. "Look at me." Something in his tone got her and she met his gray gaze, only to have him look up at the sky, then back to her. "This storm rolling in is likely gonna be nasty. The Weather Service has already issued a severe storm warning that doesn't expire until midnight. There's even a possibility that tornado watches will be put into effect. You need me to pull you out; you let me know. There won't be a single drop of disappointment. You get me? Shit gets to you, speak up, and I'll get you out." As if it heard him, a gust of wind ruffled his hair. She tucked a stray strand of her own behind her ear, even though she knew it wouldn't stay.

Damn, she had the best friends.

What could she say? "Okay. Let's go."

***

He raced across the landscape. His phone, laying in the passenger seat beside him, had finally quit ringing. Rick, his mother, Leigh, Cara, who knew who else had called? He knew he should be thankful he had their support, but he couldn't think of anything beyond the fact that his little girl was likely at the bottom of a mine. Alone. Drugged.

Beside his phone on the seat lay the letter and Kylie's scrunchie.

If you haven't yet, I expect you'll be receiving a panicked phone call at any moment, so let's cut to the heart of the matter.

Your daughter.

I have her.

For the time being? She's fine and asleep, totally oblivious. Unfortunately for you, I can't predict how long she'll stay that way. You and your friends have been a pain in our asses, MacDonald. That needs to end now.

Today?

This serves as a warning. Continue? The next time you receive a letter, it will tell you where to find her body. She'll get something a lot worse than a double dose of Benadryl.

His hands tightened on the steering wheel as he made the turn that would take him down to the old mines. He caught the familiar blur of brown and white fur in the trees and slowed a bit. It wouldn't help him get there any faster if he hit a deer or wrecked on the way.

Besides, Kylie would be mad at him if hurt an animal of any type.

Tears pricked the corners of his eyes as the old, busted blacktop ended and met a weed-choked trail. Judging by the two sets of flattened lines in the knee-high grass, someone had driven in and back out recently.

He was in the right spot.

What kind of game were they playing? What kind of kidnapper told you were to find the victim? Yes, the note said it was a warning, but why go to all this trouble? It was a lot of planning, work and risk. All for a warning.

It didn't add up.

They wanted him out of the way. Why?

For them to mount this kind of rocky scheme, there had to have been something big going down to make the drama worth their while.

The tire tracks through the grass ended near the mine's opening. The Oak Knob Mine had been deemed unsafe and sealed ages ago. Nobody was getting in through the rock wall they'd erected nearly fifty years ago. At the side of the hill, a single depressed line in the tall grass began. It followed up a gradually inclining slope around side of the mine and ended where a rocky slope began. He stopped right where the tire tracks ended and threw the shifter into park.

***

"You good?" Trent assessed her with his all too serious gaze.

"I'm good." Okay, her palms were sweaty, and she wasn't quite sure her breathing was steady, but wild horses couldn't drag her from this hillside until they found Kylie and got her out.

"Remember what I said." Trent delivered his final reminder, hitched a bag of gear over his shoulder and followed the path someone had made as they'd walked through the weeds. She grabbed her own pack out of the truck and followed, eager to get to Joe.

God, how she ached for him and poor little Kylie.

A damp, sticky wind blew by, tugging her hair as if teasing her. Dark clouds hung low and heavy in the distance. She tried not to pay attention to them, but as they'd flown through the evening, she hadn't had much else to do.

She found Rick and Trent standing at the top of the rise beside an ancient barrier of iron bars that seemed to grow out of the ground. It was about waist-high and just a couple of feet wide on three sides. Someone must have added it years ago to keep people from falling in. It reminded her of a haunted amusement park ride. Joe lay flat on his belly, looking down into the vent shaft. "Fuck me. I can't see or hear anything. I don't know whether to call out and reassure her that I'm here or stay quiet and pray she sleeps a little longer. Did you bring ropes? I'm ready to go down now. You guys just lower them down as soon as you get set up. The old entrance is sealed shut. This vent is the only way to get down there."

"Joe, that's not going to work. We're going to do this the right way. No arguments." Rick looked down, his expression firm but soft, too.

Joe stood and Cara doubted he realized she was there, which was okay. Kylie was their one and only priority. "Bullshit. The storm's coming in fast. I'm not waiting." The moment the word storm left his mouth, he seemed to realize she was there. "Sweetheart, I... I have to get her out." The devastation on his face broke her heart.

"I know. We're here to help. I think you should listen to Rick." Faintly in the distance, she heard the door of another vehicle shut. That would likely be Noah and James. Pete was out of town with his family. They were all here.

Lightning flickered dimly somewhere in the distance, far beyond the forest. She steadied herself with a deep breath and told herself for the fiftieth time that they all had far bigger things to worry about than a summer storm.

She prayed James and Noah hurried, and that they weren't needed. Rick wouldn't hesitate to lock Joe down if he decided to recklessly charge in. If it came to that, they'd need every bit of Noah's brawn. As badly as they all wanted to get their girl out, they had to play it safe.

She never hated that logic so much in her life, but she couldn't deny the wisdom of it.

Rick finally asked the question they'd all been thinking. "Any sign of her?"

Joe pointed to a pink and black cowboy boot leaning against one of the metal posts. "It was standing right here, waiting for me to find it." Grass and dirt covered the front of his uniform and his hair stood on end.

She caught movement from the corner of her eye and looked to see James and Noah jogging up the hill.

"Joe, you can't just climb down and wait for us to throw you a rope. The vent is forty feet deep and only about twenty-eight inches across. How broad are your shoulders? I'm guessing you're at least thirty inches across."

"So, if we can't fit together on the way up, I'll go down first, and send her up to you. Pull me out after." He looked to Rick, full of fear and impatience.

Light flashed in the distance. Rick took a deep breath, making his shoulders raise and sag as if the weight of the world hung on them. Thunder rolled through the sky above, a quiet, lazy beast.

"You won't fit. None of us will, but you and those broad shoulders definitely won't fit. There's no way around it." Rick looked as though his heart were breaking.

"I'm not calling in the Sheriff's Office. I don't want Hawkins anywhere near Kylie. After I get her out of this, he's a dead man." Joe looked down to the dark hole.

A damp gust of wind blew by, taunting her with the storm's threat. She shivered in the humid heat.

James ran a hand through his hair and looked sick to his stomach. "Joe, you won't fit. Pete's not here or we could send him in."

"I'll go. Get everything ready. Now. Time's wasting. Lights, gear, all of it." They all looked to her as if she'd lost her mind.

"Sweetheart, you need to be in the truck. The storm's rolling in, and it's going to be bad. They've already issued tornado warnings for the surrounding counties. I...I can't stay with you. I have to get Kylie out." The raw devastation on Joe's face only cemented her resolve. She was doing this, thunder be damned.

"It'll be a tight fit, but I can do it. There's no room for my embarrassment here. I may be a blubbering mess by the time you all pull me out, but oh well. I've survived worse and Kylie shouldn't have to. Every second we waste arguing is another second she's in that hole. Just have someone scoop me up and pour me into the back of one of

186

the trucks. Eventually I'll get my shit together. Y'all will just have to deal with me being a basket case. I can keep it together long enough to get to Kylie and get her out. The longer we wait, the harder it's going to be for me and her."

James dropped his bag and started removing items they'd need and she exhaled.

Joe came to stand in her space and cupped her cheek. She met his damp, chocolate and caramel eyes. "My badass, warrior princess. I don't want this for you."

"I don't want this for you." She heard the sound of another bag dropping to the ground. "Just talk to me. Don't leave me in the dark alone."

"Never. I'll be in your ear the entire time." The first raindrops fell.

Chapter Fourteen

Joe stepped aside to talk to Rick. He watched Cara flinch and close her eyes as lightning flashed again. This time a bright, defined bolt forked the earth somewhere in the forest beyond. None of them should be standing on the hill with lightning so close, but not a one of them pointed out the danger they were in. They didn't care.

With his gut twisted into a hundred knots, a tight fist clenching his heart and another squeezing his throat, he was a mess and at the worst possible time. His daughter, his world was waiting on him to rescue her and his fucking shoulders were too broad? He'd have never in a million years thought that his size and strength would be a hindrance.

He watched as James helped Cara into her harness and double checked that everything was secure. He chucked her chin and then pulled her into a bone-crushing hug. Joe knew that James and the other men worried about her mental state far more than they did her physical.

He did, too. Physically? She was so very strong. She was competent, smart and a quick thinker, especially when a situation went awry. Right then, she stared into the menacing eyes of her greatest fear, preparing to go head-to-head against her demons for his daughter.

She was the most amazing woman he'd ever met, and he'd be a fool to not grab hold and keep her by his side.

Fat, quarter-sized drops of rain fell, signaling the storms arrival. Another bolt of lightning struck too close for comfort. Less

189

than two seconds later, a loud crack shattered the air. Even expecting it, he flinched. Cara's knees bent and she paled, her eyes wide and glossy. Joe watched as James put his hands on her shoulders, rubbing them lightly. There was something deep and comforting about their connection. They were close, but it seemed to mirror the love that he felt for his sister.

Dear God. His sister was likely tearing apart the county. No doubt his mother would have told Leigh, and he'd left his phone in the truck. He'd have to call them both the moment they got Kylie out. Otherwise, no one in the state of Kentucky would get rest.

He looked to Rick. "I know this sounds stupid, but remind me when we're done here to call my sister. She'll be mad with fear."

Rick put his ever-present phone away. "Sure. It's not stupid. You've got one thing on your mind, Kylie."

"Actually, it's two things." Joe nodded in Cara's direction. "She doesn't deserve this. She should be locked away somewhere dry and safe, not dripping wet, immersed inside her biggest fear."

Rick assessed him until Joe felt as though he'd been met at the door with the business end of a shotgun and then passed inspection. "I've sent Leigh updates, but she'll want to hear it from you. I'll remind you to call her. Let's go get your baby." Rick clapped him on the shoulder and they walked side-by-side to the vent.

They all stood around the hole, dripping wet and grim-faced as the sky erupted above them. Water poured from the cloud blackened sky and wind whipped by them tearing at the clothing sticking to their wet skin.

He was no search and rescue expert, but he guessed they were breaking about twenty rules as James prepared to lower Cara into the shaft. An angry, brilliant flash burst overhead and thunder immediately roared.

He stepped in close and kissed her cheek. "You're not alone. I'm with you. We're all right by your side." He touched her ear and reminded her she would be able to hear him through her earpiece.

She trembled, and he felt the vibration of it against his face.

Rick gave the order to begin. "Let's do this."

James nodded his acknowledgement. "Mayhem, when this job's done, I owe you a beer. I think anther trip to the Thirsty Beaver is in order."

"I knew you were a cheap date, Holloway, but even for you that's low." Noah remarked. "I say we go all out and spring for pizza."

They lowered her down and the chatter continued.

Trent put in his suggestion. "How about burgers from the Rusty Bucket?"

Rick added his two cents, and Joe was humbled by the way they continued to speak nonsense just to let her know that she wasn't alone. "No. We'll all get dressed up and go formal. She'll love that. Though she'll have to show Holloway which fork is which and remind him not to belch and scratch his gut in public."

"Hey, I only did that one time, and we're lucky we didn't get food poisoning from that dive. What do you say, Mayhem? Are we going fancy or are we going to the Beaver?" James signaled that Cara should be at the halfway point.

There was a pause but then her answer came. Her voice was quiet and shaky, but his relief was profound. "Neither. I want one of Trent's burgers and a tall glass of sweet tea."

She was right. She'd nailed exactly what they needed, all of them. "Done. When this is over, we'll have a barbeque out at Trent's and invite everyone. He can make burgers, and I'll bring out the smoker for pulled pork. Kate, Leigh and Kylie can make desserts. Princess, what are you bringing?"

Quiet and a little breathy, he heard her voice through his earpiece. "Baked beans. Mine kick ass, and I'll have Momma make enough potato salad to feed an army. Joe? Call me princess again, and I'll make you regret it." Thunder boomed, and he heard her quiet whimper.

Joe swallowed back his worry. "We'll just see about that, princess."

"That's warrior princess to you, cop."

James signaled that she should be close to the mine's floor.

"Stop. I can see her," Cara broke in. "She's just below me. Go slow."

Impatience tore through him and he tightened his fists, tamping it down.

Lighting speared the sky and thunder cracked above them. He heard Cara's indrawn breath and swallowed a curse.

"I'm down. She's breathing and asleep, I think. Her respirations are normal." There was a pause, then another update. "Her pulse is normal, too. She's a limp little noodle. I want to get her out before she wakes up. Give me just a minute to get her secure."

The rain softened its assault but the lightning continued. Thunder cracked and Cara cried out.

"Mayhem? What's doin' babe?" Holloway stood, rope in hand, waiting.

"We're ready here whenever you are. We got you." Trent sounded, patient, rock steady, with water dripping from his too long hair.

"Babygirl, you got this. You're our Mayhem, our little ass-kicker." Noah the giant said, rope in hand, auburn hair plastered to his head, features grim in the shadows.

"I'm thinking on offering you a relocation package and permanently moving you to Bourbon County. We're not letting you leave after your mother's healed. I need you to quit playing around in that hole, so we can iron out the details." Rick said, adjusting a light.

Joe heard her shaky breath. "I've got her fastened in. Double checking everything now." The word *now* hitched on a sob.

"You're doing just fine, princess. I'll schedule you for a manicure when we're done, okay?" He teased her and waited, knowing she was doing the right thing by being cautious, but that didn't ease his impatience.

"Princess, my ass. I'll take you up on the manicure, since this climb has been hell on my nails, but I'm warning you MacDonald. If you keep calling me princess, we're gonna fight." The churning in his gut eased when he heard strength return to her voice.

"Okay. I have precious cargo. We're set. Slow and easy, bring us out."

"Will do," said Holloway.

"Go," Rick ordered.

Then he heard a small, terrified cry that stopped his heart. His stomach dropped to his feet. Kylie woke up.

"Hey, sweetheart. It's Cara. I've got you." Soft and oh so sweet, she spoke to his daughter.

"What? Wewe awe we?" Timid and afraid, his daughter spoke.

"In a cave, but your daddy and my guys are getting us out. You just hang tight, and we'll be outside in a few minutes."

"The bad man took me. I kicked him."

"Good girl. That's my little fighter." Tears pricked his eyes at Cara's tender words. He wished Kylie could hear his voice, but without a headset, she couldn't and Cara needed hers.

"Daddy's hewe?"

"He is. He's waiting right outside and helping to pull us out."

"It's dawk in hewe."

193

Holloway signaled that the girls were at the halfway point.

"It is. Does the dark scare you? It's okay, you know."

"A wittle bit. I have a night wight at home."

"That's okay. Everybody is scared of at least one thing." Thunder boomed and Cara gasped.

Joe's gut cramped.

"You know what I'm afraid of?"

"You'we afwaid?" A mix of awe and disbelief filled his daughter's voice.

"Yep. Thunderstorms scare me. They scare me a lot. Don't you worry. Your daddy and the guys will have us out of here in just a few more minutes, okay?"

"Daddy's strong."

"He is."

"He has big hands."

"The biggest."

"And they're strong."

"The strongest."

"He'll use his big hands to pull us out." His daughter's confidence in him threatened to bring him to his knees.

"You know it."

The men all stayed quiet, every ounce of focus honed on the ropes and the sweet voices connected to them as if the slightest breeze could tear them away.

"You're squeezing me tight." But Kylie didn't sound out of breath, she sounded…secure.

Cara let out something that sounded like part laugh and part sob. "I am. Can you breathe okay?"

"I'm fine. Don't cwy, Cawa. Daddy'll get us out. You got me, and daddy's got wopes around me. He's got wopes around you, too." His confident daughter was back. No longer the baby, she fussed over her rescuer.

"Yep."

The muscles in his shoulders burned, but there was a satisfaction from it and from the knowledge that they were getting closer. Complete darkness had descended, the wind whipped around them, howling through the trees and a steady rain fell.

James signaled that their precious burden was nearing the top, and it took everything he had not to rush to the vent and pull them out by hand.

When a wet, filthy head appeared at the opening, he almost dropped to his knees in relief. Carefully, they moved forward, taking up slack as they went.

He got there first and James was just behind him. "Let us get Mayhem secure then you can unfasten your baby girl."

He nodded his agreement. He, Trent and Rick held the weight steady while James and Noah did the rest. Lightning crackled overhead, an electric white arc, immediately punctuated by deafening thunder.

Cara whimpered and crumpled into herself.

"We're clear. I got Mayhem. Get Kylie." There was no judgment in Holloway's voice, just a need to finish the job and get everyone taken care of. It was natural for the other man to think that his first and only thought would be for his daughter, and it was. But right beside, burning just as hot, was worry and a need to pull Cara into his arms.

He pulled a wet, filthy Kylie from Cara and tucked her close, praying he didn't crush her with the strength of his relief.

Her little voice broke his heart. "Don't be mad. I tried to yell for help, like you taught me. I really tried. I kicked him and did just like you said, but he was bigger. He put something over my face and I think it made me go to sleep. Then he stopped his car and woke me up and made me drink some yucky juice." Kylie pouted at the injustice of it.

"You did good, pickle. I'm proud of you." His voice hitched, snagging over his words.

"You going to kick his ass?" He didn't have the will left in him to scold her for her choice of words. He figured being drugged, kidnapped and dropped in a mine gave even a six-year-old the right to curse.

Not seeing any point in lying, since she knew him too well, he murmured into her dirty hair, "I am."

"Good."

He could do nothing but smile. "Are you okay? Are you hurt anywhere?"

"I'm okay. Just sleepy. Have a headache." *They fucking drugged my baby.* He didn't care if it was over the counter meds or not. He was going to kill those bastards, but first thing's first. He had his child in his arms, but that wasn't all he needed. They still felt lacking.

Half empty.

"Awe we going home now?" She dropped her head against his shoulder like she'd done when she was smaller.

"Soon." He shifted her light weight to rest on his left arm, freeing his right. He might not have been able to go down and get his girl out of the hole, but by God, he had enough strength left that he could carry them out of this nightmare. "Make room for one more, pickle."

"You getting Cawa?" As exhaustion and the last dregs of the Benadryl regained their hold, she reverted back to baby.

"Yep. She's going with us."

"Good, she's scawed. She needs us."

"Yes, she does."

"I need my boot."

Trent stepped up to them. "I got it right here, pickle. I think it's full of water, though." It'll take some time to dry."

Kylie raised her head to answer. "It's okay. Will you cawwy me? Cawa needs daddy."

Trent blinked at the unexpected request then stepped up. "Is that what you want, Joe? Is that cool?"

"Yeah. Okay." Even knowing she would be in the best of care, a bittersweet ache jabbed him in the chest as he passed his daughter off.

The moment she settled in Trent's hold Kylie's focus turned to horses. "Is Scarlet's hoof okay?"

"I'll get her out of the rain and meet you at your ride." Trent nodded and headed down the path to their vehicles, fielding questions about his horses.

Joe waved and turned from watching his daughter to find James holding a trembling Cara, as if carrying her over the threshold to Hell. "She's bad, cop."

"I got her." Soaking wet, filthy, covered in cobwebs, she was the most beautiful woman he'd ever seen. "Can you stand for a second? All I need is one."

She nodded and James eased her down, not quite letting her go. He seemed afraid that if he relinquished all contact she'd fall. Wasting no time, he gripped her familiar waist and lifted her so her front was plastered against his. "You should be with Kylie. I'll be okay."

"She's fine, likely better than you at this point."

"The drug?" Worry clouded her weak voice.

"I know. That's why we're going to a hospital."

"I'm fine." She buried her head in his neck.

"Good, then it won't take long to get you checked out."

Rick clapped him on the back. "Go to Bourbon County. I'll call ahead and pave the way, make sure their exams stay off the electronic charts. Take your girls, and I'll call Leigh. She'll likely meet you guys there."

Joe nodded. "Perfect. Ask her to bring dry clothes?"

Rick's worried gaze focused on Cara. "We'll take care of it and pack up here. You just take care of the girls."

***

"You drugged her? I told you to kill the brat!" Hawkins got in his face as he yelled.

When Boyd felt spittle land on his cheek, he hit his limit. Enough was *e-fucking-nough.* They'd made their buyer happy, and he'd have to find a new location. Tonight had bought them a small window of time, but soon— likely very soon—Dark Horse would come after them with everything they had. He no longer needed Hawkins. If anything, he'd become more liability than asset.

Using both hands, Boyd slammed Dale against the wall. "Now, listen here, you dumbfuck. Tonight, we needed those assholes out of our hair. They were. We could have had every fucking drug dealer in the country here tonight, and they would have left us alone. To MacDonald, nothing mattered except rescuing his kid. If we had killed her? What do you think would have happened? Nothing would have stopped him from coming after us. Nothing. He would have given up his badge, his career, his anything and everything, to take us down. You know why?" He fisted his hands in Hawkins' shirt, pulled him forward and slammed him back again. "Because he would no longer have anything to lose. The only thing he'd have would be a hunger for revenge, and we don't need that kind of heat."

Hawkins lips moved but no sound came out until the third try. "I run this town." The man tried, but his spine had lost its starch.

"Oh, yeah? You're doing such a fine job. Your own deputies don't trust you. You don't even get that there was a second layer to what I did, and I did it for your benefit." Boyd watched and saw nothing but confusion staring back at him.

"Think about it. His daughter's life was in danger. Did he call you, the fucking sheriff? No. Did he call 911 or any of his fellow deputies? You can check tomorrow when you go in, but I think you'll find he didn't call in one resource."

Hawkins still didn't get it. Boyd continued explaining. "So now, you know for absolute certain that MacDonald doesn't trust you or your department. If he had, he would have called you. You've fucked up by alienating him. People like and trust him. That'll be your downfall.

"Keep it up, old man, and I'll stuff you down that fucking hole." He waited until acceptance crept into the Sheriff's eyes. When Boyd was certain he'd been understood, he let go.

He turned his back on Hawkins and looked to Sutton who stood nearby, watching with that eerie stare. "Are we through? I want out of this fucking piss-ant town."

"The Detroit buyers are happy. The east coast buyers are satisfied for the time being. But the south, it's untapped. I underestimated Kentucky's connection to Florida. So, no, we're not done yet. This county is prime real estate."

Fuck it. He couldn't take this shit any longer. He would have to find a way to take Sutton out of the picture. It was the only way to get him off his back and to remove the ball and chain from his ankle. He had to play the game for just a little longer.

"We have to move locations."

"Agreed, though I have some unfinished business to attend to." Sutton's gaze drifted to the window where they'd caught a flash of the girl watching them a few nights ago. Disgust boiled in Boyd's belly, but maybe if Sutton focused on the girl, he'd pay less attention to others.

Boyd suspected that was too much to hope for.

Chapter Fifteen

He brushed a stray curl away from his daughter's cheek and sent thanks to the heavens. Again. Bathed and dressed in clean clothes, she was tucked into a spare bedroom at Trent and Kate's. He would have preferred to have her in her own bed at home, but at least this substitution was familiar and safe. Leigh had helped her bathe and combed the tangles from her hair. Kate made her a grilled cheese sandwich and hot chocolate while he showered and put on the clothes his sister brought. Having her family close was all it had taken to set Kylie's world right. She'd clutched her ragged frog close and fallen right to sleep.

His world was far from right, but he'd be damned if it would stay that way for much longer. If the Grants didn't have something they could use as evidence tomorrow, he'd find a way to make something happen. He wouldn't rest until every one of those assholes was rotting behind bars.

He closed the door on his sleeping daughter and went to check on his second but equally as important concern. *Cara.* God, but she humbled him. He'd never be able to express his gratitude.

They'd driven from the mine straight to the urgent care that Rick had recommended. They checked both Kylie and Cara's vitals and gave them a thorough check for any injuries they might have missed in his eagerness to get them off the hill. They'd also drawn blood from Kylie to test for foreign substances. Rick had arranged to have them all charted under fictitious names just to be safe. He'd been torn between wanting to wait on the lab results and getting his girls home, clean, and dry.

In the end, he'd left after Rick and the doctor had assured him they would call results to him as soon as they came back. One thing about having obscenely rich friends with shady pasts and crazy connections? Rules were conveniently forgotten on a routine basis.

He walked into the room Cara was using without knocking. Finding it empty, he continued onto the bathroom's open door. He found her standing in front of the mirror, combing out and drying her hair. With the loud dryer blowing in her ear, she couldn't have heard his quiet approach. He took a moment to watch her. Hair still wet from her shower, and a little bit pale, she stood there wrapped in nothing but a towel.

He remembered the feel of her weight in his arms as he carried her to the truck. He'd taken her straight to the driver side door and helped her in. Trent who'd already buckled Kylie into her car seat and had been keeping her company, nodded his farewell. He'd kept Cara tight to his side the entire way to the urgent care. Fortunately, by the time they'd made it to Bourbon County, the storm had mellowed. The rain had slowed to a calm drizzle and only a few sparse flickers of lightning flickered in the distance. Against the sound of his truck driving through the night, the distant thunder didn't have a chance and she'd had time to settle.

She'd answered the doctor's questions mechanically and cooperated, but she had all the animation of a robot. He'd hated it, but couldn't do a damn thing about it.

He stepped into her line of sight. When she didn't cover up, flinch or shoo him out, he took that as an invitation and stepped into the bathroom and her space. She stood there simply staring at him.

He couldn't stand it. Other than her mechanical answers to the doctor, she hadn't uttered a single word. He didn't know whether he wanted to shake or coddle her. He took the hair dryer from her, switched it off and set it on the counter. "How are you?"

"I'm fine." She gifted him with a plastic smile.

"Let me see your hands." He tamped down his impatience and raised them himself. "You really do need a manicure."

"I got all the dirt out, but I haven't had a chance to clean up the ragged edges yet. They're not that bad." Finally, he saw a hint of her spine. He hated to play that game, but if it got him his Cara back, he'd do it. He hadn't missed the concerned looks James and the other guys had given her when she wasn't looking. They'd tried to gently coax her out, but hadn't been able to draw out their Mayhem.

He'd planned to come in here to thank her, but when he saw that spark, he changed his tactic. "Don't worry. I'll treat my princess to a manicure later."

Her eyes narrowed, and she tilted her head in that way he loved. "I'm no princess, Joe."

"You're pretty enough to be one." He leaned in and smelled the area where her jaw met her ear. "Smell like royalty, too."

"I just ran enough dirty water down Trent's drain to fill a pond." She looked up at him as if he'd lost his mind.

He picked her up and set her ass on the counter beside the sink. "Your hair is soft enough. He ran a finger behind her ear in a slow caress.

She tried to pull up her towel, but seeing as she sat on it, it wasn't budging. Her eyes shot daggers at him.

Finally, he was getting somewhere.

He touched her chin and used the pad of his finger to trail a slow path down her neck. "What about your pretty little toes? What color polish are you wearing today?"

She tried to cross her arms over her chest, but his finger got to her cleavage first, blocking her. Dipping his finger into the shallow hollow, he untucked the twist in the towel at her breasts and let the entire thing fall.

"No answer? I'll have to see for myself. Princess." He ran his finger between her breasts and down her belly. He slowed and continued straight down over the soft curls at the juncture of her thighs. She kept her legs together so he followed the seam to her knees and then down her shins. Easing down to his knees, he looked at her feet. "Just what I thought. Purple polish for my perfect princess."

"Are you trying to be a poet MacDonald? If so, don't because you stink." The tightness in his throat eased when he heard a good dash of snark in her tone.

"Nope, I'm not a poet. I'm just a plain 'ole country boy who's trying to figure out what to do with his princess." He kissed the spot where her knees touched.

"That's warrior princess to you, Mr. MacDonald." *There she was. His Cara.*

"Yes, ma'am." He eased his thumbs between her ankles the slid them up the insides of her calves until he hit her knees. There he applied pressure until her legs opened.

"What are you doing?" Suspicion colored her voice.

"Nothing much. Shhh…" Starting at mid-thigh, he licked a path up her inner leg until he reached the joint where her thigh met his heaven. Her sharply indrawn breath sounded like music to his ears. With his thumbs, he exposed her and, with his mouth, he loved her.

***

Holy shit. Her head dropped back to rest against the mirror with a thud. Joe held her legs open with his shoulders and rocked her world with his hands and mouth. Already weak and overwhelmed by sensation, she could do nothing more but tangle her hands in his hair and hold on. Exquisite pleasure washed over her in a warm glow.

Groaning against her, he tilted her pelvis, gently dropping her to rest her shoulders against the mirror. He wrapped one hand under a leg to tightly grip her ass. He used the other to aid his mouth. Tongue, teeth, fingers, and lips stirred so much sensation she didn't know where she ended and he began.

Liquid, languid arousal erupted into hurried, turbulent passion. Instinctively, she placed the foot of her free leg on the counter, giving him even more access.

He rewarded her with a light smack on her ass and a muttered, "That's my girl. Give me your all." Then he took full advantage of her shift, setting fire to her world. He rocked into her with his fingers and tongue. Sharp, powerful bliss saturated her every cell until she wanted to burst. Quivering with the onslaught of ecstasy, unable to contain the magnitude of pleasure, she exploded.

Ready for her cry, he stood, covered her mouth with his and drew the waves of orgasm out with his fingers. Muscles taught, breathless, she held onto his shoulders as his body moved against hers, blanketing it with his scent, his strength. From head to pussy, he covered her.

The moment she went boneless, he pulled his cock free of his jeans. Eager, hungry for more, she grabbed for him only to have him pull away with a curse. "Fuck. Me." He growled low and harsh.

"I'm trying to." She smiled, trying to soften his sudden frustration.

"I can't. No Condom." He pressed his forehead to hers and trailed a finger over her heavy breast in regret. His chest heaved and, even through his tee, she made out the lines of his tense, heavy muscles.

When a tendril of bliss budded in her tight nipple and spread, she understood his regret all too well. "I'm protected. I'm on the pill and clean but I understand if you don't..." Her words trailed off. She didn't want to put him in that awkward position so she changed course. "You took care of me, I'll—"

"No. I trust you. It's good. We're good." He kissed her hot and deep and dropped his jeans farther.

God, this man shook her to her core in the best ways imaginable.

With his cock fisted in hand, he fit the speared head to her entrance. Eager, needy, she clutched his hips, nails digging into the flesh of his ass and urged him on. When he looked at her, she melted.

"My princess is a hungry little thing, isn't she?" He smiled brighter then delivered with one sure stroke.

Packed to bursting with electric pleasure, she gloried in the male beauty covering her. Hers for the taking. She wrapped her legs around his waist, and let him have everything.

"Don't wanna hurt you, but I'm not sure I can go easy, sweetheart." He pulled back and pushed in with stoic deliberation. Tense from head to toe, he shook with hunger.

She couldn't bear the thought of him needing something she could give.

"Hang on." She placed a staying hand on his chest only to have him look at her like she'd lost her mind. "Trust me."

"Always." But that look hadn't left his face.

"Let me down."

He pulled out and she almost called him back, the loss so sharp. Weak from her earlier stress and the orgasm he'd given her, when she tried to climb down, she realized her problem. Her muscles were jelly. "Um. Help?"

He quirked an eyebrow, but when she held her arms out, he lifted her and set her on her feet. She held onto his biceps and steadied herself. Then she hoped she could do this without making a fool of herself.

In for a penny...

She let go and turned around, baring her ass. Bracing her hands on the counter, she arched her back, and taunted him with the view. She looked over her shoulder and found him staring at her ass.

"Ahem." It was her turn to look at him with an arched brow. He looked up and a slow, wicked grin crept across his face. Heat simmered in his gaze, branding her. Then, totally not caring, his gaze swept back to her ass. "Joe." When his focus came back to her, she replied, "Now you don't have to worry about breaking my neck. Do your worst, big boy."

His calloused hand cupped one butt cheek and the other her jaw. He kissed her tenderly but the moment his tongue touched hers, their appetite for each other surged. Charged hunger zipped along her nerve endings.

Fisting his cock, he broke away, chest heaving and moved to stand behind her. "You undo me." Taking her hips in his hands, he seated himself at her core. Then he slid in, fast and hard. Overwhelmingly full, she whimpered at the sensation overload. He hit home, pulled back scraping by her already tender tissues. Delicious, tight, burning friction scalded her with pleasure.

Draping his larger body over hers, wrapping his arms around her, he held her to him, buffering her arms from the force of his thrusts. Then he let go of his need. Holding her tightly, he pounded into her, a primal, possessive mating.

The rest of her body was an altogether different type of story. Assaulted with erotic joy, she reveled in his possession. Her body grew tighter and tighter with each pass until she didn't think she could bear the pleasure and force any longer. Unable to contain it any longer, she released the pressure, exploding in a rush of blistering ecstasy.

Biting her lip and moaning, she fought to stay silent as another, larger orgasm surged over her.

Iron bands wrapped tight around her middle as his pace doubled. Hard and furious, his body pistoned into hers.

Hot spurts jetted inside her. Growling, his pace slowed as he pulled her back, tight against his hips. He alternated soft kisses down her spine with murmured praise.

She laid her head on her hands on the counter and let her weight go. She'd barely taken her next breath when he pulled out and swept her into his arms.

***

Burdened with a mess of emotions, they met in Trent's living room. Cara watched as Joe skipped his usual chair and took a seat in the middle of the couch then drew her to sit beside him. Far too tired to argue, she did so. She had to admit, when he wrapped one arm around her, pulling her into his side, there was nowhere else she'd rather be.

Their arrival seemed to serve as a signal for everyone to gather. Always prepared, most of them kept an extra set of clothes in their vehicles and had time to change. Weariness, anger and even a thin layer of fear hung over the room like a smoky haze.

"Joe, I went out to your ride for the note Boyd left. I scanned it into our files and then sealed it in a bag. Didn't think you'd mind." Rick sat at his usual spot at the head of Trent's dining room table.

"Not at all. Thanks." Joe's voice went gruff, quiet. "Thanks for everything, again. Boyd keeps this shit up; I'll never get out of your debt."

Not taking it as the joke it was meant as, Rick met Joe's gaze head on. "There's no need for debts in this room." Rick's tone, though subdued left no room for argument. "Now that the unnecessary formal crap is out of the way, onto the most important topic. Safety. Joe, how do you feel about Kylie staying here until this is sorted? Kate's available to keep an eye on her, and we'd all rest easier knowing she is safe here on the farm."

"I was going to speak to Trent about that. I agree. After tonight? Yeah, I want her here. I'll run out tomorrow and pack some of her things. She'll think she's on a vacation and school doesn't start for another week and a half."

The tension in Cara's shoulders eased. "I can help as well, if Kate has something to do." Rick nodded his thanks. When Joe's only response was to rub his hand up and down her arm, she figured he accepted the solution as well.

Leigh came in from likely peeking in on her niece and sat beside Joe. He pulled her into his other side and kissed the top of her head. "Thanks guys. I can't tell you how much I appreciate you keeping her here. I'll come out and stay with her if needed."

"Good. It'll be a short drive for you, since you'll be staying here as well." Rick looked down at his computer and spoke as if he hadn't just delivered a shock.

Leigh's head snapped to look at him. "Excuse me?"

Rick raised his head and looked directly at Leigh. "I said that's good. It'll be a short drive for you, since you'll be staying here as—"

"I heard your words. What I don't get is why you think you can tell me what to do. I can't stay here." She sat up straight, breaking her brother's hold.

"I know, space is tight here. Tonight, we'll put you with Cara, and tomorrow you'll—"

"No, Rick. You're not getting it. I'll be sleeping at my place tonight and every other night. You may be the head of this outfit, but I'm not one of your soldiers. I'm no one. There's no reason for anyone to come after me."

"Leigh, you're staying here. End of discussion." Even sitting, he looked as though he'd turned his nose down at her, like a parent to an errant child.

Leigh stood and cocked her hip, with one hand fisted on her waist. "No. You don't get to issue me orders. No."

"Sis." With that single, quiet word, Joe had his sister's attention.

She turned to face him, but remained silent.

"Think about what happened today. If Kylie is safe behind castle walls, and they need to get me out of the picture, where are they going to look next? Every day it feels as though I'm tiptoeing around landmines. I don't need to worry about your safety too. Losing you would be just as devastating as losing Kylie. I simply can't. Please stay here, either at Trent's or at the big house."

Cara watched Leigh's will crumple and she ached for the gorgeous, willowy brunette. But Joe was right and Leigh was smart enough to know it. Caring enough to listen. "You're lucky you're my brother, you know?"

"I do know. I want to keep it that way."

Leigh softened and spoke to Joe as if his opinion was the only one that mattered. "I'll sleep with Kylie tonight and figure out the rest tomorrow." She gave him a sad little smile then went to the kitchen. There she opened the dishwasher and began rinsing dishes in the sink. She never once acknowledged Rick, making Cara wonder if something more lurked beneath the surface of their casual acquaintance.

Joe looked to the table and everyone scattered around the room. "What I want to know is why they wanted me out of the picture tonight. The note said it was a warning, but I don't believe it."

Noah spoke quietly from the table where he sat at Rick's left, facing the group. "I don't either. I mean, that was a huge risk to take and a lot of work. I would think that leaving the note and a picture would have been enough of a threat." The big man's fisted hands on the table contrasted with his seemingly relaxed pose. Cara's heart had melted earlier when he'd taken a few moments to sit with Kylie while she ate her dinner. He'd spoken softly and joked with the little girl, but his eyes had been full of worry and anger.

"They had plans tonight, likely out at the quarry and wanted to make sure all of us and especially Joe, were occupied." James spoke from the end of the table, opposite Rick. "Chicken shit assholes. I'd like to cram their asses in a dark mine without light, food or water and leave them there for about fifty years."

"Agreed. Since Joe was their focus, I'm sure Hawkins was a primary player. I get why Joe didn't want to call in rescue tonight, but by not doing so Hawkins now knows Joe is onto him." Trent pointed his beer bottle to Joe.

With exhaustion stealing the last of her strength, she leaned deeper into Joe. His chest vibrated beneath her ear when he spoke. "I'm not the only one who's lost faith in him. I'm getting hints all over town that people think he's dirty. I'm going to meet with a teen who overdosed not too long ago and her parents. They have something to tell, but don't want me to come back to their home or at the station. They insisted I come alone and that we meet out of town. His authority is crumbling."

Although it sounded like a good thing, it hinted at bigger trouble. She placed a hand on his chest and looked up to Joe. "That'll make him more dangerous, more likely to take bigger risks."

"Exactly." Rick shut the cover on his laptop. "We're all exhausted and heartsick tonight. Let's take a breather and we'll meet again after Joe has his meeting. Joe? Text me your location when you meet with the family?"

"Sure. As soon as they tell me where we're meeting, I'll update you."

"Any questions?" Rick looked to the room.

Holloway raised his hand. "I have a question. When are you going to get your own place? Or like a real office or something, at least? Nothing screams home business like having mission planning sessions in front of the TV."

Rick shot him the middle finger.

Chapter Sixteen

Cara turned her back on sweeping green pastures outlined by white fencing and dotted with grazing horses. The heavy morning mist created a picture worthy of a thousand words. When molten chocolate and caramel eyes met hers, she felt no loss at the change in scenery.

"I didn't get a chance to say thank you for last night." Quiet, a touch gravelly and far too serious, Joe's voice warmed her. She looked past the soft, kissable lips that drew her attention and focused on his words.

"Thank me for what? I didn't do anything." Baffled by his statement, she went back to staring at his mouth. Her hands found the solid muscle of his waist and held on.

"You fucking amaze me. Does braving the summer's worst storm to date and climbing down a lightless, abandoned, narrow mineshaft to rescue my daughter ring a bell?" He touched her nose with the tip of one finger.

"Joe, I adore Kylie and, I'll be honest, that adoration is sliding fast toward love, but I would have done that for anyone. It's part of the job. It's also what a decent human being does when another is in trouble." He stared at her as if he didn't know what to make of her. "What?"

"You didn't do that because you're a member of Dark Horse. You didn't get a paycheck for last night."

"Yes, I did." She touched his nose as he'd done to hers.

Anger flashed over his features. "Fucking, Rick. I'll—"

"No, Rick didn't pay me money. My payment, my satisfaction, came when I watched you carry her to bed while she chattered on about Trent's horses. I saw you kiss the top of her head like she's the most precious thing in your universe. When she spilled the last bit of her hot chocolate and you wiped it up without blinking. Then, when you got up in the middle of the night to check on her, even though she was safe in the same bed with your sister. Having a part ensuring that kind of loving relationship thrives and that Kylie lives a happy life is the only form of payment I need. She hugged me last night before you carried her to bed. The feel of her little arms around my neck will stay with me for the rest of my days. I don't give a single damn about Rick's bank account." Indignation flashed through her, hot and bright.

He relaxed and pulled her against his chest. When pressed against all that delicious masculine strength, she melted. "Cara May, you undo me. I didn't think there were many more women like Kate and Leigh—strong, capable and hiding hearts of gold. I was wrong. I found one more. I'm not letting her get away."

She pulled back and looked up at him. A suspiciously warm glow bloomed deep in her chest. "What are you saying?"

"I love you." He kissed her soft and quick then finished. "I didn't think I would ever find a woman worth the risk of upsetting Kylie's world for, but I had it backward. I was being selfish, thinking about my heart as much as I was hers. I did find a woman worthy enough, but the trick's on me. I'd be a fool to keep her out of my daughter's life. I'd be cheating Kylie. I'm not sure I'm worthy enough of that woman's love. Of your love."

"Joe." She took a deep breath and looked into the eyes she...loved. Yeah, she loved those eyes and the man behind them, didn't she? "Joe." She didn't know what to say. She owed him her honesty, but the feelings inside her swelled, overwhelming. *Love.* Honor that he considered her equal to the wonderful women in his life and awe that he felt her worthy of an important place in Kylie's life. She blurted the first thing that came to mind. "It was the jeans."

"What?" There was that look again, the one that said he had no clue where her head was at.

"The first day we met." Embarrassed, she hid her face in his chest. "Those old jeans and your swagger. Kylie was an added bonus." She spoke to the muscles beneath her.

"The jeans with the hole near the—"

"Yeah, those. What can I say? I'm a sucker for a man in well-fitting, faded blue jeans." She looked up at him and grinned, hating the heat that flushed her cheeks.

His grin matched hers then outshone it. "Well, then. I was doing housework and not planning on leaving the house." When he laughed, her heart lightened. "I'm glad to see we're on the same page."

"Absolutely." She moved her hands so she could tangle her fingers in the hair at his nape.

He shook his head and laughed again. Even seeing his amusement, she couldn't let him walk away without sharing her true feelings. His gift was far too important to let go unacknowledged.

She stopped him on the second shake by putting both hands at his jaw. Standing on tiptoe, she kissed him. Slow, sweet and tender she poured her love for him into their connection.

"I love you too, Joe MacDonald."

"I don't want leave you and Kylie, and I really don't want to go to work today." A heavy cloud of reality dimmed their sunshine as he touched her cheek with a single fingertip.

"I know. We'll be here waiting when you're finished for the day. Stay safe."

Without another word, he headed for his truck and, while she watched his walk, she prayed that he'd be safe.

She went inside and found Kylie, Leigh, and Kate in the dining room. They guys had set it back to normal before heading out well past midnight. Kylie waved a piece of toast at her in greeting. She finished swallowing her breakfast and beamed.

"Trent's going to take me to see Bonnie after breakfast." She forked a bite of eggs into her mouth and Cara heard the thump-thump of her feet hitting the chair legs as she swung them under the table.

"That'll be fun." Cara found a mug and poured herself some coffee. Kate handed her a plate and pointed to the stove where a mountain for food waited.

"Can I be done now?" Kylie asked and then took a drink of milk.

"Take your plate to the sink and go ahead. Trent's in his office, waiting." Kate pointed down the hallway with her spatula. "Cara, load up your plate. We want to talk to you about something as soon as Kylie leaves."

Curious, she did as instructed and fixed a plate. Kate must have made enough food for a small army. "Thanks. You didn't have to, but I appreciate it." She sat at the table across from Leigh who sat with her hands wrapped around a coffee mug.

"I enjoy it. I never had much family to fuss over and, now that I do, I plan to enjoy it to the fullest." At that moment, Trent and Kylie came through. He stopped by to steal a quick kiss from Kate.

"See you in an hour," he murmured against her mouth. "And don't get into any trouble while I'm away, beauty." Though gentle and seemingly playful, something dark and sad lurked beneath his words.

He met Kylie at the door where she practically hung on the door handle. He took her hand in his, opened the door with his other. Then they were gone and the kitchen filled with silence. Cara took a bite of her breakfast and waited, wondering.

Finally, Kate sat with her own plate and began. "We have two things we want to discuss with you. I'll let Leigh take the lead on the first and most important." The ridiculously beautiful brunette pointed to her equally lovely cousin with her fork.

Leigh met Cara head on, woman to woman. "Yes, first and absolutely most important. Joe. Kate and I agree that you are worthy of my brother. We already liked you, but last night cinched it. Also, Kylie thinks the world of you. If we were given the option of choosing Joe's next love, we couldn't do better ourselves. If your relationship goes down that path, we're more than happy to welcome you into the MacDonald fold. That being said, if you hurt my brother or my niece, I'll hurt you."

Oddly, despite the threat, Leigh's words filled Cara with a sense of welcome. She set her fork down and met their gazes with her own steady one. "I adore them both and hurting either of them would hurt me, too. I…thank you."

Leigh sipped her coffee and set her cup down. "Good. Now onto the nasty stuff. We need your bodyguard skills again."

"Okay." When both women gave her the MacDonald look she'd come to know well, she wasn't surprised. Like Joe, they didn't know what to think of her.

Kate spoke. "Don't you want to know what the job is before you answer?"

"Will it get me off the farm for a few minutes?" she asked.

"Yes." Leigh gave her head a little toss, much like her brother. "Okay, then." She waved her mug at Kate.

Kate set her fork down and wiped her mouth with her napkin. "Okay. I talked to Trent last night and, after some persuasion, he agreed to let me go talk with Phillip Bailey. He doesn't like me going at all and both he and Rick insist on going along. But I don't think Bailey will talk if they're in the room. The guys said they would only allow it if you came and stayed with us the entire time. I know he'll be behind glass and I'll be secure, but they hate the idea of me going alone."

"That makes sense. I agree that having a brooding Trent and Rick nearby would put anyone's hackles up. Although the inside of a prison should be safe, I understand why, after everything that's happened, they wouldn't want to take any chances. I'm in. When do we leave?"

"Mom is coming out to see Pickle for a bit around lunch time. She won't rest until she sees for herself that she's okay. She'll watch her while we're gone, if that's okay." Leigh stood and pushed her chair in.

"Sure. That'll give me time to run up to the big house to check on my mother."

***

Later that afternoon, Cara and Kate waited inside the county jail's visitation room. With a presence capable of shaming royalty, Kate took a seat in a hard plastic chair. Even knowing the former beauty queen as she did, the transformation shocked Cara. She'd even dressed the part in a knee-length pencil skirt, killer icepick heels and a prim, but very flattering, blouse. With her back straight, hands in her lap and her ankles crossed just so, she could have been royalty.

Cara stood with her back to the concrete block corner and tried to become invisible. Rick and Leigh waited in the lobby with a pacing Trent, who likely worried about far more than Kate's physical safety.

A moment later, a wild-eyed, disheveled man dressed in orange shuffled into view. His hair was a perfect milk chocolate at the ends, with a wide stripe of gray roots hugging his scalp.

Something wild and scary flickered in his eyes when they honed in on Kate. A wide smile split his face. "Katherine, it's about time you came to visit me."

Cara watched, fascinated and repulsed as Kate's mouth flattened for a brief second before her perfect smile returned. "I apologize, dearest. I've had some trouble lately. That nephew of yours is it again. He's made a mess of everything."

Rage flashed across Bailey's face. "Boyd," he spat, as if the word was the vilest potion he'd ever tasted.

"Yes. I simply can't bear his interference any longer. Can you tell me where to find him?" Cara had to hand it to Kate, she had the ice princess routine down to a science. She deserved an Oscar for her performance.

"He's hiding, always hiding. I curse the day I told Sutton to pull him out of Afghanistan. He's caused me far more trouble than he's helped. He promised me he'd take care of everything. He lied, but he should be good at it, since he's done it all his life. It's a Campbell trait. I still don't know why I married into that family."

"I want to put an end to his lies. Do you know where he hides? Or if he works with anyone we can track?"

"You and I were going places, Jackie. But you loved that Dawson and not me. No one understands my greatness." A sad and wistful look eased his angry features.

"I know, darling. We live in a cruel world." Her words were kind, but they were filled with pity for his mental illness, not the hate and greed that had twisted it into something far worse.

"I was going to the White House with you by my side. It's gone now. He took it." Bailey look down to his lap like a pouting child and his hair fell to cover his face.

"He did. Boyd took it. Where can I find him?" Kate paused and a look of guilt crossed her face. She tucked a lock of her long hair behind her ear and took a deep breath. "Maybe we can get your dream back? Tell me where to look."

Bailey looked up at her as if she were daft and should know the answer. "Campbell Hollow. He won't stay there, but he always checks on his sister at least once a week. She's so pretty to be a daft little thing. Far too pretty to be so dumb. It's a shame."

His cold words stabbed Cara in the heart.

"His sister? Why don't I remember her?" Genuine bafflement caused Kate to frown.

"Yes. She looks like a much younger image of my Marilyn, but after the girl's car wreck years ago, she was never the same. She had a major head injury and was in a coma for a month. Gorgeous, but she'll never grow up. Boyd was driving when the accident happened. He still blames himself. She's the only thing he cares about more than himself, but he hasn't been the same since the accident either."

"Of course. How could I have forgotten? Thank you." Abruptly she stood and turned. With a tilt of her head toward the door, she indicated she was leaving, a long, glorious lock of hair falling over her shoulder. Cara followed, admiring the woman's strength. Courage came in many forms and, although it was an entirely different shade than the kind she was used to being surrounded by, it was no less powerful.

They walked through the door and down a concrete hallway. Kate's heels echoed loudly, out of place in this cold world. At the end of the narrow hall, they walked through another heavy door. The instant they stepped through, Trent pulled Kate into his arms. Cara watched as she leaned heavily on him, squeezing his waist tightly. He cupped her nape with one hand and rubbed her back with the other. Over Kate's shoulder, his gray eyes met Cara's.

She gave him a thumb's up to let him know his girl had done well. At that, he closed his eyes and hugged her even tighter.

"It won't take five minutes. We'll be in and out before anyone knows we're there." Leigh, her voice full of frustration, spoke to Rick. Cara turned to see them locked in a serious discussion. Though she'd missed the first part of the debate while she'd been with Kate, she could guess what their disagreement was about.

Addie.

"I understand you're worried about her. Believe me, I can't sleep at night for the fear that tells me she's in danger." Rick crossed his arms over his chest.

"Why don't we take this argument on the road?" Trent broke in and gestured that they should take their discussion elsewhere.

Full of temper, it looked as though Leigh just stopped herself from tearing into him before pursing her mouth and nodding. She shot Rick a look full of venom.

They loaded into Rick's SUV, but before the Leigh and Rick saga could continue, Trent turned to look behind him. "So? Babe, how did it go? You weren't in there as long as I expected."

While Cara listened she watched Rick drive. His focus appeared to be on the road ahead, but she'd seen the tension in those shoulders before. From her spot in the middle seat, she didn't need to see his white-knuckled grip to know he was torn.

Leigh had put him between a rock and a hard place. Cara suspected the social worker's big heart forced her to cause trouble.

Leigh stayed silent, closing her eyes and leaning her forehead on the window.

Not knowing how to help, Cara did the only thing she could think of and took the woman's hand in hers. Leigh's gave a single squeeze, but held on.

The car stopped with a lurch making Cara look up. They were in a parking lot outside an all-in-one grocery store. Rick bit out a curse then grumbled. "Kate, stay put and keep talking. Cara, update MacDonald. Let him know we're making a stop on the way back. We'll be back on the farm later than I expected. Leigh, you're with me. Let's go." With a long-legged stretch, he climbed out and slammed the door.

Shock marked Leigh's beautiful face as she followed, shutting her door with a soft thump. Discreetly, she wiped an eye, trying in vain to hide her tears. Looking no less miserable, Rick pulled Leigh close and tucked her beneath his arm. Marked with sadness, she looked nothing like a woman who'd just gotten her way.

With a shuddered breath, Kate continued, "Bailey said that he cursed the day he asked Sutton to pull Boyd out from Afghanistan. Then—"

Trent already vigilant, straightened. "Fuck. Sutton? You're sure that he said Sutton?"

"I'm sure. Who is he?" Concern colored Kate's voice.

Something dark and sinister lurked in the periphery of her memory, just out of reach. Like a thin veil of smoke, she could just see, but not touch it. "He did say Sutton. I heard him clearly. What am I missing? It sounds familiar but I can't place the name."

"Marcus Sutton of L and S Consulting."

Recognition and nausea smacked her at the same time. "Oh, no."

***

Joe sat with his back to a picnic table at the shelter house in the state park where the Grants had indicated they'd meet him. At their request he'd met them after his shift ended and driven his truck. They hadn't asked, but when he'd stopped by his house to pack for Kylie, he'd changed out of his uniform. A few minutes early, he sat and waited wondering if something more than their child's overdose had given them reason to go to such lengths or if that single tragedy was enough.

He had no idea.

He checked his phone for messages, but nothing had changed in the two minutes since he last checked. Throughout his day, a sense of tense anticipation, a foreboding, haunted him. He'd chalked it up to the prior night's events, but couldn't let himself sweep the warning away.

He'd gone into work fully prepared for it to feel like the longest day in history. The strain of working under Hawkins had become so great; he feared he couldn't make it much longer. He'd either snap and walk off the job or lose his temper and attack the man. He'd love nothing more than to beat him bloody, but that went against everything his badge stood for.

He adjusted his baseball hat and stood just as the sound of tires crunching over gravel met his ears. A few seconds later, a silver minivan came into view.

Curiosity made him wonder what they were up to. The Grants drove a green SUV, if he remembered correctly. A moment later Brayden, Patricia and Mark Cline stepped out. They shut their doors and the sound seemed extra loud as it echoed through the forested hills.

Patricia opened the back door on her side and helped Nicholas, their youngest out of his car seat. She walked with him to the nearby playground while Brayden and Mark walked in his direction. Brayden didn't appear any more excited to see Joe than he had the last time they'd spoken.

About the time they made it to the picnic table where Joe waited, another vehicle, the green SUV he'd been expecting, pulled down the road and parked beside the van. Brayden immediately turned around and jogged back to the second car. The moment Haley Grant stepped out, he took her hand in his. She was a pretty little blond with her entire life in front of her, but she'd nearly lost it. Her parents exited and walked over to join Mark Cline who waited just a few feet outside the shelter.

A faded blue truck parked near the first two vehicles, and he wasn't surprised to see Lori and Alyssa Schmidt exit it. The teens had their little party and Haley overdosed in Alyssa's bedroom. Lori, a single mother, had been at work and devastated when she'd been notified. The girls had been close friends since grade school.

He wasn't surprised to see the families had come together, but he still didn't get why they'd been so secretive. The three teens came to meet him, leading the pack, with their parents close behind.

Brayden led the girls, with his shoulders straight. The courage didn't quite make it to his face, but Joe had to hand it to him—the boy was trying. "Mr. MacDonald, we need to tell you something."

"All right, I'm listening. What's going on?" Joe gestured to the picnic table, hoping the low-key setting would help put the kids at ease.

Silence.

Maybe a little prompting would set things in motion? "Is this about the night of Haley's overdose?"

"Uh, it's all my fault. I don't want to get the girls in trouble." Brayden sat at the table and the girls followed suit. They all hung their heads, finding the knife carvings on the scarred, wooden top fascinating.

Alyssa blurted, "We all tried it. And it was my idea."

"No." Haley looked up at him and twisted her fingers into knots. Her light brown eyes misted with unshed tears. "It was mine. I was stressing out and wanted to relax for a bit. Last year at school, Marcy talked about smoking weed and how it relaxed her. I just wanted to let go of the stress for a little while. I asked Brayden if he knew where to get some."

Alyssa tucked a strand of streaked brown and blond hair behind her ear. "He told us it was a bad idea and tried to talk us out of it."

"Then it became a game. We teased him. I begged him." Haley looked up to Brayden with a silent apology.

"Then Clint heard us talking after a movie let out and said he knew a guy and would make a call. He set everything up with Jimmy Hawkins and told us where to meet him." Alyssa met Joe's gaze for a brief moment before looking back down to the table. She traced a carved heart with her fingernail.

Brayden's shoulders slumped. He looked from one girl to the other, as if they baffled him, but Haley continued before he could say anything.

"He wanted to go alone, but we wouldn't let him. When we got to the parking lot beside the movie theatre, Jimmy was acting strange. Brayden told him, no, never mind. We changed our minds and didn't want the pot."

Brayden's eyes met Joe's. "He insisted, said we had to take it. I told him no. Then to make him go away, I told him we didn't have any money. I thought that would send him away. Instead, he took my hand, put the bag in it and said don't worry about it. The first one was on him. Then he drove away."

"Brayden wanted to flush it, but Alyssa and I wanted to try it. So we did, and then I got sick."

There was more. He wasn't sure what yet, but this wasn't enough to warrant the secrecy their parents had gone to.

"We really thought it was regular pot." Alyssa glanced up at her mother who stood close by watching with her arms crossed and a fist over her mouth.

Joe looked to Brayden. He was being as patient as he could with the kids, but he'd be doing them a favor by getting to the point. "So you didn't find it."

The boy met his eyes. "No, sir."

"All right, kids. Your parents didn't call me out here for a secret meeting to tell me that. What is it that's got you all scared so badly?"

Brayden pulled his cell phone from his pocket. "That night, after they took Haley away in the ambulance, I thought I was going to puke, like really vomit. There were still people everywhere, and I didn't want to be heard if I did puke. I went out into Alyssa's backyard hoping that I could breathe easier and so, if I got sick, no one would think I needed to go to the hospital, too. I just wanted a minute or two of fresh air. When I opened the patio door, I was quiet."

Lori spoke up for the first time and placed a hand on her daughter's shoulder. "It had a wretched squeak the week before, and my brother oiled the hinges just a couple of days prior. If he hadn't been so picky—" She covered her mouth again and shook her head. "I can't imagine how much worse things could have been." She half-sobbed, half-laughed. "When the kids finally came to us, I baked him a cake and told him thank you. Only I couldn't tell him why it had been so important. He looked at me like I had a screw loose."

Haley's mother gave Lori a side hug. "When we get this out and things come to light, you can explain. We can't let him get away with this, hon."

"I know." Lori hugged her back and patted Brayden's shoulder who looked up to her.

"It'll be okay. We're going to fix it." Then he turned to Joe. "I heard someone talking and didn't think much at first. I was going to take a minute to see if I was really going to puke or not. I think it was more for worrying about Haley than the pot... but then I realized his voice sounded familiar. Once I heard what he was saying, and realized who he was, I froze." He paused for a moment, running a hand through his hair.

His voice was steady when he continued. "I was scared. But then he said something that made me mad, really angry, and I didn't think at all. Something inside me snapped, and I started recording."

Something black and oily swirled in Joe's belly. "Who did you hear?" With dread lodged like a hot lump in his throat, he asked the question although he already knew the answer.

"It was Sheriff Hawkins. When he came around the corner, he had his cell phone in his hand."

Joe held out his hand and Brayden put the phone in his palm. Joe pushed play on the video. The backyard was dark, and the poor kid's hand shook as he'd held it. The image was virtually worthless until he heard the voice confirming everything the teen said.

"I swear, boy, if you weren't blood, I would have already put you away for the rest of your life. What made you think that pinching the product and lacing pot with it would be a good idea? You are not to touch the H again, do you understand me?" The video was silent for a few seconds but when it continued, things only got worse.

"Maybe we'll get lucky and the little blond will die." Joe flinched and he saw Haley's father turn and walk away with his hands fisted by his side, his wide shoulders tense.

Brayden reached over and paused the video. Joe looked and saw anger blazing in the kid's eyes. "That's what he said that made me mad. He said that same thing before I started recording. I mean, I know we did something stupid, but she didn't deserve to die."

"No, buddy. You're absolutely right. Can I hear the rest?" Joe watched as his words seemed to ease something in Brayden. Maybe he'd taken a portion of the boy's burden by agreeing?

He let Brayden press play and braced himself. "I know Mark Cline is a volunteer firefighter. They're a respected family. It would be easier if the kids came from the trashy side of town, but kids are easy to manipulate. If they cause trouble, I'm sure there's something I can hold over their head. Their parents need their jobs. The Clines have another kid to feed. It's easy to paint girls, even the good ones, as whores. If push comes to shove, then we can always make sure there's another overdose or two. That wouldn't be too hard to stage and everyone would believe it after tonight's mess. Just keep your fucking nose clean." The video came to the end and Joe looked to Brayden.

The boy spoke before he could say anything. "During the last part, where's the video is extra blurry, I was moving back to the door. I was standing on the porch with the door open when he came back around the corner. He saw me. I think he thought I was just coming outside. But...he asked me how my little brother was doing, and had a scary look on his face. I...I almost deleted the video, but I didn't want him to get away with it. Then again, I didn't want to cause trouble either. I just didn't know what to do."

Joe sighed. "For what it's worth, you and the girls made the right choice. It might have been scary, but you told your parents everything. You stuck together for what's right."

"What do we do? I mean he's the Sheriff, but he's wrong. Mom said that you really seemed like you wanted to get to the bottom of things, wanted to know where the heroin came from. That we could trust you, but you're not the Sheriff."

"You're right on all accounts." He handed the boy's phone back and met him eye-to-eye. "You can trust me and, yes, I absolutely want to get to the bottom of this. I don't want what happened to Haley to happen to anyone else. When drugs come to town, bad things happen. I'm going to do everything I can to put a stop to the drugs and to Sheriff Hawkins, too."

Alyssa spoke up. "He should be the one in jail, not planning to do those horrible things to us or our parents. They're good parents. We made a stupid mistake, but that's not their fault."

"You're right. And I'm going to do everything in my power to make sure he ends up in prison where he belongs. I'm honored that you kids and your parents trusted me with this. Will you trust me just a little longer?" Joe stood and looked to the adults.

Haley's father still looked ready to commit murder, and Joe didn't blame him. "What happens from here? My wife has begged me not to go after him. Shed tears on my chest because she's worried I'll lose it and go after him. I'm trying, but…"

"As hard as it is, you need to keep it together for just a little longer." Joe looked at them as a whole. "We need to take this to the right people. It sucks, but that's the way it has to be. If I set up a meeting with Judge Holt, Detective Bowie, and Commander Stephens, at the State Police Post, would you all be willing to come? All of you? I know it's hard, but when you come together, like you have, they'll listen."

Mark Cline put a hand on his son's shoulder. "We've discussed it, and we'll do whatever it takes to put him behind bars, but we have to keep our kids safe too." Worry had aged the man ten years since Joe had last seen him.

He looked to them all, humbled that they'd trusted him with something of this magnitude. "Agreed. No question, they come first. I will keep an extra eye out, run extra patrols and will talk to a couple of deputies I'm close to. I won't tell them why exactly, just that I have bad feeling. They'll help. I'll move as quickly as I can on this. You have my word.

"Brayden? I want you to keep the video and your phone. I'm not going to take that from you, but can you send me a copy?" He pulled a card with his number out of his wallet and handed it to the teen.

"Brayden, look at me." The boy did and something tugged at Joe's heart. They were all too young and far too innocent. "You need anything at all, or if you have any questions, you can call me direct at any time. Okay?"

"Sure."

"Same thing goes for you girls. And I don't want you to pay any mind to what he said about girls. He's wrong. Dead wrong." They nodded, but when Joe saw the beginnings of tears in their eyes, he wanted nothing more than to put his fist in Dale Hawkins' face.

Chapter Seventeen

Joe checked the time on his dash. They should pull in any time. He'd arrived at the Caudill's place about five minutes prior, planning to meet Cara, Rick and his sister. While starting his truck after watching the teens and their parents head out before him, he'd gotten Cara's message. She said they planned to make a quick stop, and she placed a lot of emphasis on the word *quick*. Cara and Leigh could ride with him and update him on what had happened with Bailey.

He didn't like the thought of taking Leigh and Kate virtually next door to the snake's nest, but he knew is sister. When she set her mind to something, Rick didn't have a chance. Leigh loved all kids, but something about this girl tugged especially hard on her heartstrings.

Rick's SUV pulled into the driveway and parked not too far from his truck. Joe stepped out and adjusted his hat to block out the early evening sun. When he saw the look on Rick's face, his greeting stopped before leaving his mouth.

Doors opened and shut and Rick let the orders fly. "Leigh, Cara, Joe, you're with me. Trent and Kate, stay here and keep watch." He made it about a step and a half before Leigh stopped him. Joe suspected not many men or women could keep up with or had the courage to face a pissed off Rick, but leave it to his sister. With her long legs, she caught and stepped in front of him.

"Hey." She stopped him with a tender hand on his chest. "I'm sorry to do this to you. I don't mean to be a pain in your ass, I swear. I just want—need—her to be safe. Thank you for everything you've done for her and for me. I mean it."

Rick's strain eased as he cupped her jaw in one hand. "Let's just get this done and get you out of here." The man looked like he wanted to do more, but held himself back. "Grab her things. If she sees this crowd, she may run."

"Okay." Soft and accepting, Leigh agreed making Joe wonder if Rick was a miracle worker.

After his sister grabbed the grocery bags bags, Rick led the way. Joe let Leigh, then Cara, follow behind them. He brought up the rear. They followed Rick around the back where he opened the door and went in first while Joe surveyed the backyard. Everything looked the same as it had each time he'd been there with his sister. The grass was getting too high again, making the place look twice as neglected.

Something set him on edge and he told himself that it was Rick's tension. He stepped inside and shut the door. The interior was dim as always, but surprisingly cool. He looked around and saw that a small refrigerator had made an appearance and so had a small writing desk.

Rick had been busy.

Apparently his rule forbidding anyone from coming out here alone applied to everyone but him.

"Anything new?" Rick and Leigh stood close together in the corner where Joe guessed a miniscule dining room might have once been. It was hard to tell where one room should end and the next began. Nothing remained except bare floors and naked studs.

Joe paced to the front room then turned when his sister spoke.

"I don't think so. Only a new set of drawi—"

Crack.

A shockingly loud report blasted the house and everyone flinched. Joe heard Cara's whimper and saw Rick wrap his arms around Leigh and tackle her to the ground. He and Cara both dropped to the ground a millisecond after them. As he crawled across the floor toward her, four more shots blasted the house in quick succession.

He made it to Cara's side. She answered his question before he could ask it. "I'm okay. Scared the shit out of me, but I'm okay." Her golden eyes met his and he was relieved to see they were steady. "You?" Then she called her friend's name a little louder. "Rick?"

"I'm fine. Sis? You okay?" Joe's gaze never left Cara's worried but steady eyes as he waited an eternity for his sister's answer.

Rick spoke for them both. "We're good. Mayhem, you armed?"

Cara didn't hesitate. "I am. My Beretta, loaded with fifteen plus one in the chamber. You?"

"I have my Wilson Combat .45 with nine total. Joe?"

"G22 with fifteen and my backup G27 at my ankle with nine."

"Oh no. Trent and Kate." Just then, an engine roared to life and then quickly faded into the distance. Joe's concern matched Cara's exclamation. He loved Kate like a sister and Trent had earned more than his respect this past summer. Joe had come to think of him as a friend.

Rick spoke. "Windows are bulletproof glass. As long as they were inside, they should be fine. Fuck!"

Leigh's soft voice spoke up. "I'm so s—"

"Not now," Rick said coldly, all business. When Joe noted his hold on his sister seemed no less gentle, he chose not to interfere. As long as the man kept his sister safe, Joe would gladly accept the added debt.

Joe braced and readied to chance a quick peek out the front window when the back door burst open. Dale Hawkins walked in and swept the room with his rifle and a cocky sneer. When his focus landed on Joe he froze, his expression full of condescension and hate. A split second later, the front door crashed open with a curse. Jimmy Hawkins stepped in and fired wildly.

He, Cara and Rick all returned fire. Like a puppet on a string, Jimmy's body jerked and he went down just outside the doorway. Something crashed just outside the opening and he disappeared from view.

Dale fired, and Rick cursed. Joe didn't have time to worry about the meaning behind the tell-tale jolt he'd seen rock his friend's leg. In response, Joe shot, hitting the Dale in the chest. He jumped up and walked over to disarm him, trusting Cara to cover them all.

"Too damn righteous to see the bigger picture." Hawkins spat blood at Joe's shoes.

Joe held his gun on Hawkins wishing like hell he had a pair of handcuffs or zip-ties on him. "Drop your gun, Dale. Now."

"Why, so you can get all the glory? Big, bad deputy taking down the corrupt Sheriff? I don't think so." He raised his gun and pointed it at Joe.

Not having any choice, he shot again, hitting him in the right shoulder. Hawkins dropped the gun and went silent. Joe kicked it away.

"Rick? How are you man?" He chanced a glance at his friend and saw his sister with her bloodied hands on his thigh. An alarming amount of blood coated her hands and already seeped to the floor.

"I'll be fine." His voice sounded weak and all kinds of strained.

"Sure you will. Let's get out of here. My phone's in the truck and we need an ambulance. Cara? Cover me while I run out to the truck?"

"Yeah, I'm on it."

"That's my girl. Sis, stay on Rick. I hate to leave him in here, but I don't want to move him. He needs an ambulance yesterday."

"I can walk, MacDonald. I'm not dead." Rick tried to stand but didn't fight it when Leigh used only a single hand on his chest to stop him.

Another shot fired outside and they all flinched. Then another answered.

"Joe." He heard the torment in his sister's voice and understood her unvoiced thoughts. She feared for Rick's life, but didn't want him to head out into danger either.

"Love you, Leigh. I'll be back. Promise."

"Love you too, Joe." He tucked her quiet words into his heart and headed out.

***

Cara watched Joe leap over the front step ruins and run to his truck. Staying out of sight as much as possible, she scanned the area. She couldn't see where the other shots came from. Standing in the open doorway, she chanced a quick glance down and saw blood on the collapsed front steps. Maybe Jimmy had fired a couple of wild shots as he fled?

Another shot sounded and Joe hit the ground. She carefully stepped out and on the busted wood and readied to provide cover fire. He crawled to the driver side of his truck and stayed low. She couldn't see any blood, but that didn't stop the panic from clawing at her throat.

Visions of Justin, lying in the sand, so close but so far away flashed before her eyes. She closed her eyes and tried to blink it away.

A hand gripped her arm in a bone-crushing grip and turned her, her ankle twisting in the rubble beneath her feet. She tried to cry out but a sweaty hand covered her mouth.

Boyd hissed in her ear. "Finally got you, bitch. Let's go." The scent of heated gun cleaning oil and sweat filled her nostrils. Something warm and metallic pushed against her temple, and she closed her eyes in shame. She was supposed to be Joe's backup, and she'd failed.

Another gunshot blasted through the still air, and she flinched. Then she heard a voice that eased her fear. Trent called out. "Yo, MacDonald! You got any cuffs in your truck?" Trent marched a stumbling, bleeding Jimmy Hawkins out from the tree line.

He froze when he saw her and Boyd. Joe must have seen the look on Trent's face, because he turned and looked directly at her. She wanted to weep for her stupidity.

"Let's go." Boyd spoke quietly in her ear, then he raised his voice for the guys to hear. "Boys, Cara and I have some unfinished business to attend to. She'll catch up to you later. Or not." He tugged her and the hem of her jeans caught in the collapsed front steps, knocking her off balance.

She fell and the world around her erupted in gunfire.

***

Leigh's alarm grew as the flow of blood from Rick's thigh leaked at a steady, horrifying rate. She knelt on the hard floor beside him and placed both hands on the dark spot on his inner thigh. The dark crimson stain spread faster and farther by the second.

"Leigh, baby. Take my gun. I know Joe had to have shown you how to use one." His words came out in a slow, stuttering pace that terrified her more than the blood loss. Rick, always so strong and capable, he'd seemed invincible. He was so big and domineering—to think that something as small as a single bullet could knock him on his ass went well beyond sobering.

"You hold it. I've got to keep the pressure on." She pressed even harder on the wound with both hands, making him groan in pain.

She would have thought it impossible, but his handsome face paled even more.

"You need to protect yourself. There's no telling who's out there. Take it." Her heart lurched when she saw determination stamped in granite across his features.

"I'll be fine. You'll protect me. I trust you." She locked gazes with him, willing him to hang on just a little longer. She held pressure and hoped and prayed with everything she had that he could hold on until help came. The spread of blood met the floor and crept toward her knees.

"I'm not strong enough." Each word that left his mouth grew weaker than the last. "You have to protect yourself. I can't do it." When shame flickered in his eyes, her heart broke.

She shifted her position so she could leverage her body and put more of her weight into her grim chore. "Rick, you hang on. I—we need—" A broken sob tore from her chest. *I can't lose it now.* She had to remain calm. "Addie. Me. I need your help to find her. She needs you." She took a deep breath and fought the hitch in her chest. "You're the only one capable of finding her." He'd done so much for them both. In his weakest moment, he deserved the truth. "I need you." Her voice broke.

Then his eyes closed. The gun fell from his hand, hitting the floor with a loud thud.

Joe would want her to take it and be prepared to defend herself. Rick was right, she knew how.

She watched, concentrating on the subtle, almost invisible rise and fall of his chest. The choice was easy—as long as there was a single ounce of blood in his body or one small breath, she would continue to hold pressure.

The door opened behind her, and she sighed with relief, yet she couldn't pull her concentration from the rise and fall of Rick's chest. "Please, please tell me there's an ambulance on the way." *Joe? Cara? Trent or Kate?* She didn't care if it was Santa Claus behind her as long as they brought some sort of hope.

"Don't know my dear, but neither one of us will be here to find out. Let's go." An unfamiliar, sinister voice spoke behind her, chilling her blood. She closed her eyes and continued to press all her weight into Rick's wound.

Something sharp and cold touched the back of her neck. Electric pain whipped through her, burning her every cell with agony.

The last thing she saw was her blood-soaked hands falling away from Rick's wound as the world faded to black.

***

Something heavy fell on top of Cara, knocking the air from her lungs. She struggled to breathe and fought to untangle her arms from beneath her. Only a few heartbeats later, and the weight was gone and familiar hands ran over her body.

"Fuck, sweetheart. Are you okay?" Joe asked.

"I'm fine. My ankle's screaming, and he knocked the wind out of me, but I'm fine. I promise. Get Trent something to restrain Jimmy before the idiot does something stupid and gets himself shot again. I'm surprised he hasn't passed out by now. Hand me your phone, and I'll call the ambulance."

"Yes, ma'am." While she called 911, he jogged back to his truck and came back with a handful of extra-large zip ties and tossed a few to Trent who immediately restrained Jimmy.

"You sure you're good?" He looked her over with a world of doubt on his face.

"I am. Go do your thing. I'll be right behind you. I need to assess Rick's wound." She took a set of ties from Trent and set to work on an unconscious Boyd. She prayed for all she was worth, that her friend wasn't injured too badly. In all the chaos, she hadn't been able to get a look at his wound.

With a single, long-legged step, Joe hefted himself up and over the crumbled steps. She relaxed. *It is over. Thank—*

Something crashed inside. "Rick! Rick, where'd she go?" Joe's voice was loud, part anger, part panicked shout.

She didn't hear any response until Joe cursed a blue streak and the back door slammed. Dread settled in her belly. Something was wrong. Way wrong.

Trent rolled a crumpled Boyd over to his side who groaned and opened his glossy eyes.

"He got her, didn't he? Fucker likes pretty women and girls." He coughed and blood bubbled from his mouth.

"Got who?" Trent asked as he patted Boyd down, checking for weapons.

"The pretty one that looks like your Kate. He wanted the blond little girl, but said he'd settle for the sexy brunette instead."

Icy fear crept its way up Cara's spine.

"Make you a deal." Boyd coughed and there was a hint of desperation behind his cocky words.

"We don't deal with scum. Ever." Trent stood over Boyd, his expression full of disgust. He looked as though he wanted to scrape something from the bottom of his boot.

"You will this time. Sutton took her. You want her back, you'll deal."

Trent glared and said nothing.

Finally caving, Boyd spoke, his words barely intelligible. "Promise me that you fucking do-gooders will watch over my sister, and I'll tell you where to find her. Keep Sutton away from my sister."

***

Joe walked back into the little house to find both Rick and Hawkins lying flat on their backs. His sister was nowhere to be found. He shook Rick who'd barely been able to open his eyes then he'd bolted out the back door, but had no idea which direction to run. His every instinct was telling him to run like he'd never run before, but the woods which were only a short distance away hid a hundred different options.

Fuck. Fuck, fuck, fuck!

He stalked back inside, praying they could get something useful from Jimmy or Hawkins, *if* they survived.

Checking on Rick, he found that he was still breathing, but his pulse was weak.

I need to get my head together or I won't do anyone any good. God, Leigh had been taken, and Rick was so much worse than Joe had thought. *Fuck!*

Cara. She was a nurse. He need to get her in here. Maybe she could do something he couldn't. What, he had no clue, but he had to try.

He restrained the barely breathing Hawkins just to be safe before he went back out front.

Trent tucked his phone into his back pocket and looked to the driveway with his hands on his hips. "I called Kate to come back. There should be a med kit in Rick's ride. She's not far and will be here any minute."

"Cara, I need you to look at Rick. It's bad. Come here." Not giving a fuck, he let his grief into his voice. If anything happened to his sister, he'd never, ever forgive himself. Without waiting for her reply, he swept her into his arms and carried her inside.

Fuck.

***

Silent and careful, she followed them through the woods. How Addie wished she had one of her grandfather's old guns. But no, her good for nothing father had sold them all at the pawn shop.

She had the phone the do-gooders had left her in her pocket. She'd been playing with it, learning how to use the camera and flashlight things on it. She hoped it would be of use now. She didn't know what else to do. She just knew she had to do something.

The pretty lady who always left her stuff dangled limply over the creepy guy's shoulder. Her hair was so long that it almost dragged the ground. Addie thought she knew where he was taking her, but didn't want to make any noise by calling for help on the phone. And by all the gunfire she'd heard, there still might be trouble at her house.

Her home.

She knew it wasn't much more than a shithole, but it was all she'd ever known. Now she wouldn't be able to stay there ever again. She didn't know where she'd go.

The guy slowly stepped out into the clearing where her aunt used to live. Her trailer had burned down not long after she died and no one ever did anything about it. With his gun in one hand and the other arm around the lady's legs, he walked to a shiny black car. He opened the passenger door and put her inside then quietly shut the door. Then he got in the driver's side and started the engine.

A picture. She could take a picture of the license plate. Her shaky fingers fumbled over the buttons until she found the right one.

She waited until the car turned around to pull out. Then she snapped a picture. Then another.

She blinked and the car was gone.

***

Cara sat in the chair next to Joe and ran her hand up and down his back. She felt utterly useless as the man she loved worried. Kate sat in the chair on his other side, silently offering her support, yet her fear was likely every bit as strong. From what Cara understood, the two women were more like sisters than cousins.

She leaned over, kissed his shoulder and sent another wish into the universe. She knew this man. He'd never forgive himself if something happened to his sister. Long hours had passed since she'd been taken and they had virtually nothing to go on. Unfortunately, Boyd had passed out before he gave Trent anything useful. He was in intensive care and still unstable.

Trent came out through the emergency room doors and ran a hand through his hair. "Fucking stubborn asshole. He sent the nurse to get AMA papers. He's always gone his own way, but this takes the cake. I want her back too damn it, but he lost a ton of blood. They just removed a bullet from his leg and has over twenty stitches."

Cara stood and walked to her friend. "Do you want me to talk to him? It can't hurt." Sometimes her softer touch made more progress than the males' chest thumping tendencies.

"Thanks, but it won't do any good. He grabbed my phone out of my hand and called in the rest of the crew. They'll meet us back at my place in a bit. The way Rick lit a fire under their asses, they might even beat us there."

This would kill Rick. Always one to shoulder the weight of responsibility, he'd likely see this as his biggest failure. Because of Addie, he and Leigh forged a deep connection and sparks ignited whenever the two entered the same room, yet they both denied being in any sort of relationship.

She wondered what would happen between them if the girl wasn't their focus.

Joe scrubbed his hands over his face and sat up straighter. "You're certain he'll be fine?"

Trent answered. "They just finished giving him a unit of blood and a ton of fluids. They want to give him one more unit, but he's refusing it as well. He's still a little pale, but he'll be fine as long as he does what he's told. You can guess what kind of fight that's going to be."

"Okay. At least that's one good thing. The sun will be up soon and I need to call mom and dad. They only know there's been trouble. I have to find a way to tell them their daughter has disappeared and was most likely kidnapped. I'm going back to your place. I want to be there when Kylie wakes up." Tired, heartsick, he stood and patted his pockets.

Kate stood and gave him a tight squeeze. "Sure. You and Cara go. Trent and I will stay here and try to sit on Rick. We'll catch up with you in a bit."

Cara's heart split in two as she watched Joe's arms clench tight around his cousin. He tucked her head under his chin and held her for a long moment before releasing her. He held his hand out for Cara and she gave it to him. They walked side by side into the wee hours of the dark morning.

When they came to his truck, he pulled her tight against him. "I need you." The pain and grief in his voice made her weep. She wished she could take every ounce of his misery from him. He'd been through so much already. The sight of this incredibly strong male crippled by his love for his family would never leave her.

"You have me. I'm not going anywhere." With her face pressed to close to him, she spoke to his heart.

"Oh yeah?"

"Yeah. If I have to, I'll climb you like a tree."

Though his smile was weak, when it came, she tucked it into her heart to keep forever.

Epilogue

Two months later.

"Yay!" The rapid *stomp-stomp-stomp* of boots clattered through the house, warming Cara's heart. "We're going to a barbeque!" She caught a flash of a pink and yellow swimsuit and cowboy boots speeding down the hall as she put the lid on her baked beans.

Joe walked in from loading a cooler full of drinks into his truck and his shoulders slumped. "Cowboy boots and a bikini? No. Just no. She's six, for cryin' out loud."

"How about you load this and the others into the truck? I'll get her straightened out." She smiled and handed the dish to the baffled man that she loved.

"Works for me." He leaned in and kissed her long and deep, making her heart sing.

Her life was gloriously full.

Full of love, laughter, friends and family. At Joe's insistence, or more accurately order, she'd moved more of her things to Riley Creek. She still planned to finish her degree and, though it would be tough, she had no doubt that their relationship would make it through the semester and come out stronger on the other side.

A flash of sadness marred his handsome features, and she wished for all she was worth that she could take his troubles away, but some things not even love could erase.

But eventually, with a love as strong and true as theirs on their side, they could conquer anything that life threw at them.

The End

About the author

As a teen, International Amazon Best Seller, Amy J. Hawthorn, fed her reading appetite with fantasy and horror stories. Then she stumbled upon a pretty book cover—complete with a bare-chested, sword-wielding, Highlander. That Highlander and his author showed her the magic of a Happily-Ever-After.

She has read her way through Kentucky, Arizona, Southern California, and then back home to Kentucky, where she's living out her own Happily-Ever-After. The only person surprised by her Best Seller title? Amy. Her friends and family are laughing and saying I told you so.

For more information on Amy's other books visit
amyjhawthorn.com

www.ingramcontent.com/pod-product-compliance
Lightning Source LLC
Chambersburg PA
CBHW050506260626
47157CB00004B/1206